NOBLE ULTIMATUM
JACK NOBLE BOOK THIRTEEN

L.T. RYAN

Copyright © 2021 by L.T. Ryan. All rights reserved. No part of this publication may be copied, reproduced in any format, by any means, electronic or otherwise, without prior consent from the copyright owner and publisher of this book. This is a work of fiction. All characters, names, places and events are the product of the author's imagination or used fictitiously. For information contact:

Jack Noble™ and The Jack Noble Series™ are trademarks of L.T. Ryan and Liquid Mind Media, LLC.

contact@ltryan.com

http://LTRyan.com

THE JACK NOBLE SERIES

For paperback purchase links, visit:

The Recruit (Short Story)
The First Deception (Prequel 1)
Noble Beginnings (Jack Noble #1)
A Deadly Distance (Jack Noble #2)
Ripple Effect (Bear Logan)
Thin Line (Jack Noble #3)
Noble Intentions (Jack Noble #4)
When Dead in Greece (Jack Noble #5)
Noble Retribution (Jack Noble #6)
Noble Betrayal (Jack Noble #7)
Never Go Home (Jack Noble #8)
Beyond Betrayal (Clarissa Abbot)
Noble Judgment (Jack Noble #9)
Never Cry Mercy (Jack Noble #10)
Deadline (Jack Noble #11)
End Game (Jack Noble #12)
Noble Ultimatum (Jack Noble #13)
Noble Legend (Jack Noble #14)

PART 1

CHAPTER 1

"Why did you murder Frank Skinner in broad daylight, Mr. Noble?"

The man gripped his pen between his teeth as he slipped one arm free from his blue blazer, shifted his notebook to his other hand, then let the jacket slide onto the Victorian-era couch. He pulled the pen from his mouth, dabbing the end against his tongue. With it hovering over the blank page of his notebook, he stared unblinking over his gold-rimmed glasses at Jack Noble.

Jack held the man's gaze for several seconds before attempting a reply. When he opened his mouth to speak, he couldn't find the right words.

The man, whose name was Schreiber, tapped the end of his pen against his pad. The thump-thump-thump of a waltz. He glanced toward the narrow part between the drapes.

"That make you nervous?" Jack asked.

Schreiber nodded, tight and terse. His hair was pulled back into something akin to a man bun, only a little lower. "If you don't mind?"

Jack planted both palms on the hand-carved wooded arms of the chair he occupied and pushed himself off the seat. He took note of the other man stiffening. Jack would have been concerned if the guy hadn't. Schreiber's occupation was that of a journalist, not a soldier or a spy or a lawyer or a cop. He wasn't used to dealing with this element of society.

He didn't want to acknowledge people like me existed, but he sure as hell slept better because of our existence.

The meeting had been secured through back-channel communications. The risk in reaching out had been great. Jack trusted *maybe* six people enough to call upon while in his current predicament. The Agency knew the names of all six. The Agency presumably monitored all incoming and outgoing emails, messages, and phone calls of the six.

And that's what made the favor he phoned in all the more valuable. An old friend's mentor, who had nothing to do with the life Noble led, had arranged for Schreiber to book a room at the Hotel D'Coque in Luxembourg City. Noble spent three days tailing the man, first in his home city of Dresden, Germany, then as he made the trip to Luxembourg. If anyone else had followed Schreiber, they deserved to get the jump on Jack because he had failed to spot them.

Noble spread the blinds open another inch with his scissored index and middle fingers. Dark passing clouds diffused the light streaming through the window. Gusts of wind whipped dead leaves on the sidewalk into mini-cyclones, a hint of a late-spring storm brewing.

The busy street below was lined with four- and five-story buildings. Shops and lobbies on the ground level. Offices and apartments above. From a hundred-fifty feet up, the meandering pedestrians were nothing more than flat representations of themselves. Not real. Maybe that's what made dropping a bomb from thousands of feet up so easy to do. Noble scanned the passing throng for anyone who looked out of place. An individual overdressed for the heatwave. A guy lingering under an awning. Someone staring back at him from one of the many windows nestled in the steel and brick facades across the street.

The numbers offered anonymity. For Jack and for *them*. And make no mistake about it. The people hunting him were out there. Since he'd left Clarissa's hideout in Italy, the place she insisted no one knew about, they'd been a day behind him. Had she informed someone higher up the food chain about his presence? Or had they been watching her? He watched her sleep and told her where he'd be for a little while longer. She never showed, and he hadn't spent more than twenty-four hours in one location since.

A chance existed a few of the faces of his hunters would be recognizable.

But agents came and went and died in the line of duty. Fresh recruits stepped up to take their place. The cycle repeated, depending on the state of the world, which, face it, had been shit for almost two decades now. Jack would lay odds it'd be some twenty-two-year-old fresh-faced kid wearing black glasses and carrying a Glock while possessing orders to kill on sight who would do him in.

"Mr. Noble," Schreiber said. "I was promised a story, an exclusive story. A CIA Director was murdered in the middle of a city street. *By you.* Are you going to answer my questions, or should I press the send button on my phone to have the police sent to my position?"

Jack let the sheer curtain fall shut and lingered there for a moment staring at the now-hazy street. They were out there. Somewhere beyond the veil. The room darkened after he pulled the right side of the drapes over the left.

Schreiber sulked back to the table and half-rested his ass on it. The guy didn't fancy getting too comfortable. At the moment, nothing stood between him and the door. As long as he wasn't too relaxed, he might be able to get to it before Jack felt like stopping him.

"Frank Skinner recruited me into the SIS in the days after I left the Marines and the CIA-sponsored program they forced me into before I had completed recruit training. He found me outside a dive bar in Key West. My first inclination was to turn him down. It's funny. A nagging feeling tells me that's what I should've done."

Schreiber dragged his pen across his notebook. Sounded like leaves scraping the street. A few seconds later, he stopped and glanced over his glasses again. "When was this?"

"Spring, 2002, I suppose."

"And what was your opinion of Skinner then?"

"Any opinion I had of Frank Skinner circa '02 has been affected by the events of the past decade. And those have been washed away by what's happened this year."

Schreiber focused on the tip of his pen for a few moments before asking another question. "A man with your skills, you could have done this at any time. Why in the middle of the day? In the middle of a street? Why in front of so many witnesses?"

Jack had relived that moment thousands of times. Truth drenched Schreiber's words. A planned hit would have served Noble better. He could have returned to the shadows, tracked Frank to his next destination, and taken the man's life in the middle of the night.

"Hate."

"Excuse me?" Schreiber said. "Hate?"

"Hatred. Pride. Hubris. Arrogance." Jack rose from his chair and walked back to the window, eliciting a groan from Schreiber as he pulled the curtain back again. Noble squinted against the sunlight knifing through a slit in the clouds. "Take your pick, man. If I could go back to that day, I'd kill him again, same place, same manner."

The room darkened again as he turned and let the shades fall in place.

"What specifically did Frank Skinner do to you?" Schreiber perched atop a stool with his right leg crossed over his left. His foot bounced.

"What didn't he do? I don't have all the evidence. OK? For all I know, every negative event that's taken place, every person I've lost, every time I've been in danger, I can attribute it all to Frank Skinner."

"So that's why you did it, then? That's why you murdered him."

Jack stuffed his hands in his pocket. The mousy man across from him again reacted by straightening up, eyes wide, pen clutched tight as though he could use it to knock away a bullet.

"I did it because the guy was a traitor to his country. He'd been working against the States for a decade, maybe more. I didn't murder him—and when I have all the evidence, everyone all the way up to the President will agree with me."

"Surely you are aware you can't act as judge, jury, and executioner, Mr. Noble."

"Surely you are aware I can snap your neck easier than you can a pencil, Mr. Schreiber."

Schreiber produced a tablet. He turned it horizontally in his palm and tapped on the screen several times. The muffled sound of a crowd of people speaking French floated out of the speakers.

He held the device up for Jack to see. There Noble was, in the middle of the road. Frank Skinner on his knees. A pistol aimed at Skinner's bloody head. The quick flash of muzzle blast followed by the eruption of gunfire.

People screamed and raced past the cameraman, who only stood there for a few additional moments before running off. The image jumped and panned all around. The last thing Noble saw before the footage cut off was Frank Skinner collapsing on the ground.

Dead.

CHAPTER 2

"WHAT WERE YOU THINKING AT THAT MOMENT?"

Schreiber rose from the stool, pen pressed to paper. He sucked his bottom lip into his mouth. His dangling mustache touched his chin.

Jack stared at the footage, now frozen on the image of Frank's slumped body. Noble stood over him, eyes cast down at the lump that used to be a man he trusted at one time. How long ago had that been? Had he ever fully trusted Skinner?

And what was he thinking after he killed Frank?

"I can't recall."

"You can't recall?" Schreiber deflated with a heavy sigh. "So, all I have from you is a confession? Should I call the authorities now?"

"You know you won't make it out of the room alive if you do."

He leveled his pen at Jack as though the thing were loaded with 9mm rounds. "That is exactly the reason I didn't want to take this meeting. You reached out to me, Mr. Noble. You wanted to tell your story."

Jack took a second to consider this and nodded at the guy. It had been Jack's idea. He wanted the truth out there. Schreiber needed to ask the right questions though.

"Look, you're wanting me to tell you what I was thinking at that time? I have no idea. Probably good riddance, Frank. Countless moments led up to me playing judge, jury, and executioner that day. I suppose I knew if I didn't do it then, Frank would get away with it. He'd find a way to silence me for good. Christ knows he's been trying for years."

"Can you explain what you mean there?"

Jack revealed a few events from the past. Things that were classified, but even the classified docs didn't tell the truth. "None of this happened during my time with the SIS. But that was a couple years later. Afterward, I worked on a contract basis. The first time I believed Skinner wanted me dead is when he offered me a job to take care of a supposed rogue agent named, Brett Taylor."

Schreiber listened intently as Jack listed events, frequently holding up a finger asking for time to jot down his thoughts on the matter. When Jack had finished, Schreiber set his pen and notebook down on the weathered coffee table between them.

"And what about the evidence that Skinner was working against the United States?"

Jack swallowed back the lump in his throat. This was the most he'd spoken at once in a couple of months. Clarissa had left shortly after he arrived at her hideout, and she hadn't come back. Everyone in the little village spoke Italian. Jack could get by with a few phrases, but that was it. They welcomed him into their homes, their bars, their cafes. But hardly anyone attempted to communicate with him.

"You have to take me at my word."

Schreiber scoffed. "At your word? I can't print any of this based on what you've told me. Your country thinks you are a murderous traitor. My country thinks this. The whole world thinks this, Mr. Noble. I need hard proof."

"I know you do. That's why I arranged our meeting."

"Whatever do you mean?"

"I need your help."

The slim man shifted his pen to his other hand and brushed his mustache inward with his thumb and forefinger. "I can't begin to understand what you mean by that."

This was the risk. Jack understood that when he first made contact. Schreiber was at the top of his game. He had contacts globally who could trade in favors and provide him with the intelligence Jack would use to piece together his case against Frank. Noble's word would never be enough. Not after the life he'd lived. But if this benign-looking journalist could gather the evidence, it could get Jack off the hook.

"I'm a wanted man. You know that. And with technology today, I can't get within a mile of the places I need to without being caught on a surveillance system. Facial recognition, license plate readers, they'd have me surrounded before I knew they'd spotted me."

Schreiber nodded at this. "I presumed that's why you chose Luxembourg. An assumption they don't have that kind of tech, when, in fact, you can't escape it unless you stick to the smallest of towns. That is how you've managed so far, isn't it?"

"More or less."

"Have you remained in one place the entire time you've been off the grid?"

"More or less." Jack smiled. The gesture seemed to influence the journalist.

Schreiber took a deep breath and let his shoulders slump and head fall forward an inch as he exhaled.

"What is it I can do for you, Mr. Noble?"

Jack proceeded to tell Schreiber the names of five individuals placed in high-ranking positions in intelligence agencies in the United States, Great Britain, France, Russia, and Israel. Schreiber committed each to memory as well as the information he needed to procure from them. His reward for this would be uncovering one of the greatest intelligence scandals the world had seen.

"Why can't you go to these men directly?" Schreiber asked. "It's not like years ago where you'd have to expose yourself in order to do so."

"To get close enough, I'd have to. I can't take that risk."

"These men, they'd vouch for you?"

"It's not about vouching for me. Exposing the truth. That's what we're after. I can live the rest of my life on the run if need be. Prefer not to. Each of those five men hold a key. I also hold something over them. As soon as you mention my name and Frank's, they'll know what your meeting is about."

Noble returned to the window. He parted the drapes and curtains a foot or so. The sun had again retreated behind a silvery veil of racing clouds.

Lightning flashed far off over the city skyline. The storm would arrive soon. Jack had use of the room for another night, but he wouldn't stay. Not here. Too exposed. Too much risk now that he'd met with the journalist. He had to work on a plan to get to the small country's border with Belgium. A friend there would allow him passage.

Schreiber cleared his throat.

"Our meeting is concluded now?"

Noble turned his back on the window. The thought that he hadn't studied the windows across the street passed through his mind, and he stepped out of the line of sight. He gave the journalist a slight nod.

"What if I don't do this?" Schreiber asked. "Suppose I go to MI-5 or MI-6 and hand all this over and let them do what they wish with it?"

Jack eyed him for several seconds, offered a shrug. "Then nothing changes. Skinner remains a hero gunned down by his onetime protégé. No one will investigate his dealings over the past decade. Those who profited from those dealings will remain unnamed, planning God-knows-what against my country." He paused a beat, then added, "Yours too, I suspect."

"No repercussions from you?"

Jack felt his lip twitch into a slight smile. "You won't know that until it's too late."

The color drained from Schreiber's face as he fumbled his navy-blue bag open and stuffed his pen and pad inside. He retrieved his cell phone from the table.

"Don't turn that on until you are two blocks from here," Jack said. "They'll eventually figure out we were here. But we need as much of a head start as possible."

Schreiber stuffed the device into his back pocket. Like most phones Jack saw people handling, Schreiber's was too big for his front pocket with his keys and wallet shoved in there.

"How should we do this? Leave together? Separate?"

"There's one security camera on this floor. Turn left and go to the end of the hallway. I'll be right behind you. There are three doors in the lobby that lead outside. You take the one on the left and keep going that way down the street."

Schreiber nodded as he threw his bag over his shoulder and started toward the door.

"One more thing." Jack pulled a burner cell phone from his pocket. He handed the phone and two disposable SIM cards to the journalist. "It already has one in it. After our first call, you melt the SIM and replace it with the card marked with a red X. Got it?"

Schreiber took the phone and went to place it in the same pocket as his own cell. He handed it off to his other hand behind his back and tucked it away. "When will you call?"

"Two days. That should be enough time for you to make contact."

The journalist turned without responding. Noble grabbed his arm.

"Don't back out now, Schreiber. That phone rings, answer it."

Schreiber nodded without looking back. He headed straight to the door and exited the room. Noble didn't linger behind. He followed the journalist out and down the hallway to the gunmetal grey door leading to the stairwell. The sound of it opening echoed throughout the twenty-story steel and concrete chamber. It sounded as though there were an entire company of soldiers racing up or down the steps.

A few minutes later, they entered the lobby. Schreiber first, then Noble ten seconds later. They avoided eye contact, but Jack remained a few steps behind and to the right so he could keep the journalist in his peripheral. He lost a few steps when a woman looking the other way bumped into him. Once outside, he'd lose that view, and if the man decided to call it off, reach out to the authorities, Jack would be unaware.

He paused at the tinted door and inhaled the disinfectant-laden air. It carried a hint of lemon. The street outside was mildly busy. Enough people milling about that he would be able to absorb himself and become anonymous. He thought of his longtime partner and best friend Bear Logan. If the big shaggy man, who stood six-and-a-half feet tall, were there, they'd stand out amid the clean-cut pedestrians.

Jack pulled the door toward him. A rush of cool air whispered past. The incoming rain drenched the breeze. He stepped through the opening and was met with the crack of a gunshot.

CHAPTER 3

RILEY "BEAR" LOGAN GRIPPED THE COLD METAL RAILS SPANNING twenty feet with both hands. Sweat-soaked palms threatened to slide off. He squeezed with the tips of his fingers.

Fingers that at one time could snap a man's arm in two. Gouge eyeballs out. Hold Sasha close.

Now they could barely flex.

His weight bearing down on useless legs that no longer knew how to walk became too much for the big man. His right hand slipped off the rail. His pinky flexed back two inches further than it was meant to. Sasha or Mandy gasped. He couldn't see either, not as his right knee buckled and he began the long fall forward, twisting at the waist in an attempt to come down on his side.

If the left hand could keep its grip, then maybe, just maybe, the landing wouldn't be so rough. But the left one functioned worse than the right. It had been the palm press than kept Bear's left side supported. And so, as he went down, his left hand slipped outside the railing, resulting in an awkward bend of his elbow, but he didn't feel it.

The side of Bear's head collided with the floor. That floor with the dated parquet design that made him dizzy when he stared at it. Did it do that when he toured the facility before his surgery?

He couldn't recall.

Bear couldn't recall most things these days.

Sweat coated his face, dampened his hair and his shirt. He lay on his side, on that damn parquet flooring, a warm trickle of salty blood seeping from his lips, down his cheek, onto the ground.

What next? How do I get up?

"Bear, are you OK?"

He felt the hand, delicate, soft, on his thick forearm. The one stretched beyond his head that his face rested on.

"It's gonna be fine," Mandy said. "You'll get back to the way you were."

Would he? Would he ever?

"Get the hell away from me!"

It was more than a growl. And the sharp intake of breath from both Sasha and Mandy, plus the nurse and therapist, told him his words had hit harder than any physical action he could have taken.

The high-pitched squeal morphed into a buzzing drone that faded in and out. He turned his right hand down so the palm planted on the floor. Pushing through his fingertips, his upper arm rose. Using his forearm for support, Bear pulled his right knee up, rolled over into a sorry-looking child's pose, his cheek pressed against the floor.

Through his heavy panting, he heard Sasha consoling Mandy, who tried to conceal her sobs, choking them down.

Good girl.

He had trained her to hide her emotions, no matter the situation.

"Sweetie," the nurse said—or was it the PT gal? Bear couldn't be sure. They all had the same French accent. "Come with me. We'll get a treat."

Did treats work anymore? Mandy was hardly a child now.

Bear lifted his head high enough to turn it. His other cheek slapped the floor with a thud. The small puddle of blood was inches from his nose. He inhaled the acrid smell.

"Go with her." Sasha had an arm draped around Mandy's shoulder. She turned the girl toward the PT gal and gave her a little push to set Mandy on her way.

Whoosh, whoosh, whoosh.

The blood pushed through Bear's head hard enough his vision pulsed. Sasha closed the door and spun on her heel. She gazed at something beyond him. Her lips tightened, a slight shake of her head. She slipped out of his view. Her footsteps echoed around the silent room, rising above the whoosh.

And then she was there. Crouched in front of him, head turned sideways to match his. Looking him in the eye. Her eyebrows almost knitted together, separated by a crinkle above her nose.

"You bloody asshole."

She rose, turned, headed toward the door.

"Sasha." He knew it sounded like he had spaghetti in his mouth, wrapped around his tongue. Probably came out more like "masha," but what could he do?

She stopped, her hand on the knob. She debated whether to stay. Whether to hear him out again. These outbursts had been a daily occurrence since the surgery. The operation to remove the tumor. Partially successful, the surgeon had said. Best he could do, under the circumstances, considering Bear couldn't travel to where the doctor routinely practiced.

They had removed eighty-five percent of the tumor. The rest, they said, was too deeply rooted. However, there was good news. As good as could be in such a situation. There were two tumors, and the one they could not fully remove was benign.

For the time being.

Recovery had not gone as expected, though. By this point, Bear should've been on his feet, talking smoothly all the time. Instead, he could hardly support himself. And his words at times came out well, and other times presented themselves as a miss-mash mush-mouth sounding plate of scrambled eggs.

"I'm waiting," Sasha said, her fingers grazing the handle. She looked over her shoulder at him. He could see the pity in her eyes. That damn look she'd worn since the surgeon said this might be the new normal for Bear. "Do you have nothing to say for yourself?"

Bear's head felt like a boulder attached to his neck by a prehistoric hinge. He fought to keep his cheek an inch or two off the floor. He'd shuffled over enough that the puddle of blood and drool was beneath him.

He forced the word out through his dry mouth. "Sorry."

"Yes, you are." She turned and walked back over. Staring down at him, she continued, "The man I knew, that I fell in love with, would not allow this to get him down. Yet look at you. A defeated mass lying there."

"I'm trying."

"Then try harder. And I don't mean keeping yourself up. I mean getting your ass back up off the ground after you've fallen. Not lashing out at the one person in this world who looks up to you and trusts you completely."

Her biting words did not miss their mark. Bear fully absorbed what she said.

"For Christ's sake, Bear. If you need to lash out, then you save it for when you and I are alone. I'm a big girl. I can handle anything you can say. But Mandy is still a child in a lot of ways. You need to show her how a real man handles this problem."

"I'm scared, babe. Frightened that I might—"

"You might what?" She folded her arms over her chest. "Stay like this forever? Not be able to control yourself? Die?"

A chuckle escaped Bear's lips. A foreign sound that took both of them aback. "I haven't feared dying in years. There's ways I don't want to go, sure. Hell, if I want to pass on wearing a diaper, shitting and pissing myself. But no. It ain't death."

She dropped her chin and let out a long sigh. Eyes closed, she lowered herself to the ground. A silent nod to the nurse sent the woman hurrying to exit the room.

Bear eased his head down as she stroked his hair. He was careful to avoid the blood on the floor.

"I know this isn't easy, Bear. Probably the toughest battle you've ever waged. But you have to relish in the love and support. Fight for us when you can't muster the strength to do it for yourself."

"What if they're wrong? What if this thing burrowed into my brain continues to grow or turns cancerous?"

"Then we deal with it."

We.

An amazing word. Since the age of eighteen, he'd had few *we's* in his life. It came down to the trio of Jack, Mandy, and Sasha.

"Why don't you go find Mandy?" he said. "Bring her back so I can apologize after I get my big ass down this walkway."

Sasha reached out with both arms. Bear grabbed her hands and together they got him back to his feet. Through laborious breaths, he latched on to the railings. He'd never been this out of shape in his life. A man who remained on the move with a quickness that belied his size and frame.

Sasha watched as Bear sucked in breath after breath, steeling himself for the short trek. It might as well have been miles. He hadn't completed it yet.

"Help me back to the start," he said.

"You don't have to," she said.

"I want to."

She held his gaze for a moment, hers growing as steeled as his. With a single nod she returned to his side, helped him do a one-eighty and move back to the other side of the room.

He started instantly. One hand sliding down the railing. His feet dragging on the floor. First his right, then left. The other hand joining the rest of him.

"Go find her." He almost choked on the words. His lungs burned from the effort and exertion.

"You'll be OK alone in here?"

"What's the worst can happen?" He offered a smile that did little to unfurrow Sasha's brow.

"I think we saw that earlier, didn't we?"

"If that's the worst, then I'll be fine all alone."

She shook her head, raised her hands so her palms faced him, and spun on her heel. A second later the door shut behind her.

Bear pushed on, his will driving him forward, the only way he knew to go. He'd beat this.

He passed the center point, where he'd had his fall. Another foot and he'd have gone further than at any time during his rehabilitation. Two months and he still couldn't walk more than a few steps on his own. If these people couldn't figure it out, he'd do it himself.

The overhead lights flickered a few times before shutting off. Fluorescent yellow gave way to the midday sunlight streaming in through the parted blinds. Bear glanced through the window at the duck pond. He had a view of it from his room and spent many mornings watching the fowl as the ducklings grew.

Right hand forward. Left foot. Right foot. Left hand. Again. His sweaty palms slid along the cold railing.

All at once he stopped and swung his head toward the door at the unmistakable sound of gunfire.

CHAPTER 4

SCHREIBER SPUN TOWARD JACK, HOVERED THERE AS THE LIFE drained from his body, his brain no longer capable of telling his heart to pump. The perfect black hole in the center of his forehead looked like a third eye for a brief moment. He collapsed to the ground in a heap.

The woman behind him caught not only blood and brain matter, but the remainder of the round that tore through Schreiber, and dozens of skull fragments. Some large enough, they penetrated and protruded an inch or two. She fell a few seconds after Schreiber.

An innocent bystander who should've hit the snooze button one more time. A husband, three kids, and the family dog will wait anxiously for her return. It'll be nightfall at the earliest before they stand beside her lifeless body at the morgue.

Jack processed the information in a split second while the crowd surrounding them ran and screamed and knocked one another over in an attempt to get to safety.

A single round, likely fired from a perch. This wasn't a bolt-action Winchester either. The shooter used a high-powered, high-caliber sniper rifle. A pro, cloaked in shadows looking for Noble.

He took cover behind the thick stone middle pillar which offered an escape route into the lobby. The lobby that contained several security cameras that would surely be pored over by detectives and analysts from multiple foreign agencies once someone identified Jack.

He chose Luxembourg and specifically Luxembourg City because the streets remained surveillance-free. He only had one eye in the sky to contend with. Unfortunately, that one likely peered through a scope in search of his face.

The chaos died down in the absence of further shots. A crowd of five or six people hovered over Schreiber and the dead woman. Fools, all of them. They were likely to suffer the same fate. And they offered Jack cover from the sniper.

Noble dropped to a knee, worked his way around the pillar and scurried across the void to the bodies.

"I'm a doctor," he said. The people standing there reacted to his commanding tone by backing away. He was about to lose his human shield. "No, stay put."

Jack peeled back the man's sport coat, the one he had complimented when they first met. He tugged the notebook free from the inside pocket and jammed it into his own.

"What are you doing?" a man with thinning brown hair and an uncomplimentary haircut said, taking several large steps back and placing Noble in view of the shooter. "You're no doctor. Police!"

"Shut up," Jack said. "You'll get yourself—"

The warning couldn't come fast enough. The sniper fired another round and hit the man with the thinning brown hair in the middle of the back. The bullet exited on his left side, just under his armpit. Naturally, his humerus should have absorbed the shot, but he had his hands up. The round hit an old man standing there in the abdomen. The worst possible place. A soft spot incapable of deflecting the weakened fragment. A crimson bloom formed, and the man bowed forward as he clutched his gut.

Another life taken. A wife, kids, maybe grandkids, old German shepherd, all without a patriarch. And the old man didn't look promising either.

"Everyone get down!"

Without hesitation, Noble rose and sprinted behind the columns, drawing the attention of the sniper. Chucks of concrete exploded into plumes of dust. Windows erupted sending glass shards everywhere. Several pelted Jack on his right side. The expected pain remained at bay. Safety glass. Dull on the edges.

The sniper would anticipate Jack's next moves. At the final pillar, he'd have three choices: stay put, head inside, or venture out into the open. Remaining in place was not an option. The police would arrive soon. Noble would be taken into custody. He'd be easier to kill in jail. The sniper knew this and would be happy to keep Jack pinned down.

He eased around the column, keeping it between him and the sniper. Beyond the landing, the wide sidewalk stretched over ten feet and met the road. Two lanes of traffic and parking on either side. Not quite to the standards of the US, but not exactly an alley either.

He had no chance. A quick peek in the shooter's direction confirmed when a round slammed into the column inches from his face. Fragments of concrete pelted his left eye, reducing his vision to muddy clouds.

Getting back inside would prove simpler but had the potential to be life-ending as well. He leaned against the column. There was no door directly in front of him. Right or left. Five feet of travel, minimum. To the right, he'd be exposed the entire time.

But the other door left him in view for a second at most. For some men, that would be enough time to adjust, aim, and make the kill shot. Was this guy that good? Jack glanced at the four bodies forever interconnected. The crowd was gone. Some hid behind the other columns. Some had headed inside. Others had vanished, as they should've from the beginning.

Pinning his left eye shut, he used the remaining windows as mirrors. The deserted street offered no cover aside from a few parked cars. That cemented the decision.

He had to go inside.

The question remained, what waited behind the building? Little chance the sniper worked alone. A team could be waiting on the other side. Jack checked his pistol, a Beretta 92FS he'd procured from an old man in the village he'd hid out in. He was the only one who'd ever fired it. He'd performed all the maintenance and cleaning. Loaded the magazine in the weapon and the two in his pockets.

If anyone waited for him behind the hotel, the Beretta would decide their fate.

Jack untucked his shirt, pulled the pistol free from the compression holster, and fired at the window in front of him.

CHAPTER 5

Isabella Cavallero, known to most in the group as Isa, tapped on her mechanical keyboard, sending off a round of rapid-fire clickity-clacks that drove the other analysts insane. But today there were no complaints. Even if the others did mind—face it, they did—they were too busy deciphering the tsunami of information pouring into the command center.

On the three thirty-four-inch curved monitors lined up side by side in front of her, Isa opened window after window featuring news feeds, still images, and live security footage from a hotel in Luxembourg City.

A shooting had occurred.

Shootings happen across the globe. Every single day. What made this one special?

That was Isa's job. Figure out what the hell made this a headlining event.

First was the method. A high-powered rifle fired from above. A sniper. Four bodies slain close together, but not shot at the same time. Other shots that didn't find their mark. Why? They were following someone. The shooter had a target.

The other reason this had her and the rest of her team's full attention was they had specific intelligence that something was going down in Luxembourg City. The sleepy city was, as they say, on their radar.

All other open windows faded into oblivion as Isa focused on the image of a man's face partially obscured by a wide stone or concrete column. Chunks were missing from one side.

"It's him," she said.

She and her team sat in a circle, all chairs facing inward, six feet of desk space, massive monitors, phones, cell phones, burner phones, multiple computer towers, iPads, MacBooks. None of it existed for a few seconds as the other three analysts rose and stared at her.

"Who?" Petrovski, a man thirty-three years of age who had been imprisoned at the age of fourteen by the Russian government for hacking into a database full of political enemy information. Rights workers managed to free him by the time he was seventeen. He soon after found employment in Germany, a private firm that put his skills to use under the guise of GIS. He would find himself in trouble again, but the penalty this time was to be offered a quarter- million-dollar salary working for the group.

A few clicks later, the rest of the team had the image front and center on their main screen.

"Him," Isa said.

"You found The Ghost," Petrovski said.

The Ghost was the nickname they'd given Jack Noble after searching for months and turning up zero leads. They knew he'd been in the small Italian town, yet no one claimed to have seen him. Were they looking out for Noble's best interests?

From the town, the trail went cold. No one had ever evaded the trackers, the analysts, the handlers, and Clive Swift like this. Frankly, it was impossible to do so unless they were hiding in a hole in the desert.

Oh wait, someone tried that and still couldn't evade them.

Everyone left a trail.

But not The Ghost.

The net was pointless if it never closed in on the prey.

Isa felt the others' eyes drawn toward the presence behind her. She pulled a cool breath through her partially separated lips. It chilled the roof of her mouth, her tongue, and tonsils.

"Is it him?"

Clive Swift placed his hand on Isa's shoulder. The tips of his thumb and index finger applied counter pressure, sending a jolt of pain down her arm.

She let the sensation pulse through her own fingers and leave her body. "Look for yourself." Isa pushed away from the desk. The casters on her Herman Miller Aero chair gliding on the concrete floor. She gestured to the enhanced image of the man on the screen. "But I'm pretty confident we found our ghost."

Clive nodded his approval to Isa as he moved forward to occupy the space she had vacated. He placed his hands on her desk. The feeling cool and electric at the same time. He had waited for this moment for over two months. Two long months, lying awake at night, absorbing everything he could find on Jack Noble so he could begin to think like the man.

Problem was, Noble had done so much, been involved with so many organizations and agencies, performing a multitude of tasks, there was no psych profile to rely on. Clive couldn't simply tell himself to *think like Jack* and have it be so.

He grazed the screen with the tip of his right index finger. A little over half the man's face appeared. The beard hid a portion of it, but they'd seen pictures of Noble with a beard.

Clive pulled his iPhone from his pocket, a monstrous thing that his daughter couldn't even hold when she wanted to watch a video. He entered the twelve-digit password to wake the screen, navigated across three screens, two levels into a folder, and pressed a simple blue icon for an app. When prompted, he entered a twenty-character password. A few more taps on his screen and he had what he was looking for. Pictures of Noble. He opened each, compared them to the screen.

"Satisfied?" Isa said.

He liked the woman. She had been a hell of an analyst since coming on board with their organization. But she could be bloody pushy, and he had a bad habit of letting her do so.

She pushed up against him. He caught a waft of her perfume or body gel or whatever the hell women wore these days. Since the passing of his wife and daughter in the train bombing, he had yet to take a lover, let alone date someone long enough to understand today's grooming habits of females under thirty-five.

"Well?" She swatted his hand out of the way and pointed at the image on the screen while glancing at his phone. "Looks like a match to me."

The room hummed with the sound of the fan. These people were professionals. And every one of them sat anxiously waiting to be told the news.

Clive straightened, tucked his phone in his pocket. He glanced at Isa and started nodding, slow jerky movements at first growing to full blown bobbing of his head. A smile nearly formed. He felt his lips twitch and stifled the emotion. They'd found the guy. So what? It took far too long to accomplish. How much longer would it take to bring him in?

That bloody smile spread.

It wouldn't take long at all. Not with the folks he had working for him.

"OK people, listen up. We've found The Ghost."

CHAPTER 6

THERE WAS LITTLE DOUBT IN BEAR'S MIND WHO THE ATTACK team had come for. The shots fired now only took care of people who had the misfortune of being in the way. He chose this life. It had its consequences. It put those he loved in danger. Something he had always been prepared for.

But nothing could ready him for this situation while in this condition.

He scanned the empty PT room in search of potential weapons. Against an armed man in the open hallway, the items he catalogued would do little to help. His thoughts quickly shifted from attack and defend to get out of there.

Sasha and Mandy…

Bear shook the thought free from his mind. He'd trained the girl to react without trepidation in situations such as this. And Sasha, the woman had managed for years as a British Intelligence agent. She knew what to do. He pictured her at this moment leading others to safety.

He had one mission. Get himself out.

Gripping the cold metal railing tight, he pivoted, switched his hands, and started back to where his walkers rested against the wall. Both positioned underneath tulip decals.

Three more gunshots. Closer. Bear moved faster. Risked collapsing on the floor and becoming a statistic.

Getting to the crutches was half the battle. They'd recently moved him from a wheeled walker. He hated the damned contraption while using it, but right now it would double his speed.

He locked the braces around his wrist and headed to the door. For the first time, he attempted vaulting himself forward by planting the canes onto the floor in front of him, then whipping his legs forward in unison. It tripled his travel speed.

Next to the door was a laminated printout of the fire escape route. Two rights and out through the exit door. The same direction the gunshots had originated.

Bear imagined the layout of the wing. To the left of the room was an intersecting hallway. One direction led back to the main lobby and an exit. The other to the cafeteria. He knew which way he'd go.

A whistle of wind snuck into the room carrying a fresh antiseptic odor as Bear pulled the door open an inch. Someone screamed in the distance. People shouted. Shuffling steps echoed down the corridor. And the distinct sound of a two-man tactical team communicating rose above it all.

The men were close.

Bear changed tracks. He cut the overhead lights, pivoted, and vaulted to the other side of the room. Hand over hand he lowered the darkening blinds, made from dense fabric and blocking out most of the light. It might as well have been night. If he didn't know the rails were in the middle of the room, he'd have smacked into them.

Taking position on the hinge side of the door, Bear leaned back against the wall. The overhead vent piped cold air down. The sweat at his hairline chilled. He loosened the brace on his right wrist. The crutch didn't weigh but two pounds at most. Not quite the force he wanted in a weapon, but with it he could strike quick.

The lever clicked and moved downward. The same whistle of wind sounded as the guy eased the door open. Probably with his right shoulder, his left hand supporting the barrel of his sub-machine gun. The tip of it protruded through a narrow opening into the room. A burnt odor followed, overpowering the disinfectant.

Bear waited with his hand choked up on the crutch, ready to use it as like a baseball bat. At most it'd buy him three seconds before the other guy realized where the attack came from. Plenty of time for Bear to take him down.

Old Bear, at least.

Could this new and less improved version keep up?

He breathed in slow and deep. It could be the last full breath he ever took. Might as well enjoy it. His lungs expanded to the point they burned. The smell of gunpowder lingered in his nose. A smile formed. Thoughts of brain tumors, non-working legs and muscles, and the fear of leaving Mandy behind faded.

The door jerked open a foot. The guy's black boot slipped in. His breath was short, ragged. He didn't like the situation. Bear wouldn't either. Too dark. No control. Like stepping into a grizzly's den.

Bear pressed his left foot against the wall. He cocked his right arm back.

The door moved another six inches. The MP5 or 7—same weapon, slightly different capabilities—silhouetted against the light filtering in through the opening. The man's full arm came into view. His left leg. The edge of the door rested against his right shoulder. He began to sweep the room, starting on the left, where the hallway's lighting bathed the floor.

Another inch. Then two. The door slipped off his shoulder.

And Bear attacked.

He brought the crutch down with tremendous force, all he could muster. It hit the guy's arm. Two loud snaps filled the dark space. The crutch bent and the guy's ulna split in two. The guy howled. It faded to a grunt as he stepped back with his right foot and swung the firearm in Bear's direction. His broken arm wouldn't allow his fingers to follow the command to squeeze the trigger.

Bear pushed his left foot against the wall with everything he had and propelled himself through the gap that existed between him and the attacker. He flew at the man with reckless abandon, using his sizable cranium as a weapon. What difference did it make? There was still a tumor growing inside.

He slammed into the guy's chin and mouth with a thud and several cracks. Teeth snapping and breaking free. Warm blood spread across Bear's forehead. His own? The guy's? A mix?

Didn't matter.

As his momentum carried him forward, he reached down with both hands, sliding them down along the guy's hamstrings until they hooked behind his knees. He jerked both up and toward himself. The man came off the ground. If Bear's legs worked properly, this is where he would've driven the guy into the ground. It just so happened it occurred without Bear making it so.

He landed square on the man's chest with his shoulder. Ribs and sternum broke. Both lungs were punctured. A gurgling gasp escaped the man's mouth. He lost his hold on the H&K on the way down. The strap twisted around his neck.

Bear felt along the floor until he found the weapon. He tugged it around and held it over the guy's head. Then he sat up and began twisting the firearm. The strap cinched tighter around the man's neck. He gave up trying to gouge Bear's face and attempted to free himself from the noose.

Seconds dragged on for what felt like hours. The attacker's movements slowed, became jerky, then stopped altogether. Bear felt for a pulse. Found none. He freed the H&K from the guy's neck and then searched his pockets for identification. It proved useless. After flipping the lights on, he inspected the firearm and found the MP7 ready to roll.

The screams and shots taking place in the hospital found their way into the room again. Bear looped the strap over his head and attached his crutches to his wrists. The one he'd used to assault the man was bent, but usable.

He pulled the door open, ignoring the cool draft the room sucked in. There was something else to worry about. The guy's partner. The search didn't take long. The man was near the room. His eyes widened at the sight of Bear. It wasn't out of shock that his partner wasn't the one standing there. And probably had nothing to do with Bear pointing the MP7 at him.

He recognized Bear.

Without hesitation, Bear pulled the trigger. Three rounds burst through the muzzle and smacked the guy in the chest. The first an inch to the left of the sternum. The next two an inch above the previous shot.

The hallway remained frozen for the few moments it took for the man to crash to the ground. Bear scanned for any others, then made his way over to the guy. It would take a production to get down, check his pockets, then get back up. What happened if another attack team came along? He'd be an easy target on the floor.

His thoughts changed from attack to flee. Get out. Over and over. His one mission now. He hustled to the intersection, where the exit was on his left.

Gunfire erupted in the opposite direction. From the cafeteria. The last known location of Mandy.

He took a long look at the bank of glass doors, opened, people fleeing through them.

It wasn't an option.

Bear pivoted and turned toward the cafeteria. A throng of people streamed in his direction. Some had wounds to their arms, necks, heads. Glass. The gunman had made a show out of it, scaring them, sending shards of shattered glass raining down.

"What happened?" he shouted as three dozen people pushed past him.

Responses were in hurried French. Bear was fluent, but at that moment, he couldn't decipher their panicked words.

Another round of gunfire echoed through the corridor. It was close. The sound disorienting. He propped himself on one crutch, lifted the MP7 up in the other. As each person emerged around a corner or stepped out of a doorway, Bear quickly deciphered their intent.

All were innocents who he waved past.

Until the guy dressed in black emerged, dragging Mandy along with him.

CHAPTER 7

JACK PLACED FOUR ROUNDS THROUGH THE WINDOW. THERE HAD been no movement behind it. He angled the shots upward hoping to embed the bullets in the ceiling. Aiming down would have worked to avoid innocents inside. But how would the solid flooring affect the ricochet? The ceiling offered some dampening.

He pushed back against the column, filled his lungs with the cool humid air, and exploded forward. The sniper unleashed a torrent of fire. He'd switched weapons, choosing an automatic capable of spraying the area Noble chose to flee into. The sniper probably didn't anticipate Jack taking this route until the four gunshots.

The weakened glass gave way as he left his feet and drove his shoulder through it. It felt like slamming into a fence. The resistance smacked his arm, cheek, side of his head, then it all gave way. Glass skittered across the smooth marble floor. Noble tucked his chin to his chest, extended his arm, making his body long to absorb the impact across the longest stretch possible. After making contact, he balled up and let his momentum carry him through.

Bullets continued to spray. Windows blew out. Rounds smacked into the floor. Chunks of marble flew through the air. Some hit Jack in the back.

He had one hand planted on the ground, the other wrapped around his pistol. He got off his knees, which lifted him higher, pushing his torso up.

The layout of the lobby had been ingrained in memory in the week before his meeting with the late Schreiber. He knew which hallway led to a dead end, and which would deliver him outside.

Left and straight. Those were the options. Straight led to the back alley, which fed out to two roads and several branches that snaked between buildings. To the left was a smaller alley, one of those branches.

Most would consider the choice a tossup. The sniper had a partner or two out there. No way he worked alone. Either alley likely led to a trap. But through the back offered a better chance of escape. He wouldn't be completely blocked in.

The empty lobby fell silent. The sniper had lost sight of his target. No point in wasting rounds. By now his roost would be easy to determine by the authorities who were beginning to arrive. They remained at bay. Their blue lights reflected off the spidered and shattered window glass. Looked like a disco club inside the lobby.

Jack sprinted past the first corridor, hung a left at the next, then a right. Daylight streamed in through the double doors that offered a slice of view of the rear alley. That view broadened as Noble chased down the gap.

How many people were on the ground supporting the sniper? Had anyone entered the hotel yet? A smart wager said at least one team waited across the street to catch potential fallout. The hit hadn't gone as planned. Too drawn out. Authorities had arrived, making it too late for that team to mobilize.

He stopped short of the doors and found the right wall. His elbow grazed it as he approached with the Beretta and the remaining eleven rounds at the ready.

The alley stood bare to the left. He darted across the hallway to the opposite side and moved as far forward as he could before being seen from the upper windows across the way.

Again, empty. And no way to tell beyond his visuals. If there was a way to hole up in the hotel, down in the boiler room or in a maintenance closet, he'd take it. But he'd finally broken his cardinal rule of the past two months. He'd been caught on camera. Every lobby camera filmed his face. In less than twenty-four hours, the CIA would have their closest agents on site, reviewing, investigating. He had to go now.

The door caught the wind and slipped free from his hand, clattering as it hit the stop bolted to the ground. Jack swept the first and second row of windows on the other side of the alley then dashed across. He paused to decide on the best route. Didn't let the decision linger. He chose right and ran to the first intersection.

A darkened walkway led to the next street. Sitting there, a parked yellow car offered a potential escape option.

Sweat slid down the bridge of his nose and settled into his eye at the tear duct. A film of wetness formed in response to the stinging. He wiped his face with his sleeve, then brushed his damp hair back, off his forehead.

Noble cut down the alley, wary of obstacles in his path that appeared the nearer he got. Trash cans. Bags of refuse that had missed the cans, either by laziness or just piss poor aim. Bottles and cans. A mattress cut in thirds, each laid out longways. The alley was someone's home. Were they around?

The view broadened slightly as he neared the end of the corridor. No occupants sat in the front seats of the little car. And as luck had it, the damn thing was shaking a little. Vibrating. *Idling.*

He hesitated only a moment before dashing beyond the safety the confines of the alley provided and hurling himself through the open air to the vehicle. The chipped chrome overlay on the door handle sliced at his palm. He ignored the stabbing pain and found the release button with his index finger. The door popped open with a satisfying click. The air that met him smelled like stale cigarette smoke and Polish sausage. Jack folded his body as he climbed in through the opening. Semi-cool air piped through the warped plastic vents. The seats were frayed and torn.

With his chest against the steering wheel, he reached between his legs for the slide lever. He had it all the way back and the car in first gear peeling away from the curb before he registered a woman in the back seat screaming at him.

He shifted into second while glancing into the rearview, which was duct taped to a bible perched on the dash.

"What are you doing?" The woman grabbed the top of the passenger seat and leaned forward. She had a blanket draped over her chest, pinned behind her right shoulder. Her other arm was hidden underneath.

Jack ignored her as he wove through the streets in a right-turn-left-turn pattern. Distance from the hotel. That was the name of the game now.

Sirens wailed all around. Every cop and ambulance in Luxembourg City must've been on their way to the site of the shooting.

"Let me out!" The passenger seat shook under her tight grasp.

Noble had a wide swathe of road ahead. He looked over his shoulder and took in the cramped backseat. The woman. The blanket covering her chest and stomach. The empty baby carrier strapped in next to her. He felt the blood drain from his head.

"Where's the baby?" He took in the road, then looked back at her, alternating, wondering why she looked so confused. Finally, he reached back and snagged the blanket. Her shirt scrunched up around her abdomen. Her stomach was trim. A butterfly tattoo adorned her bellybutton.

"Watch out!"

He jerked his head forward and the wheel to the right. The little car crunched as it took on the curb and found the sidewalk. A man pushed his wife into a brick storefront and then dove after her. She smacked her cheek against the facade. Jack whipped the wheel to the left. Tires screeched and the suspension, what was left of it, groaned. They fishtailed on the asphalt.

After he regained control, he glanced back again.

"Where's the baby?"

The woman sat with her mouth agape, both hands gripping the seat in front of her so tight her fingertips disappeared into the fabric.

"The baby?" Jack said. "Where?"

"M-m-m-my friend," she stuttered out. "My friend's b-b-baby."

"This her car?"

"Y-y-yes."

"Where is she?" Jack waited a moment, but the woman didn't respond. He pulled over to the side of the road and turned in the seat. "Where's your friend and the baby?"

The woman met his gaze. She grabbed a long lock of blonde hair and tucked it behind her ear. Her grey eyes looked translucent with the sun hitting them.

"She went back inside to feed the baby. I waited in the car. Closed my eyes and took a little nap."

"Nap? How the hell could you nap?" Even behind the building she had to have heard the gunshots, the chaos from the hotel.

She reached to her lap and lifted a set of headphones dangling from wires. "Why did you steal her car?" She narrowed her eyes and began looking around. "You know what, I think I should get out."

He was caught on camera at the hotel. But it could be hours before they reviewed the footage and ID'd him. If he let the woman go, she'd report the auto stolen, prompting the police to review the tapes. He had to clear the border before they knew he was there. Otherwise, the net would close in on him.

"Please," she said, leaning forward, face inches from his. He caught a whiff of lemongrass. Her hair fell from behind her ear, over her shoulder. The last inch or so was brown. "Let me go."

Jack shifted into gear. They lurched away from the shoulder.

"Afraid I can't do that right now."

CHAPTER 8

CLIVE SWIFT POSITIONED HIMSELF UNDERNEATH THE BROAD vent delivering cold air to the room. He ran hot. Always had. Most people in his position would come to work in a suit and tie. Not Clive. He didn't look unprofessional, but his light chinos and cotton oxford kept him from overheating.

The dozen people gathered around Isa's desk followed his lead. They weren't at Langley, Legoland, The Aquarium, or The Farm. Clive started Global Associated Tracking, Limited eight years ago after being forced out of his director position with MI6. He found a niche in the marketplace. A need for a group that kept up to date with technological advancements in the tracking field. He had staff in four other locations: Chicago, Buenos Aires, Singapore, and in England.

Located on the southern outskirts of Paris, the building looked like any other office. If someone were to mistakenly walk in off the street, thinking they were at their chiropractor's office, they'd find a lovely receptionist waiting behind a knee wall and sheet of plexiglass. Two rows of chairs facing each other had a rotating cast of occupants, usually from the field teams. Had to give them something to do when not out tracking a fugitive.

Beyond the receptionist's desk, a supply closet contained a hidden door, which led down two flights of stairs to a bunker outfitted with bleeding edge tech. The main room consisted of six pods typically occupied by one to four analysts. The walls were lined with fifty- to eighty-inch monitors displaying newsfeeds from around the globe, live feeds from big brother cameras when an active investigation was taking place, and general monitoring of places and people of interest.

But right now, all eyes were on him.

They'd had their first hit on The Ghost since accepting the contract.

"Capture him by any means necessary, but we must take him alive."

Those were the instructions. Clive didn't need them. That's how they operated on a day-to-day basis. At any given time, they had ten two- to six-man teams in the field working upwards of five active investigations. Some were dead ends. It was not infrequent that they rode out the six-month contract, knowing they'd forfeit the majority of the upfront payment.

He thought that would be the outcome with Jack Noble. In fact, he'd thought that the moment they took the job.

"Moments ago, we got our first solid lead on Noble," Clive said. There were nods and looks of acknowledgment amongst the analysts. These folks put in sixty hours a week at the office searching through every shred of evidence, which in this case hadn't been much and had led to them reviewing the same data over and over, looking for any single detail they could pursue. It became a wearisome game after a while.

"Where at?" Eddie Kiefer asked. The guy was former CIA and had confided that this job had special meaning for him.

"Luxembourg City, Luxembourg. Picked him up on city surveillance."

"They don't have a system there, though."

Isa spoke up. "They do now. Installed not three weeks ago. Only a few cameras, but we lucked out." She tapped her keyboard and the feed appeared on the largest monitor in the room. All attention fell upon the video footage of the shooting. They grimaced at the sight of the slain innocents.

"Who is that guy?" Eddie asked. "If Noble is there, why was that man targeted?"

"Waiting on confirmation," Isa said. "I'm with you, though. Something about him must make him important."

Eddie swept his hand out. "Or the shooter didn't know—"

"There he is by the column." Clive placed his hand on Isa's shoulder. "Freeze the footage."

Isa tapped three times on her keyboard, stopping the footage and zooming in close on Noble. She advanced frame by frame, then let it roll forward, rewound, and stopped again.

"He never moves," she said. "Went behind and stayed put."

"Let it roll." Clive leaned forward, hands on the back of Isa's chair to support him. He no longer stood in the jet stream of cool air. Sweat seeded along his hairline. He stifled the urge to finger-comb it into his hair.

"The glass." Isa pointed at her monitor. Clive glanced between it and the large screen. "It's shattering."

A blur of the man hiding behind the pillar burst through the cracked window. Chunks of it broke free and spilled inside and out. Shards danced along the concrete walkway and down the stairs like a waterfall.

"Get me the footage from inside the hotel," he said.

"Already on it." Isa cycled through several windows until she had four set up in a box on her monitor. They took over four adjacent screens on the wall.

Clive wove through his people, all pressed tight and close to Isa's desk. The padded flooring sunk under his steps. He reached the tile track circling the room and went to the first widescreen. Jack Noble was frozen in time.

"Any doubt in anyone's mind this is our ghost?"

Several heads shook in response. Stares flitted from screen to screen, taking in the sight of the man they'd been hunting.

"Lacy, who is closest to Luxembourg?"

"Sadie," she said without thinking. "In Montpellier, north of the city. She's still without a partner."

"Not for long." Clive stuffed his hand in his pocket and gripped his phone. He had someone in mind for this. Had been waiting for the right moment to call him up. His attempt failed. The line had been disconnected. "Isa, let's keep this footage rolling."

They watched the feeds through a single cycle, lasting all of twenty seconds. Noble slipped through a rear door and was lost.

"Get me that alley," Clive said.

For once Isa didn't respond by tapping on her keyboard.

"What is it?"

Her nose scrunched up and the center of her forehead wrinkled as she looked back. "There's no footage from back there. Luxembourg City only recently installed surveillance, and it is quite limited. We were lucky the hotel is situated close to the bank."

The mood in the room evaporated like helium in a popped balloon. Faces wrought with excitement grew sullen. For every minute that passed, the net grew exponentially. If Noble gained a mile of separation, that meant their search radius was now ten times wider than it had been. After an hour, they'd have lost all chance of picking the man up.

"Lacy, get Sadie mobilized now. Tell her she'll have her partner soon enough." Clive knifed through his people and positioned himself under the monitor showing the empty rear lobby. The double doors parted slightly, the result of a wind tunnel from the shattered glass in front. "There's only so many places he can go from here. What do we know about this guy?"

Lacy Evans brushed her strawberry blonde hair out of her face and said, "He's been off the grid for over three months. At some point he'll need to tap into his funds. If he managed to get a car, it's about a five-hour drive to Switzerland."

"We're assuming he has accounts there?"

"I've dug extensively into his past," she said. "He's done a number of for-hire jobs, and these are the types of operations where an employer"—with her fingers making air quotes—"wouldn't simply hand over a check."

"OK, what are the chances we can get verification on this?"

"Impossible." She pulled at a single strand of hair that had glued itself to the corner of her mouth. "That's the whole point."

"Who do we have near Geneva?"

"Bravo team is in Nice, France."

"Mobilize them."

"Wait a minute." Isa spun in her chair, smile on her face.

"What is it?" Clive said.

"Police report that just came in."

"And?"

She spun again, her dark hair billowing up and falling back down like fallout. "A vehicle stolen from the alley behind the hotel."

"Please tell me this happened recently."

She looked back, nodded while biting her bottom lip. "The woman went inside to feed her baby, leaving the auto idling with her friend inside. After the fracas, she went back out. Vehicle was gone."

Clive tempered himself. "And this woman, she was wise enough to carry something with her that lists her license plate?"

Disappointment spread across Isa's face, and he knew the answer.

"Dammit."

A new smile formed. "But I've already located her records in Germany's motor vehicle database."

"You've got the plate?"

"I've got the plate."

All the major highways in Europe have license plate readers. They scanned the plate of every vehicle that passed. When a plate matched a record in a database, the authorities were notified. Isa could bypass the system so no one knew they were monitoring, and if the vehicle Noble had escaped in hopped on the motorway, any motorway, they'd have his location. The net would shrink and tighten.

Renewed, Clive positioned himself squarely in front of the group. "Call in every analyst who is off this week. I want all field teams briefed and ready to move."

"All?" Lacy said. "Even other regions?"

"Everyone. We're going to eliminate any chance he slips past us." He walked over to Isa's station again, placed his hand on her shoulder. "Activate the LPR across Luxembourg, Belgium, Germany, France, and Switzerland."

"Already done," Isa said.

CHAPTER 9

BEAR SUNK INTO THE RECESSED DOORWAY. HE EASED HIS LEFT shoulder against the wall. The MP7 pointed in the direction of the man taking Mandy hostage. The guy's eyes swept the corridor wildly, his head turned as though it were on a swivel with no tightening nut. No doubt he searched for someone. He was looking for Bear.

Which meant he knew who Mandy was.

Bear risked leaning forward enough to take in a full shot of the hallway down to the cafeteria. Scanning the faces rapid-fire in search of Sasha. He couldn't locate her and took that as a sign that she and Mandy never found each other. No way Sasha would stay behind while some asshole dragged Mandy through the hospital at gunpoint.

Unless...

He didn't want to consider that thought. He'd lost so many people in his life. Friends. Family. Lovers. Sasha had become all three. And she'd become a mother to Mandy. Everything to Bear. God help these people and whoever sent them if either Sasha or Mandy were killed.

Mandy yelped as the guy yanked her hard to the left. Looked to be forceful enough to dislocate her shoulder. Bear squeezed his crutch, lifted the tip off the floor. As the last glimpse of Mandy's blonde hair slipped out of sight, Bear emerged from the alcove. Even with the crutches supporting him, he wove through the mob at a speed most would have found unbelievable if they weren't already in a situation they could not believe.

Bear's momentum carried him into the opposite wall near the intersecting hallway. The hum of activity rose as another group emerged from the cafeteria. They screamed out names, or in fear, or pain. Sasha wasn't among them.

Where the hell was she?

Bear closed his eyes and let the noise become background. He tuned in to two distinct voices. Sasha's never materialized. But Mandy called out.

"Let me go! Bear! Help!"

He filled his lungs with sterile air, noting the distinct smell of fear emitted from those streaming past him. That sweet-sweat sensation lingered on the back of his tongue like jalapeño.

A choice had to be made. Control and balance? Or immediate firepower?

What good would he be fallen over on his side?

Perhaps the sight of him would be enough to persuade the other man to let Mandy go.

Bear released his grip on the MP7 and let it dangle from the strap wrapped around his thick neck. He started forward. The firearm bounced off his chest. There was something reassuring about its weight thudding against his sternum.

Mandy hadn't been taken far. And Bear saw why. The guy had stopped and bound her wrists together with long zip ties. They looked like the soft-flex type, made from nylon. Less painful for her over time, he supposed. And if he had his way, she wouldn't find out. Mandy and the man had their backs to Bear, but they weren't moving. What was the guy doing? The man turned about ninety degrees, sort of facing Mandy. He had long, dark hair, and it hung in sweaty clumps, covering his face. His head bobbed up and down. The hair moved. The guy's eyes darted from a device in his hand to her face.

"Yeah, I'm sure it's her."

American. Probably former military. Definitely a mercenary.

Mandy stiffened. She was about four inches shorter than her captor. She'd grown quite a bit the past year, standing five-foot-six now. In a lot of ways, she was still that little girl Jack Noble had rescued off a street corner in New York City. But she was also on her way to becoming a woman. Stuck in that awkward place between girl and grown. Bear had to make sure she'd get through it.

Mandy had taken to the training Bear had provided her. In more recent months she'd had a healthy interest in martial arts, studying Brazilian Jiu Jitsu (Bear's favorite), Muay Thai (Sasha's favorite), and Krav Maga (Jack's favorite). Bear figured if she could master all three, there wouldn't be a situation she couldn't fight her way out of, as a last resort, of course.

This is one of those situations, girl.

Her chin lowered to her chest, but her gaze didn't settle on the floor. As the man holding her makeshift shackles turned away, she looked back. Toward Bear.

Her eyes widened. A smile formed. He put a finger to his lips and shook his head slightly. She gave a single nod, turned her head, and lowered her chin back to her chest and then she did something unexpected.

"What are we waiting here for?"

Finally, she put that attitude to good use.

The guy looked up from the cell phone. His eyes narrowed. His lips were drawn so tight they might as well not have existed. The look caused her to pull back as though she'd been physically assaulted. He lifted his right arm up and threatened to backhand her.

For months Bear's anger had been directed inward. Guilt, pain, ire over the life he'd lived, things he'd done, all of which he blamed his current condition on. There's no such thing as coincidences, he'd told himself on more than one occasion. His choices led to the tumor. He accepted one-hundred percent of the blame, no matter how much the people he loved told him otherwise.

Shit happens.

But not today.

That anger built up and something snapped inside him—he heard it the moment it happened—and all the pain, frustration, rage, hate, self-pity and loathing, it all exploded into white-hot fire burning in his gut, through his chest, exploding from his head.

He barreled forward, only half-using the left crutch for support. A renewed strength filled his ankles, knees, and hips. They didn't move fluidly, but they worked well enough to get him across the hallway faster than he'd traveled by foot since the surgery.

The new group of people streaming down the hallway posed no threat, and no obstacle to Bear. They moved around him. Why wouldn't they? No one was going to stop and ask the six-six mountain of a man if he needed help getting out. For damn sure not when he was carrying a submachine gun.

The guy uncocked his arm and grabbed Mandy by her bound wrists. He spun, started walking away from the crowd, dragging her along. No one other than Bear noticed.

Bear picked up the pace. A mistake. His right knee buckled. He let go of the MP7. It dropped and slapped him in the diaphragm. He caught the wall with his large mitt, digging into the slight grooves with his fingertips. A pair of hands gripped him above his hips.

"You OK?"

He half-glanced back at the orderly. The guy stood almost as tall as Bear. About half his width. He had long fingers that wrapped around Bear's side onto his abdomen. Was this how a ballerina or figure skater felt before liftoff?

"I'm good," he said, noting that the orderly had taken note of the weapon strapped around Bear's neck. "Best you get these folks out of here now."

"You one of them?"

Bear held the guy's gaze for a moment. "I'm the one taking them out."

"Bear!"

The call came from beyond the corner. He brushed the good Samaritan aside and tried to ease around. He ended up stumbling into the open hallway in time to see Mandy's fingers pried free from a doorway.

Crutch and right foot hit the tile. He propelled his left foot further than his regular stride. It planted hard, sending a shockwave up his leg. He felt it in his kidney. Ignoring the sensation, he vaulted forward, repeated the process.

Mandy's screams continued. Was she in danger? Scared of Bear losing her whereabouts?

"Damn you, girl," the guy shouted.

Bear was caught between thinking *that's my girl*, and *holy hell wait for me before you get yourself killed.*

The plaque for the room came into view. The morgue. Fitting. It would be someone's resting place today, and Bear had no intention of dying just yet.

He dropped the crutch. His left hand supported the small barrel, while his right wrapped around the grip and threaded the trigger guard.

Mandy grunted at the same time Bear heard a pop. He stepped into the doorway, his frame filling it. The guy stood over Mandy, who now lay on the floor. His right hand crossed his chest, and he held it up around neck level, ready to strike again.

"I told you—"

That was all Bear let the guy say. He flipped the MP7 to single shot and fired a round into the man's upper back. The guy bowed forward at the waist, then his knees buckled and he fell like a towel left to hang in the air after a strong wind gust faded.

The shot proved not immediately fatal. The man worked his mouth open and closed as his face turned deep red, then blue. The bullet had exited through the right side of his chest. Probably severed the spinal cord on top of destroying the right lung. His eyes pleaded with Bear to help him.

"I could end this for you now. But it's best you use these last few moments to think about how messed up your life choices have been that you ended up like this."

He nodded at Mandy, who got to her knees and searched the guy's pockets. She came up empty handed.

"Get the phone," Bear said.

She spun on her knees and located the device underneath a steel table with wide swirls of leftover disinfectant glimmering under the overhead lights. She hopped up and handed it over to Bear.

"Thanks," he said. "Now, we gotta find a way out of here."

"This is the morgue, right?" she said.

Bear nodded as he swiped his thumb across the phone's screen.

Mandy pointed to the back of the room, next to a bank of lockers three high and five wide. Fifteen bodies, max. What would they do if there was a disaster, natural or manmade? Maybe something like today's assault.

Bear followed her outstretched digit past the row of human coolers.

To the door with light seeping in from around the bottom.

Mandy said, "Then there's gotta be a way to transport dead people on the other side of that door."

CHAPTER 10

Luxembourg offered Jack passage to Germany, Belgium, and France. After the meeting, he had planned on traveling to the Netherlands via Belgium. The itinerary was compromised. They knew he'd been in Luxembourg City. They'd know his next destination.

He had motorways sprawling out like a spiderweb memorized. The 12 and the A6 to Belgium. The A1 and the E29, north and south, to Germany. And the A3 and A4 south to France. He knew where each went, the best places to stop, the intricacies.

And they were all worthless now.

By this point the woman with the baby realized that her car and friend had been stolen from behind the hotel. Amid the chaos of the scenario, it would take time to get a police officer or detective to listen to her. But they eventually would. If the local authorities placed no stock in what she said, surely someone sitting at a desk in front of a large monitor scanning for news from the shooting would pick up on the stolen car report. They'd take the license plate number and feed it into the EU's network of license plate readers on every major motorway.

Noble fumbled his phone out of his pocket and entered a series of thirty-six numbers he knew by heart. The call would bounce around Singapore, Japan, and the Philippines before making the trek across the Pacific where it would route through several public and private switches until it hit a bank of computers Langley had long forgotten about before finally ringing through to Brandon Cunningham.

Jack didn't want to involve the man. He'd gone through enough, according to reports Clarissa gave him before leaving her little hideaway in Italy for good.

Everything that had happened to the guy was Jack's fault.

"Pick up, buddy," he muttered. "This is the last thing I'll ask of you."

But the line rang several times. After a minute, Noble hung up.

"What's wrong?" the woman said. He glanced at her in the mirror. She had one knee drawn up and wrapped her arm around it.

"It's nothing." He eased to a stop at the light, craned his head forward to catch a glimpse of the camera perched atop the pole.

"You're worried about the videos," she said. "I saw a report on this recently, how they scan every car that drives now. You won't be able to get far, will you?"

Jack shook his head, said nothing.

"What happened at the hotel?"

"Someone tried to kill me."

"Why?"

"Why does anyone?"

She eased her cheek onto her knee and shrugged. "Did you do something to them?"

"I know something about someone very powerful, and if that information was revealed, it would cause problems for many people in several countries."

She arched her eyebrows. Her eyes grew wide. She set her foot on the floor and leaned forward. The lemongrass smell washed past Jack.

"Who are you?" she asked.

He turned his head. They were eye to eye. Her lips parted slightly.

"I'm nobody anymore. Dead man walking." She pointed at the light, which had turned green. He kept his foot on the brake. "You should get out. This isn't going to end well. I don't need any more collateral damage weighing on my soul."

She didn't move to either side. Instead, she pressed even closer to him. "Can you be trusted?"

Jack lingered on her question for a few moments before fielding a reply. But he didn't manage to get it out.

A loud bang followed by the crunching of folding metal and shattering glass sent the small car lurching forward.

Jack's head and torso snapped back then forward. He caught the steering wheel on the side of his head, an inch above his ear. The pain wrapped around his face as though someone had taken a buzzsaw and tried to lobotomize him.

The woman didn't fare much better. She'd been resting against the front seats, her arms draped over them. The impact propelled her forward to the windshield.

Instinct took over, as it often did for Noble. He stretched his arm out. Her chest smacked into it. His elbow held for a moment, then gave a few inches. She veered off course, her trajectory sloping down a few inches. He couldn't prevent her from impact, but he spared her the pain of having her face shredded by glass.

Her head hit the dash with a smack. Her body went limp for a moment as she slid down like a bird flying into a window.

In the mirror, Jack saw smoke rise from the black sedan's tires as the driver peeled back in reverse. They weren't trying to get away though. Another attempt was incoming.

Jack jostled the woman off the shifter and put the transmission in gear. The light had turned red again. A line of cars crawled through the intersection. Behind him the sedan lurched as the driver shifted to drive before braking.

There was no time to wait. They'd be hit again, and the impact would drive them into traffic, pinning them in.

Noble lurched forward, peeling the tires of the small car and laying on the horn. Startled drivers slammed on their brakes, even though their vehicles were larger and likely to not sustain any damage at their slow rate of speed. He wove through two lanes of traffic and sped off.

Their pursuer had less luck getting through the muck of autos. The passenger door popped open and a man in black wearing black gloves emerged. He rushed forward, brandishing a pistol at oncoming traffic.

Enough of a hole formed for them to get through. Before they did, Jack made a right turn.

Into a dead-end alley.

He slammed his foot down on the clutch and brake and slipped the transmission into reverse. Both feet came up. The right went back down on the gas pedal. Pivoted at the waist, he looked back through the rearview and saw a woman and child had stepped into the alley entrance. The kid grasped strings attached to half a dozen balloons colored yellow, red, and blue. The little boy glanced over. His mouth dropped open. His hand released the strings. The balloons went sailing. The car screeched to a stop a few feet from them. The woman scooped up the kid who had diverted his attention from the near collision to his balloons which soared over the tops of buildings. Sailing to the clouds.

Which was where Noble would be heading if he didn't get out of the narrow roadway with no escape at the other end.

He took the corner blind, reversing onto the main street. He went wide hoping to clear the oncoming vehicles he couldn't see. It didn't work. Another car roughly the same size clipped the rear passenger fender. Sent Noble into a swirl. He corrected halfway through a turn, faced the sedan barreling toward him.

The other car had power.

Jack's had some nimbleness.

He charged ahead, veering toward the sedan.

A game of chicken he had no chance of winning.

"What are you doing?" Her fingernails dug through his shirt. Probably left marks.

He shrugged her off, jerked the wheel hard enough to snap his head to the side. The car popped up on the sidewalk. He laid on the horn to warn pedestrians. In his peripheral, he saw his passenger slide along the seat until she was bunched up in the corner. He half-wished the door would pop open and dump her into the street.

The other driver attempted to mirror Jack's hard turn, but the bigger vehicle could only cover a lane in the same distance. They came close enough that Jack made eye contact with the driver. The image of the guy burned in his brain.

Did he know him?

From the past?

Movement ahead drew his attention forward. People frozen on the sidewalk, unsure what to do. The smart ones butted up against the buildings, taking cover in open doorways and alcoves. Some might consider the ones still standing there deserving of the Darwin Awards. Survival of the fittest, and all that.

Noble jerked the wheel again. This time he braced himself. His companion did not, though, and she tumbled toward the middle of the rear seat, reaching out and catching his arm to stop herself.

A couple yanks on the wheel corrected course. A look in the rearview saw the sedan starting a wide U-turn. Jack saw a road ahead and took it, even though it led back toward the shooting.

"Turn left," she said, pointing at the next intersection.

Noble didn't ask for further instructions. He guided the small car left.

"Now right."

Again, he turned.

"Right again."

He hesitated. In the rush to get away from the hotel, he hadn't considered the car's perfect placement. The woman concealed in the backseat. The story of the friend and baby left behind. What better cover to use? Jack wouldn't get rid of her under such circumstances. Too much risk.

The turn approached and they risked blowing past and entering a busy intersection.

"Do it." She slapped his arm on the bicep. Her fingers gripped his muscle.

Noble hit the brakes after he turned into the dead-end alley. "What the hell's going on?"

She lifted her hand off his arm and pointed at a narrow opening at the base of a six-story building. "Parking garage."

He eased the car through the opening and stopped in front of a white lift gate with yellow and black stripes painted on it. She shifted in his peripheral but did nothing to cause him to react. He stared at the sign attached to the middle of the gate. Didn't understand what was written on it, but figured it contained a universal message.

The woman threaded one leg between the two seats, then the other and slid into the front passenger seat. She leaned over Noble and rolled down the window and pushed further forward. Her hair brushed against his face. Amid the stale garage air and the smell of sweat, he picked up the scent of lemongrass again. His eyes closed, and for a second, he imagined himself and the woman on a beach somewhere. Then the possibility that she was an assassin crept back into his mind. He had one hand on the middle of her back. The other freed his pistol.

The keypad emitted a small chime with every button press. She punched in an eight-digit code. The gate lifted as she returned to the passenger seat. Strands of her hair caught in his beard. Felt like bugs crawling on his face as they snaked their way free.

He gave her a quizzical look, to which she shrugged.

"Look for a gray BMW."

CHAPTER 11

Minutes passed with no new information. Clive's analysts combed through every news and government report. They tracked trending hashtags on Twitter, Facebook and Instagram, weeded through the garbage and isolated firsthand accounts. A few blog posts already had surfaced. Shocked responses filled the comment sections of pages, posts, tweets, and images.

The room became a living, breathing organism of its own during moments like this. Each person fed off the next. They became tuned in to one another. These were the moments breakthroughs occurred.

Clive chewed his bottom lip as he waited for one of his people to speak those glorious words. *I've got something.* But so far, five minutes—three hundred individual seconds Clive had counted—had passed, and no one had uttered a syllable.

He paced the walkway, winding around the pods. Isa's workstation always his starting and ending point. He stopped behind the woman again, resting his forearm on the rigid plastic seatback of her Herman Miller chair. She had twenty-two windows open on her monitors that he could count. Probably more tucked away behind them or minimized into the taskbar.

She glanced back at him, offered a forced smile that said *we'll figure it out.* He couldn't find any confidence in it. He took a step back and filled his lungs with the cool air piping down from the wide vent. He exhaled and made his way across the room. When he reached the end, he would tell half of his team to take a break. Get some coffee. A baguette. Bring him back something. He pivoted on the hard sole of his Tom Ford wingtips. It made a slow whooshing sound. He opened his mouth to speak.

"I've got something."

His lips remained parted, though nothing came out.

The click-clack of fingers on keyboards ceased. Not all at once. More like the trailing gunshots as a firefight settled.

Chairs hummed along the carpet. Dull footsteps echoed and died as everyone made their way to the central walkway.

Only Isa remained seated.

Clive made it halfway before she piped footage onto the larger displays of what appeared to be the inside of a hospital.

Pandemonium.

"What's going on?" he asked.

"Getting this out of southern France."

"Confirm that is a hospital, Isa."

"Yes."

"What's happ—" It was all he could say before the image of armed gunmen dressed in tactical black appeared from the far edge of the screen. They carried submachine guns and did not hold back on using them. Muzzle blasts shone obscenely large on the feed like those close-up pictures of sun flares. One of the attackers went to reload, letting the magazine drop to the ground. He kicked it out of his path and it bounced off a lifeless body as he gunned down a nurse who held up both hands and pleaded for her life.

"Why in God's name are terrorists attacking a hospital in southern France?" Eddie said. He looked back at Clive. Was that fear in his eyes? Couldn't be. Not Eddie. "There's nothing important within a hundred miles of there."

"There's your answer," Clive said.

"Gotta be more to it than that," Eddie said.

Clive nodded; he'd already surmised as much. "Isa, distribute the hospital information and those feeds to the entire team. I need the name of every employee, patient, and visitor in that hospital today, yesterday, last week, and pending admittance for next week. I want the name of every person who lives in that town. I want any surveillance footage we can find from outside the hospital. These guys didn't walk five miles to get there. Let's get their vehicles."

For a moment everyone remained frozen in place, stares glued to the displays. People continued to drop. The gunmen were relentless. Why shoot up a hospital?

"Let's go, people. Who's closest in the field?"

Lacy spoke up as she hurried to her workstation. Her limp only slowed her lightly. "Sadie. I can reroute her."

Months of nothing. Now Noble was within their grasp. And then…this. A shooting at a hospital. Had to be connected. Clive would bet his life's savings on it.

"Get everyone moving in this general direction. Send Sadie to the hospital. I need her there within an hour, so if you have to call up a heli to move her, do it."

He heard his blood whooshing in time with the seconds on the bank of LED clocks that stretched along a wall. New York. L.A. London. Calcutta. Beijing. Tokyo.

"Here we go," Eddie said.

Clive stopped counting the seconds and walked over to his desk.

"Sasha Kirby. MI6."

"What is MI6 doing there?"

"They're not," Eddie said. "Kirby is. Got caught up in the middle of it. Fortunately, she was armed, and managed to take one of the shooters out and lead several people to safety."

"Any word on how many there are?"

"At this point? No."

"What do we have on Kirby? It can't be coincidental that she's there." Clive knew her name in passing but had never worked with the woman. What he knew was good, but that meant nothing. Her placement at the hospital raised the proverbial red flag and he would regard her as a suspect until she wasn't one. He considered making a phone call to one of his former associates at Legoland to see if they knew anything about this yet.

Isa waved him over to her station. When he arrived, she hunched forward, gesturing for him to do the same.

"Should we go to my office?" he asked in hushed tones.

"I can't leave my computer," she said. "Are you getting the feeling that this Kirby has something to do with this?"

He gave her a terse nod, then singled out the three analysts who shared Isa's pod. "Drop whatever you were doing and find everything you can on Sasha Kirby. Banking, family, close friends. I want it all. Isa, you delegate who does what."

The group morphed into a cohesive unit as Isa put each person on a specific task.

"Sir."

Clive stepped back and turned. Lacy stood a foot away. Small beads of sweat glistened at the edge of her hairline. She had an Army background, enlisted at first and then a warrant officer, and it showed in the way she stared at him. Rather, not looking him in the eye, but past him. She spent eight years as an MP. An investigator. Her CO recommended her to Clive. Her initial assignment in his organization had been in the field, where she excelled. The job was the perfect match for her skills and temperament. She had a mean streak and a tenacity about her that meant she stopped at nothing to get her man, or woman. The team referred to her as their Pit Bull. A nasty fall from the ledge of a five-story building after she'd miscalculated her jump across an alleyway left her with a femur broken in two places and a shattered pelvis. The accident resulted in a six-month rehab and spelled the end of her time in the field. But she was a damn good investigator, and Clive couldn't let her talent go to waste, so he brought her inside. Due to her op experience and familiarity with the other operatives, she naturally assumed the duty of handler when the previous team member left.

She smoothed her pulled-back strawberry blonde hair, wiping away the perspiration at the same time. Perhaps she'd caught him looking at it. "Sadie is less than thirty minutes away from the hospital."

He glanced over at the monitors. "Do we have a live feed from the scene?"

"Coming," Isa said.

A few seconds later the monitors all appeared to glitch at the same time, and the images were replaced. The scene could have been lifted from Aleppo. Bodies strewn about the hallways. Doctors and nurses with bloodstained scrubs hurried past the fallen to attend to the wounded. No better place to triage, he supposed. Then again, how many of the patients now were their own co-workers?

"Confirmation that the activity has subsided?"

"By all reports the perimeter is secured, but the hospital has not been cleared. It will be some time before the GIGN, the French version of a SWAT—"

"I know what they are."

"Right, well some time before that team will arrive. No gunshots reported recently, though."

Lacy lifted her cell phone and raised an eyebrow at Clive. "It's Sadie."

"Patch her through."

The call rang through to his cell. He answered.

"Clive, what's going on?" Sadie said. "I'm being re-routed to a hospital? Did our mark wind up there?"

"Hardly," he said. "From what we can tell, someone orchestrated a terrorist attack."

"At a small regional hospital in France?"

"Doesn't sit well with me either."

"Is it still ongoing?"

"We think they've got it under control."

"So, what am I supposed to do there?"

"Find a woman named Sasha Kirby." He snapped and pointed at Lacy, signaling for her to upload an initial dossier to Sadie. "She's MI6, or was. We need to know what she's doing there. I can't accept that it's coincidence that the same day we locate Noble because someone tried to take him out, there's a random attack in the middle of France and Kirby happens to be there."

"You think she's involved?"

"I'm not making that leap." He paused a beat. "Yet."

"And if she won't talk?"

"Then I suppose I will be making that jump." He caught sight of Lacy wincing at his words. He turned his attention back to the call. "We'll have everything we can on her by the time you arrive."

CHAPTER 12

Jack tucked the beat-up little car into a corner of the garage out of reach from the sunlight streaming in through grime-stained windows. The engine ticked after he cut the ignition. Exhaust fumes mixed with the smell of gasoline and oil crept in through the vents. Shadows danced across the concrete structure. More to do with the trees outside the building than any possible inhabitants.

"We shouldn't stay here too long," the woman said.

Jack didn't respond. In part, he wanted to make sure no one else was present in the garage. He also wanted to see how the woman reacted. She'd gone from sleeping in the backseat to offering him a potential getaway. If he had picked her up right behind the hotel, he'd have reason to be more suspicious. But it took work to find the idling car at the end of the alley. Could the hit team have predicted his escape route? Possible. But doubtful.

She exhaled, pulled her knee to her chest and her foot on the seat and shifted to wedge herself up against the car door.

The engine settled into a silent lull. The garage remained still, with only the sound of a wayward tree branch scratching against a window.

Noble pulled the latch slow enough it didn't click too loud. But the door banged as it fought free from the frame. The sound echoed across the cavernous space. He remained still for a moment, his right hand rested on his pistol's grip. He caught the woman throwing a glance at the Beretta.

"Would you really use that in here?"

He scanned the three rows of compact and mid-sized vehicles in search of movement. "I'd use it anywhere."

"You think someone in this building would be a threat to you?"

"Everyone's a threat to me."

"Even me?" She arched an eyebrow and tapped that soft spot beneath her pronounced clavicle.

He thought it over for a second, shrugged, and exited the car without answering. A moment later, the other door clicked, banged, and squealed on busted hinges. She cursed in German, a harsh and hushed sound that might as well have been a tirade by a drunk with a megaphone. She fought the trunk hatch open and continued cursing. At least she didn't slam the lid shut after grabbing a black nylon duffel and tossing it over her left shoulder. The bag rested against her hip. She adjusted the strap for balance. Her footsteps clanked against the concrete and bounced off the walls as she hurried to Jack's side.

"Wanna take out a billboard and announce we're here?" he said.

"I think rolling that shitty tin-can through the entrance was announcement enough." She shrugged the duffel's strap back onto her shoulder and pointed at the gray BMW. "That's it. Fob is in the cupholder."

Jack took in the space again, then turned toward her. "How do you know this?"

Her cheeks turned two shades of red and she glanced away. After a sharp inhale and a couple of false starts, she said, "I met him last night."

"Where?"

"A club."

"What kind?"

"What?"

"A strip club?"

"Dance."

"Drugs?"

She shook her head.

"Drinks?"

She nodded her head.

"Lots?"

She shrugged and looked like she wanted to bury her head.

It all came together for Jack. "You came back with him."

"We've got a real genius here."

"Never met him before?"

She flashed a hardened glance at him. "Don't judge me."

"I couldn't care less what you do and who you do it with. I'm wondering what this guy's patterns are. How long we'll have before he reports his car stolen."

A slight smile formed on her full lips. "He was into some heavy stuff. I turned it down, otherwise I'd still be in bed. We've got at least six hours until he's back in business."

"So, there were drugs."

"Pills," she acknowledged. "Like I said, I didn't take any."

"Wait here."

Jack noted that the only security cameras in the garage were positioned by the entrance and exit lanes and they faced the street. Everything they'd done since parking had gone unrecorded. It would only be a matter of concealing his face when leaving. Maybe the license plate, too.

He found the driver's side door unlocked. The fob in the cupholder. A six-pack of bottled water with labels written in a language he didn't understand on the backseat. The picture made it clear enough they came from some glacier millions of years old, so the water had to be pure.

He slid in behind the wheel of the M5. Looked like any other Beemer, but this one had some power to it. It started with the push of a button. The low growl of its 500-plus-horsepower engine was ready to roll. He eased out of the spot and directed the car toward the exit and offered a quick nod and two-finger salute to the woman whose mouth dropped open as she realized he was leaving her behind.

So, she sprinted forward and jumped in front of the car.

Noble hit the brakes. The car squealed to a stop, the bumper inches from her knees. He pressed the button to roll down the windows.

"The hell are you doing?"

"You're not leaving me here."

"You're not coming with me."

"Please." She glanced over her shoulder, licked her lips. "I can't stay here."

Jack got the sense that the woman was as desperate to get out of Luxembourg as he was. Her troubles didn't amount to what he faced, but she was running from something.

"I don't have time for this shit."

She jerked her head a couple inches. Her eyes locked in on something. Noble checked the rearview. The door held open for a second, then swung shut. The yellow cone of light turned black. And in the darkness, he saw a figure.

The woman ducked and rushed to the side of the BMW.

He leaned over and opened the passenger door, waited for her to get in.

"We should find your friend," he said.

She shook her head. "I don't want to get her in trouble."

He stopped and waited for the gate to raise. "What kind of trouble?"

She looked toward the window, said nothing.

He took a last look in the rearview. Whoever had entered the garage was out of sight. "You got a name?"

"Ines." Then she turned her head toward him. "You?"

"Jack."

"You look like a Jack."

"Doesn't sound like a compliment."

"It's not." The words were not accompanied by a smile or wink or any other gesture indicating what she had said was meant to be taken in jest. Instead, she turned back to the window and stared at the dark corner of the garage. "Can we get out of here?"

They covered their faces as they passed the security camera, then worked their way back to the main road.

She held her hand to her head where it had smacked the dash when the sedan hit them.

"How's it feel?" he asked.

"Like someone took a sap to my face."

"Let me have a look." He switched hands on the steering wheel, then reached over to feel the lump near her hairline. "Feel dizzy? Nauseous? Headaches? Anything like that?"

She shrugged the question off. "I'll be OK."

"We should stop once we're outside of the city."

"Don't. Let's get across the border before the car is reported stolen. We can get a lot further in France or Germany." She noticed his concern. "They aren't going to stop this car for a border check. This thing signals middle-to-upper management. Another boring corporate asshole making his way back home to continue his dull life."

"Who hurt you?"

"Shut up."

Jack brought up his mental map of the area. He preferred to go to Belgium. Less restrictive. Could get to the coast. Easier to get to England where he had at least one friend. Plus, the beer in Belgium was better there than anywhere else in Europe. But it was also the furthest drive from Luxembourg City. Every minute they were on the road, they risked being found. For the moment they had a vehicle they could take on the highways. The quickest route out was south to France.

He picked up the A3 inside the beltway and made the drive south toward the border. They settled into the traffic pattern, keeping pace with a red Mercedes coupe.

"Why're you so desperate to leave?" he asked.

She took her eyes off the rolling green scenery for a second. She chewed the corner of her bottom lip. "That guy was an asshole."

"Makes sense."

"No, you don't get it."

"So, help me get it."

"He tried to drug me. I saw him do it. So, I played his game. Changed the rules up on him."

"That's why he won't be ready to go for a while."

She nodded.

For a moment he wondered if he should've let her in the car. Everything he'd assumed about her was wrong. Who was she? "Doesn't explain why you needed to leave."

"I knew I was heading out this morning anyway, so I took a parting gift." She hugged her bag to her chest.

And there it was. A thief.

"What'd you take?"

"He pulled a picture, a painting, off the wall, and there was a safe. So, I asked him to open it, and he did. I had no idea it was even there. And he starts talking crazy about how I can never blow his cover."

"Ines," Jack interrupted. "What did you take?"

She turned her duffel sideways on her lap and unzipped it, then angled it toward Jack. He eased his foot off the accelerator, widening the gap between the Mercedes. In the bag he saw a stack of bills in various currencies, at least three passports, a pistol with two spare magazines.

"I didn't know what was in the bag. He opened the safe, shuffled a few things around, took out this book to show me. It was filled with pictures of people. Some famous. Some regular. By that point, he was mumbling. It didn't take long until he collapsed face first onto the book, eventually sliding off his stool onto the hard tile floor."

Opportunity had presented itself, and Ines took advantage.

She continued. "I grabbed the duffel and hurried back to where me and my friend were staying. Locked the bag in the car. My friend had balked at leaving, but I pressed, and she gave in."

"I hardly slept last night, which is why you found me asleep in the car you stole." Her expression changed to one of shock. "The car you stole. My friend's car, with me in it. And here I am, worried about petty theft."

Jack held up his hand. "One, I borrowed that car, and it's safely parked in a garage not far from where I found it. Two, what's in that bag is hardly petty theft. Not to the guy you took it from."

There was more he wanted to say but refrained. Few people had belongings stashed away like the guy had. Who needed three passports except for someone like Noble? He tossed a quick glance up at the sky. A sky full of faceless spies hovering above the stratosphere. Was the car being tracked by one of them?

Before ditching the BMW, he planned on copying the registration information.

They passed the border without incident. He didn't even notice until Ines pointed out they were in France. Thank God for the Schengen Agreement.

"You know this area?" he asked.

She shook her head. "Never been here before, but I need to stop. Haven't eaten since six yesterday."

"Bound to be a decent-size town here soon. We'll stop first place we have options."

What he didn't tell her was leaving her behind with the vehicle was *his* first option.

CHAPTER 13

THE SUNLIGHT KNIFED THROUGH BEAR'S EYES AND STABBED HIS brain. It felt like it had swollen to twice its regular size in a matter of seconds. He clenched his eyelids shut, then blinked a few times. The blurry haze lifted and soon all he felt was the warmth on his face cooling a second later as a gust of wind whipped past and lifted dead leaves off the grass and deposited them in the alley.

Mandy slammed the hospital door shut. She freed a slat from a nearby pallet and wedged it under the door handle. The wood grated against concrete until she couldn't move it anymore.

She grabbed Bear's hand and tugged him to the left. "See, like I said. A way out."

"What about the—"

"Keys?" They glinted in the sunlight as she dangled them in front of him while forcing a smile.

"Where'd you…"

She hesitated, allowing him time to finish. When he didn't, she said, "They were on a hook. Grabbed 'em. Figured if there wasn't a *dead-people-mobile* out here, they'd fit a car belonging to a doctor or whatever."

Bear took the keys from her and depressed the lock button on the black fob. The taillights of a hearse parked thirty feet away blinked red.

"Did good, kid."

That didn't seem to be any consolation to her. "Sasha?"

"She never found you?"

Mandy shook her head. Her gaze cast down at a muddy puddle confined to a pothole a foot from the building.

"Look," Bear said. "Sasha's as competent as I am. Probably more so. She'll be fine. But right now, I gotta worry about you. Someone is after us."

They both jerked their heads back toward the morgue as someone slammed against the door from inside. They hustled across the alley. Bear pressed the unlock key several times and yelled at Mandy to get in.

She climbed into the passenger seat as Bear used the roof to steady himself. He hadn't done anything close to attempting to climb in behind the wheel during his rehab. Wasn't even sure he could bend that way yet.

Bear yanked the door open and failed to get his foot over the threshold. He reached down, cupped his hand behind his knee, and lifted his leg into the air.

Mandy winced at the look on his face. "I can drive us out of here."

The banging against the door continued. Another gust of wind chilled his skin near his sweat-drenched collar as he lowered himself through the opening. He tightened his grip to steady his shaking arms.

"Bear," she said. "Climb into the back. I'll get us out of here."

The morgue door crashed open, slamming into the concrete wall like a crack of thunder. Bear fell back into the wedge between the door and frame and gripped the MP7 with both hands. The Black man who emerged from the opening lifted his hands in the air.

Bear recognized the orderly, said, "The hell are you doing?"

"I'm trying to help you," he said. "Thought they took you, or the girl."

"What's your deal, man? Why you so hell-bent on this?"

The guy took a couple steps forward. "She's too young to drive. You're not ready. Let me help you. Get you out of here. Come on. What do you say? Lower the gun."

Bear gripped the H&K tighter. His index finger grazed the trigger. Could he trust this guy? He couldn't come up with a single reason to do so.

"Stay put," Bear said.

From inside, another round of gunfire erupted. Sounded close. The orderly flinched, looked back, hopped to the side. He mouthed something, but Bear couldn't figure out what it was. Had to be some kind of warning.

There was shouting from within the morgue.

"Man down."

"Forget him, he's dead."

"They gotta be out there."

Bear waited for the first guy to emerge through the doorway. He didn't hesitate this time. Three rounds, all dead center. The guy went down in a heap.

The orderly whipped the door shut. He threw his shoulder into it and sprawled his legs out. "Go on. Get her out of here."

Bear looked inside the car. Mandy leaned over her armrest; tears slipped past her eyes as her gaze darted between Bear and the orderly.

"You gotta save him," she said.

Bear thumbed the fob again, and the liftgate on the rear of the vehicle rose. Shutting the driver's door, he told Mandy to scoot behind the wheel and get them out of there. Then he pulled the rear door open and leaned back against it.

"You," Bear yelled at the orderly. "Get in back."

Sweat beaded on the man's shaved head and slid down like streams. He was thin but strong. His forearm muscles rippled. "They'll get through."

Bear gestured with the MP7. "Let me worry about that. OK?"

The guy bared his teeth as though one final massive push would prevent the men on the other side from escaping.

"Now," Bear said. "For all we know half of them are looking for another way out."

The orderly looked toward the opening in the rear of the vehicle, presumably sizing it up. He pushed off the door, took two long lunges, and dove headfirst. Bear mashed the button again to close the liftgate before the guy had taken his second step. A beep signaled the gate's descent.

The morgue door crashed open. Bear didn't wait for someone to appear. He squeezed the trigger three times, hitting the door twice and the exterior wall once. A plume of decimated concrete rose and covered the area like white smoke.

Bear fell back into the vehicle and yelled, "Mandy, go!"

The girl hit the accelerator hard enough to spin the tires for a few seconds. When they began moving, the rear end fishtailed. For a second it looked like they would collide with the building. Before Bear could tell her how to correct, she figured it out and they raced down the alley behind the hospital.

Bear rolled his window down. Sirens approached. Finally. How the hell weren't they already there?

Mandy looked from the road back to him. "You take over."

"We can't stop," Bear said. "Hear those sirens?"

"They're here to help," she said.

He shook his head. "Not us. Not me, at least. We gotta roll, sweetie. And we gotta get past here before they block us in."

"Turn right here," the orderly said, threading his leg over the seat and plopping down next to Bear. "Then make your first left. That'll wind us through the woods. Cops won't come in that way."

Bear studied the man. How was it he had come to be so close when Mandy had been taken, and then again as they attempted escape? Was he one of them?

The orderly gripped his left hand with his right. He'd been shaking. Fresh sweat formed on his head. This wasn't a man used to this kind of activity.

"Really are a bleeding good Samaritan, huh?"

The orderly squinted back at Bear, had to process the meaning of the words. "I-I could just tell you were the kind of man who could get out alive."

"All those people racing down the hall got out alive."

"Did they?"

Mandy looked up at them in the rearview, her eyes wet and red. "Sasha?"

Bear held up a hand, in part to calm her, but also to block her penetrating stare. "Watch the road, sweetie. I'm sure we'll run into Sasha soon enough."

The orderly cast a look back at the hospital. "We're almost far enough. I can take over."

"Take over what?" Bear said.

"Driving."

"Nah, I'll do—"

"Are you kidding?" The orderly shook his head, pressed his thumb and middle finger against his closed eyes. "You can barely walk."

"I'm improving by the second," Bear said. "Besides, driving isn't walking."

"You don't know the roads here."

"You can tell me."

"What if we're chased? I can—"

"You know how to drive when being chased?" Bear watched the man for any tells indicating a lie.

The orderly lowered his head. "I just want to help."

Bear grabbed the driver's seat and leaned closer to Mandy. "How're you feeling? Think you can keep going?"

She nodded.

"How far to a train station?" He glanced over at the orderly.

"Five minutes, max." He pointed at the upcoming intersection. "Turn right here, then it'll be on the left in a couple kilometers. You can drop me off ahead."

"Nah, you're coming with us."

"What? Why?"

Bear couldn't answer that. Everything with the guy had been a coincidence, and he didn't like that. He had to keep the man close until they were in touch with Sasha again.

He bit down on his index finger and turned toward the window.

If they saw Sasha again.

CHAPTER 14

Clive stood at the rear of the room and watched his team move like a finely-tuned orchestra. The conductor of surveillance. Months of struggle and pain had led to this moment. And this moment was not without its difficulties. Was it ever? The hospital shooting had been unexpected. And after reflecting, he had no doubt it was related.

Who else was involved?

Lacy had moved a team into position at the hospital where they would meet up with Sadie, who Clive knew would not be pleased. She'd prefer to work alone rather than with a team she was unfamiliar with. She'd cite operational integrity or some other such nonsense. Clive would let her give her speech, then tell her tough luck.

The scenes played out on the big screens mounted across the walls. The crowds had thinned outside of the hotel in Luxembourg City. Yellow police tape blocked the entrance. Detectives had moved on and had been replaced by crime scene investigators who were taking pictures and collecting samples. Another monitor displayed a scrolling log of license plate numbers. The search net widened with every passing minute. An initial group of fewer than four highways available for escape had grown by several dozen, as every tributary became part of the search territory. Within a few hours the number of square kilometers they had to cover would reach a total too high for the team to effectively manage. They would be back where they started.

Despite this, Clive had little concern. There was no awful feeling gnawing at his gut. Why? Because they had Noble. They had him on tape. The most current version of him. And they could feed that through the system, and facial recognition software would pick him up the moment he showed up on a networked camera. They also had the license plate of the car he escaped in, which Isa located in a garage not far from the hotel. It took her less than thirty seconds to determine Noble had left there in a BMW M5. "Nice ride," had been Clive's comment. "Hope he enjoys it."

There hadn't been any hits on the vehicle. Yet. But it was only a matter of time. And the moment the license plate pinged or Noble's face was detected, the web would shrink again.

Clive turned his attention to the hospital. The situation was under control, but the cost had been severe. He surmised the body count would be upwards of twenty dead, and at least four times that many wounded.

He walked down the middle of the room and came to a stop in front of a fifty-five-inch Samsung, the screen split into eighths. Each rectangle played a video feed on a loop. He was sure there were dozens more cameras in the hospital. Someone had chosen to use these, though, so he watched with two of his analysts nearby. Was there something recorded they could use? He noted the reason for these specific feeds, and turned his head toward Isa. She glanced up in time to see him offer her a quick nod. Her half-hearted smile indicated his assumption was correct.

Each stream focused on a member of the hit team. In seven feeds, innocents fell. Some dead when they hit the floor. Others writhing in pain. He felt a knot in his stomach. Death was more a part of Clive's world than most. He had no qualms issuing the order to terminate a terrorist or rogue agent they'd hunted down. If his team showed up, you had done something to bring them there. He drilled that into his people, analysts and field operators alike. But innocents...he couldn't tolerate that.

"Lacy," he said. "If you can get the resources together, and if any of the hit team are left behind, we need to gather as much intel as we can from them. After this is all over, I want to hunt down the people behind this. I don't care if it's out of my own wallet."

The click-clack of keyboards and low hum of chatter ceased as his team focused on him. Had his conciliatory tone, which was always even, caught them off guard?

He ignored their stares. He watched the scenes on the Samsung one more time. When he reached the eighth feed, Clive froze. What had appeared to be footage of a throng of people streaming down the hallway like they were swept up in rapids contained something else. As the crowd thinned, a scene played out. A girl, maybe thirteen or fourteen, being dragged by one of the attackers.

And someone hunting them.

"Zoom in on that."

"What?"

He rushed to the display and placed his finger on the small feed. "This one. Hurry."

The other feeds gave way as the one that caught Clive's attention took over the screen. A large man stumbled across the hallway in pursuit.

"Can you get any closer?" Clive asked.

The image zoomed in on the big man. Clive's breath caught in his throat as he waited for the right moment. He didn't want to assume who the man was. The crowd had thinned. Stragglers continued to hurry down the hallway. They avoided the man. Then the guy turned his head.

"Freeze it!"

The video went still.

"Riley Logan," Clive said. He jabbed his finger at the nearest monitor. "Get his picture up now."

A few seconds later, three images of Riley "Bear" Logan were posted, all face shots.

"Got a profile?"

And there it was. The profile picture matched the still image from the video.

"What the bloody hell is going on?" Clive stepped back until he butted up against a cubicle wall. "Can anyone tell me what is happening here today?"

The team knew the history between Noble and Bear well. They'd studied it, from the two men meeting in Recruit Training at the age of eighteen, to their most recent business dealings. And now, not even four hundred kilometers apart, they were both involved in shooting events.

Isa stood next to Clive, disbelief on her face. "This can't be a coincidence, right?"

The reality of what was happening began to set in. "Someone is more than a step ahead of us." He turned toward Isa. "I need live feeds from the hospital. If they aren't gone, we need to pull our people back."

She called out to one of her team and multiple monitors began to pipe in the current streams from the hospital. The hallways looked like war zones, bodies strewn about, blood streaks across the floors. There were cops in tactical gear clearing the hospital room by room.

"I think they're gone," Isa said. "Who do you think is behind this?"

"Could be any number of people or groups or governments. Clearly what we've witnessed is a coordinated attack meant to take out both of these men. While we've been struggling to locate Noble for months, someone else had not only him in their sights, but Logan as well. First guess would be multiple government agencies, but I can't fathom them giving the go-ahead for the carnage at the hospital."

"So, who's that leave?" Isa asked.

Clive shook his head. There wasn't enough time to list all the possibilities. "Doesn't matter right now. What does is that we get these men off the streets. Whoever found them is not going to stop until they've completed the job."

Eddie alerted them to a new development. "You need to see this."

They all focused on the monitor as a new feed ran showing a scene behind the hospital.

"That's Logan," Clive said. "The girl must be the one he fostered."

"Mandy," Isa said.

"Do we have anything on her?"

"Very little. He's done well to shield her."

They watched as a second man joined them as Bear killed one of the attackers, and as they finally fled the alley.

Clive looked at Isa. "Get Sadie on the phone. Now."

CHAPTER 15

THE GAS-STATION-MARKET COMBO LOOKED LIKE ANY OF THE nondescript gas-station-market combos Jack would find on any exit on every highway back in the States. It provided an odd comfort. The cameras everywhere didn't. He glanced at Ines. Her hair draped over her shoulder. Her face angled toward the side window. It was best she was oblivious. But a nagging feeling had him wondering if she actually was.

The gas station offered six pumps. Four were occupied. He opted for the outside pump and pulled to a stop.

"Here's some cash." He handed Ines forty euros. "Grab some coffee and snacks." She reached for the money; he didn't let go. "Make sure it's fresh coffee. Don't bring back stale shit."

She rolled her eyes, slipped the cash in her pocket, and jogged to the store entrance. He kept watch over her even after she slipped inside. The sun reflected off the windows, making it difficult to track her movements after she moved past the first row of shelves.

The air carried that sweet smell of fresh-cut native grasses. It was a fragrance that fescue and Kentucky bluegrass just didn't produce. Thoughts of his childhood home filled his mind. Him and his brother nearly drowning trying to pet a manatee. His sister... He pushed the thought away before heading down that dark tunnel.

The pump clicked off and Jack shielded his eyes against the glare to catch a glimpse of the woman. She wasn't at the register or anywhere near the front of the store. The coffee must not have been fresh. Go figure.

He pulled open the rear door and moved the duffel bag from the backseat to the front. He just needed to get a few miles down the road, then he could check out the contents. Maybe figure out who the guy really was. Might be an asset Jack could use to get out of this mess.

Noble slid in behind the wheel, pushed the start button. The engine purred, ready to be put to the test. "Bad idea," he muttered to himself.

The entrance door swung open. Ines stood there, holding two cups of coffee stacked one on the other, and a white bag filled with snacks and whatever else she could get for forty euros. He had to move, and fast. He grabbed the passenger headrest and twisted in the seat to scan the area behind him. When he swung his head back around, Ines stood there with her mouth open, eyebrow raised. One cup of coffee tumbled to the ground, then the other. They crashed on top of each other, a puddle spread out at her feet. She didn't move. The bag fell next. Jack looked back again.

"Son of a bitch."

The first of three vans hopped the median and then the curb and into the parking lot. It veered to the right. The next to the left. And the third was heading straight for the BMW. Jack had the pedal to the floor before shifting into first gear. The tires squealed and spun and the car drifted right then left before gripping the asphalt and charging forward. Everything played out in clips as time slowed. Jack whipped the wheel and spun in a tight circle. The first van nearly caught his rear end. The van jerked as it came to a stop. Ines screamed loud enough he heard it over the commotion surrounding them.

The second van pulled to a stop next to him. The third van went from thirty to stopped in an instant. Two hooded men were up front. One produced a pistol that glinted in the sun.

He was pinned in. Stuck in a corner. The worst place to be. And the worst place to put Jack Noble. He stepped on the accelerator and veered to the left. The van couldn't mimic the BMW's movements. Their only chance was to shoot.

And they did.

The first bullet smashed the rear driver's side glass. It shattered into a thousand small fragments which rained across the interior. Aside from a small flinch, the shot failed to faze Jack. He glanced over, meeting the closest man's stare. It wasn't long enough for him to even recall the guy's face, yet there was a hint of recognition there. Who was the guy? Who were these people? Questions for later. For now, he had to get out.

Another shot.

The rear window shattered. The bullet blew through the passenger headrest and embedded in the dash.

Jack reached the road. Crossing into the flow of traffic was impossible. The steady stream of cars was equivalent to a class three rapid. He did the only thing he could do and turned into oncoming traffic. The nimble M5 handled the herky-jerky driving style as though it were the dirt bike his father had given him and his brother Sean when Jack turned ten. But the traffic thickened ahead. Worse, a three-foot railing occupied the median. He'd have to pull into another parking lot or take his chances with slamming the brakes and spinning halfway around in the middle of the road. One glance in the rearview told him that was a bad idea. The van was gaining ground.

Ahead, the traffic light remained stuck on red. A line of cars coming off the highway were approaching the intersection, about to turn in his direction. He veered toward the median, added thirty kilometers to his speed and tried to outrace them. It became obvious he wouldn't be able to. Coming off the highway, there were two turn lanes. He laid on the horn as advanced warning. Best case scenario they'd move just enough for him to cross the intersection and switch to the right side of the road, while causing enough congestion behind him to slow the van down.

It only took a few seconds to reach the underpass. Flashing high beams and laying on the horn, Jack scraped against the median to avoid the first car in his way. And then the worst happened. Everyone stopped.

He slammed the brakes. A second car clipped the BMW's fender. It fishtailed and the opposite fender hit the median rail hard. Jack struggled to regain control of the vehicle. The impending collision from behind loomed large.

For a moment, he was on the field again, holding the ball with three receivers out, draped in coverage. A blitzer coming free from behind. A hole, ever so slight, opened up between the guard and tackle, and Jack took it.

The sound of the van slamming into an innocent's small Citroen was enough to make even Jack cringe. But he didn't look back. His path to freedom had been cut off by a refrigerated box truck that took up the entire intersection.

One option remained. One window of opportunity to escape.

The offramp.

Riding the shoulder, Jack hugged the curved road doing fifty, which was twenty more than a safe speed. The cars he passed honked and jerked to the opposite narrow shoulder, giving him just enough room to skate past. At the top, he merged with the flow of traffic on the motorway and did his best to blend in for five miles. The upcoming exit offered nothing of value to him other than a chance to get off the road, roll down the windows, and catch his breath.

A few minutes later, he was a quarter-mile down a road that was little more than a dirt path overgrown with brush. A slight breeze wafted through the sedan, carrying with it the sweet smell of those native grasses again. Wiping his brow, he could've killed for a beer, but had to make do with the last swallow of lukewarm water. The crumpled bottle found its way under the driver's seat.

He stepped out, stretched, scanned his surroundings. Nothing but fields and woods in every direction. Even the road was out of sight. For the first time all day, he felt anonymous, that no one was watching. And because of that, he took his first deep breath in hours.

He reached into the passenger side and grabbed the duffel bag. Guessing at the contents, he estimated it weighed around twenty pounds. A computer for sure. Some cash, visible and hidden. Passports, IDs. The pistol and spare magazines.

"Only one way to find out."

The zipper caught and gave way after a minor struggle. He reached in and pulled out three stacks of money. Euros, US dollars, and Great Britain Pounds. Something he might have in a safe deposit box. Next, he fished out four wallets, followed by an equal number of passports, all of which he laid side by side on the BMW's hood.

"Who are you?" he muttered. "Why would you drug the girl?"

He dumped the remaining contents, a scarf, a jacket, some snacks, onto the hood and sorted through it quickly. He retrieved and inspected the H&K VP9. It was ready to go with one in the chamber. He aimed down the sights, assumed they were good to go, too. The duffel still had some weight to it, so Jack went to work finding the hidden compartment. It didn't take long. He found more cash, promissory notes, and a steel wallet with twenty-four words etched on it. Cryptocurrency. Might be a good amount, might be nothing. He'd get Brandon on it when they next talked. If they talked.

Satisfied he had removed all of the bag's contents, he turned his attention to the wallets and passports. The one that caught his eye looked like a standard issue United States of America passport. That's where he started. He peeled back the wallet, thumbed the first page over, and then he dropped it on the ground.

"Son of a bitch."

He grabbed the next.

"Gotta be kidding me."

He went through the other two, then the wallets. How could this be? These weren't off some douchebag. They were…

"Jack, it's over. It's time to come in."

He looked over his shoulder, dumbfounded that the woman standing in front of him was Ines.

CHAPTER 16

THE SERENE COUNTRYSIDE COMPRISED OF ALTERNATING COW pastures and lavender fields lulled Bear into a false sense of security. His pulse, which had been near maxed out since the first gunshot, had leveled off at a respectable eighty beats per second. Until his thoughts turned back to Sasha.

Had she made it out of the hospital? He had her cell phone number memorized, but this wasn't the time to call. They might have her, and any call would tip them off to his location.

"Why are we going so far?" Mandy asked. "It's been twenty minutes. I thought you said the train station was only five minutes away."

The orderly glanced at Bear. The man was part of the reason Bear chose to go to the next town. The group that had coordinated the attack at the hospital likely had the train station staked out. Presumably, they'd have someone at the next station, too. But the train schedule worked in Bear's favor. He'd take out the orderly and ditch the car, and he and Mandy would keep switching trains until they were on the other side of France. There they'd lay low until he could make arrangements to get them to England. Sasha would be there. He knew it.

The orderly slowed the vehicle down and started veering toward a narrow shoulder bordered by a deep ditch. He kept his gaze fixed on the road ahead.

"The hell you doing?" Bear said.

The orderly didn't answer.

"You might think I'm incapable of taking you out—"

"I saw what you did back there," he said. "Look, I just want to get out. The train station is ahead. If those people are there..." The man's eyes misted over. "I don't want to be there." He jerked the car to a stop, turned in his seat, pointed at Mandy. "She shouldn't be there, either. Why would you put the girl in this position?"

"She's safest with me."

"How is that possible? You are a dead man walking."

Bear chuckled. "I have been for the past two decades. Doesn't mean she's not safest with me."

The man started to speak. Bear cut him off.

"What are you gonna do to defend her? Help her? Get her to safety? Do you have contacts in the DSGE or MI6? Nah, they'll wreck you, then they'll take her, and make her bait. Then they'll finish the job they failed at the hospital. And guess what? You die. She dies. We all die."

The man wiped his sweat-soaked forehead and dried his hands off on his pants.

Bear continued. "You want to bounce, do it, bro. I doubt you're any use to us anyway."

The guy opened the door and stepped out. Bear met him around the front of the car.

Bear put his hands on the guy's shoulders. "Look, I appreciate you getting us this far. You can give me your name and a contact number, and I'll make sure you're taken care of."

"I don't know if that's a good idea."

"Those people, they wanted me dead because I did the right thing. They'll have footage. They'll know you were with us."

"Are you trying to convince me to give you my info, or stay with you?"

Bear wasn't sure anymore. His thoughts of ditching the orderly didn't seem quite right now. "How important is living to you?" Bear waited for the guy to respond. "Let me rephrase that. How important is a quick and painless death to you? 'Cause if they get a hold of you, you're dead. But I guarantee it won't be quick, and it won't be painless."

The orderly nodded and went back to the driver's side of the vehicle.

Five minutes later, they pulled into the lot for the small train station. There were few cars outside of a section dedicated to a couple of car rental companies. Activity outside the terminal was minimal. An elderly couple waited on a bench, their canes nestled together in between them. A mother watched her kids play. The girl with pigtails was doing cartwheels.

The trio remained in the vehicle for a few silent minutes. Mandy spoke first.

"Does it look OK to you?"

"You tell me," Bear said. He'd been training the girl for a while. Her instincts were on point, but her mind got in the way. Most people suffered from this. It's what separated people like Jack and Bear from the rest of the population.

"The only possible threat comes from within," she said.

"How so?"

"The old couple, they aren't a concern. And that lady is watching her kids too intently to be any danger to us."

"Who is then?"

"Those car rental kiosks." Mandy pointed at the Hertz Sixt and Europcar signs. A single building away from the station housed all three companies. One person patrolled inside. "But he looks weak. I could take him out."

"You could." Bear paused a beat to see if she would continue. "So, what's that leave us with?"

"Whoever is inside the station."

"Good girl, Mandy." He opened his door and hefted himself out. He felt steadier than he had all day. Whether adrenaline or confidence, he hoped the effects didn't wear off any time soon. "Now let's go see what's waiting for us inside."

The orderly was there the few times Bear stumbled, keeping him upright. As they approached, the elderly woman looked up, smiled, then went back to her crossword puzzle. The cartwheeling girl ran up to Mandy and asked her something French. Mandy blushed, unable to reply quickly enough. Her French wasn't terrible, but she hadn't reached a point of mastery yet.

Inside, they purchased a rail pass good for six rides. They had just missed the last train. The next would arrive in ten minutes. Depart in twenty. Too much time. Bear imagined a dartboard, with the hospital at the bullseye. There would be surveillance showing the direction they had turned when leaving the hospital. From there, every mile, every right or left turn, expanded that circle, but they were still within an inch of the bullseye in the grand scheme of things.

The orderly plopped down in a chair, folded his arms, tucked his chin to his chest. Poor guy had no idea his day would turn out like this. But he couldn't turn into Jell-O yet. Not until they were on the train. Bear planned to keep him around for one or two changeovers. Then it would be time to put him to sleep. For a bit.

"Eyes up," Bear said.

The man didn't look up.

"Eyes up," Bear repeated. "Can't let our guard down yet."

"What am I supposed to do?"

"Just look for anything suspicious."

The orderly shook his head as he struggled to get out of the chair. The moment of respite had sapped him of his strength. Bear had seen it hundreds of times before. He'd experienced it plenty himself, even before his surgery.

"There's the train," Mandy said.

Bear glanced at the clock. "Ahead of schedule. God bless the French."

The orderly chuckled. "Haven't spent much time here, have you?"

"Let's go." Bear grabbed Mandy's hand and started toward the platform. A couple hundred steps stood between them and the chance to expand that circle. He had it mapped out in his mind. They just had to get on that train.

The train squealed to a stop. A warm gust of wind blew past carrying with it a myriad of smells that conjured up images in Bear's mind of Yankee Stadium. The train hissed as it settled. The doors opened. A handful of people exited and walked off in a line. No one took notice of the odd threesome making their way toward the train.

Each step felt lighter than the last. A hundred feet. Fifty. Twenty. They'd be at the door in a moment. He felt his knees weaken and stumbled. The orderly swept in and caught him. An employee took note but stopped short of coming to help. Bear pushed forward. The orderly held him back.

"What is it?"

"Anything suspicious, right?" the orderly muttered.

Bear didn't wait for him to continue. He followed the man's gaze down the platform toward the front of the train.

He couldn't believe what he saw.

Who he saw.

The tanned skin.

Dark hair that hung in curls.

Eight or nine years older than the last time he'd seen her.

Beautiful as she had been a decade ago.

She paused and gasped. It hit her the same way it had him. Only she knew what she was about to run into.

"Bear," Mandy said. "What is it?"

Bear struggled to speak. He didn't have to take his eyes off the woman to know they were done. He heard the shuffling of feet coming from behind the station entrance and from the other end of the train. In his peripheral, he saw two armed men exit the train just feet away.

They were done.

"Bear?" Mandy pleaded now. "What's wrong? Why aren't we going?"

"We're not going, sweetie."

"Why?"

The woman tried to smile, but it came across as a grimace rather than whatever she might have meant. Mandy finally saw her.

"Who is that? Is she a friend?"

"She was."

"Was?"

"Yeah."

"Who is she?"

"Sadie."

PART 2

CHAPTER 17

THE OLD WOMAN HANDED CLARISSA A FOLDED NOTE. THICK, heavy stock paper that felt more like a paperweight. An amazing thing, she thought, how a single piece of paper was so flimsy and easy to damage. But if folded over a dozen times, the sharpest blade could do minimal damage.

Mrs. Calabase failed to greet Clarissa with her trademarked smile connecting her mouth and eyes. She didn't offer the familiar Italian proverb as she had every other day when Clarissa stopped by her stand. Fear basked in her watery eyes when she grabbed Clarissa's wrist in a death lock, turned her hand over, and dropped the paperweight-note into her palm.

Clarissa had attempted to open it there, not understanding that the contents would be life-altering. Her first thought was the old woman had finally decided to give up her lasagna recipe. Mrs. Calabase shook her head and mouthed, "Get out," before turning away and leaving her shop unattended.

So, she left with her nightly vegetables and chicken and took a roundabout way to her nondescript apartment in the nondescript little village perched atop the northern Italian mountains. The sun dipped behind the highest parts of town. Shadows stretched until they encompassed the alley. Many stands along the narrow roads had already been converted into outdoor dining for the dozens of small restaurants. How they managed to stay open in a place that had long ago seen its best days kept Clarissa guessing. There were no jobs. No youth remaining behind. No money. Yet everyone seemed happy.

Except for Mrs. Calabase on this day.

Clarissa wound her way to her apartment. The smell of pasta and fish saturated the air. She almost stopped at her favorite place where a plate of food cost five euros, and a full carafe of wine even less. Many nights had been spent there. Most of them alone. Some of the best had been when Jack Noble had found her months ago while he was on the run. They lived the way she had always dreamt they would if they could have ever survived as a couple. It never lasted. Not in New York. Not in Italy. It was always the same. One day, she'd wake up and he was gone. Her logical mind understood it was for the better. But you know what? To hell with logic. She would've gone with him.

She had been awake when he left. She heard him say to her, "If you're hearing this, I'll be in one town over for the next ten hours."

She never went.

Why should she? He assumed she was asleep, and that's the only reason he said it. Besides, he'd become toxic. Hurt and pain followed him everywhere. Bear knew it. Clarissa knew it. Hell, even Jack knew it.

The earlier interaction with the old woman left Clarissa apprehensive, so she hung back for a bit and monitored her front door. The old building had tiny windows, making it impossible to see inside.

She looked down at the note. Curiosity was getting the better of her. But knowing it could contain anything, she decided it would be better to open it in the relative safety of her apartment.

Crossing the street, Clarissa was on high alert. Every noise coming from every open window sent her spiraling. Was that a gunshot? Or someone slamming a door shut? She hurried the final twenty feet, unlocked her door, and went inside.

The still air lingered, still fragrant with the candle she had burned earlier that day. A quick glance indicated nothing had been disturbed. She dropped to a knee and lowered her head until her cheek was an inch off the floor. There she confirmed the tripwire was in place. The only way in and out was through the front door. No one would miss disturbing the thread. There were still times Clarissa missed it and tore it free from the wall on her way out.

Rising to her feet, she dusted her elbows and knees off. "Now get it together, girl. Maybe a glass of wine would help?" she muttered, and added, "Can't hurt."

She poured a glass of a local red table wine. The anticipation of that first sip made her face flush, her mouth water. She pulled it in, held it in her mouth for a moment, then tipped her head back. The wine warmed her throat, chest, stomach.

"Now, time to see what you are all about, my folded friend."

She set the note on the table and went to work dismantling the intricate locking system the writer had used. For as heavy as the paper was, the contents were quite minimal. Clarissa's throat caught as she tried to read it aloud. She took another sip of wine.

"You have approximately forty-eight hours from the time Mrs. Calabase hands this to you. Get out and get far away much sooner than two days from now. They almost have you now. Their movements thus far indicate they will know your general location very soon. Once they reach the town, you will never escape. You should leave tonight. Pick a direction and go. The further you can be from here, the better. They will track you down. They will find you. They will take you. They will kill you."

She held the unsigned note for five minutes, repeating the words until they had turned into a mantra of sorts. Her glass had spilled over during the second reading. Wine dripped off the edge of the table onto her lap.

Banging on the door ripped her from the meditative state. Clarissa shifted into the person she had struggled to abandon. She inventoried the kitchen, the one she had spent months in and could barely remember which drawer had the knives. But in that instant, she knew the weight and size and location of each one. She grabbed two, one for attack and the other to defend, and headed to the door.

The banging persisted. What was the point? They'd get the attention of everyone around. The guys here might be old, but they loved Clarissa and would band together to protect her.

"Who is it?"

No answer, just more banging.

"I can kill you."

No answer, just more banging.

"For Christ's sake." She unlocked the door, pulled it open, jumped back three feet, landing at the ready.

The old woman retreated a step before emboldening herself and entering the apartment.

Clarissa let the knives drop to the floor as she reached for the woman. "Mrs. Calabase, what are you doing here?"

"My dear, I had to bring you this." Her accent was thick, but her English perfect. She pulled her shawl off her arm. Resting on her forearm was a weathered wooden box. She shoved it toward Clarissa. "These were my husband's. The last ones he purchased before he passed on. I have no idea if either works."

Clarissa didn't immediately reach for the box. "Either of what? Mrs. Calabase, what is going on? Who gave you that note?"

She waved the younger woman off. "This is of no concern. It does not matter who gave me the note. What matters is I saw the souls of a thousand dead killers in that man's eyes. They were black, the color of his soul."

Clarissa wanted to reason with the woman, but she wouldn't stop.

"He won't take you or kill you. He will devour your soul, and you will be lost forever. Your energy will never move on as he will feast on it for the remainder of his eternal life."

The old woman had lost it, Clarissa was convinced. Maybe she had even penned the note herself.

"Take this." Mrs. Calabase jammed the box into Clarissa's stomach hard enough Clarissa coughed. "I must go now. I have to leave this place."

"Leave? Where will you go?" Clarissa reached into her pocket for loose bills. It was the only thing she could think to do.

"My daughter... No, this is none of your concern. I shouldn't tell you, and you must not tell me where you are going. Do you understand?"

"No." The whole situation was getting weirder by the moment.

The old woman let go of the box and retreated backward to the door. She reached behind and grabbed the latch. Before disappearing into the darkening night, she said, "Please, dear, leave tonight."

Clarissa rushed to the door, but Mrs. Calabase was already out of sight.

The town felt as though it had thousands of eyes, all focused on Clarissa. She closed the door and locked it, went back to the kitchen, placed the box on the table. A worn string wrapped in figure eights served as a latch. She unwound it, being careful not to pull too hard, then opened the lid.

The pistol caught her attention first. Mr. Calabase had upgraded recently, and the 9mm Beretta was a perfect fit for Clarissa. She removed the magazine, broke it down, inspected it, and put it back together. It was a well-maintained pistol with only a hint of ever having been shot. She fitted the inside-the-waistband holster and laid the additional magazines out on the table.

Next to the pistol was a key to a Vespa she'd never seen Mrs. Calabase riding. She hoped it was as recent a purchase as the Beretta. Clarissa ran to the door with the pistol in hand and stepped out into the night. Silvery wisps of clouds raced overhead, blocking out the moon for seconds at a time. She stepped around the corner of the building and saw the scooter waiting there. The gas fumes lingered in the air. Not wanting to wait until the final minute to find out her mode of transportation was a lemon, Clarissa hopped on and started it on the first key turn.

"Perfect," she whispered.

On her way inside, she debated that word. How could this situation be perfect? The past several months had seen her friendship, which was more of an on-again-off-again relationship with Beck crumble to the point he told her to get away and stay out of his life or he'd have her arrested for what went down.

She locked herself inside the apartment again and returned to the kitchen.

"One more glass, kiddo."

Her thoughts turned to what had happened. She still couldn't figure out why Beck turned on her. Why he believed she was at fault. That she could even do something like take the money. She cursed him for putting her through this and realized maybe it was better that she run now. At first, she had hoped it was Beck who had delivered the letter. But the way Mrs. Calabase spoke of the man who had, Clarissa knew it wasn't him. The man had his flaws and could be more intense than anyone she knew, even Jack.

But his eyes were kind. Even in their darkest moments, his eyes were a beacon of light.

She glanced around the kitchen and decided there was nothing worth bringing, so she headed upstairs to her bedroom. A small backpack was already packed. Her bug out bag should something bad happen. That's what this was, right? Something bad about to happen.

Before leaving her room for the last time, she grabbed one last memento. The jacket Jack had left behind. She pulled it on and felt swamped in it. And she loved how that felt.

CHAPTER 18

As far as prison cells went, this one ranked top two. The comfortable cot could have been mistaken for a Tempur-Pedic. A bookshelf hung overhead, filled with a few bestsellers from various genres. The toilet had a lid and a rolling writing desk sat next to it.

"What the hell do people do in here?" Noble muttered. He rested against the wall; his legs stretched out on the mattress. A day had passed since he'd been detained by the one person in Europe he hadn't suspected being out for him. Hell of a ruse that woman pulled off. *Ines.* Had that been the only truth to come out of her mouth? Was it even a truth? One of the passports had the name, but that meant nothing. Jack had a dozen passports stashed in various banks and deposit boxes and at his properties.

None said *Jack Noble*.

He felt a slight twinge in his gut at the thought. Years ago, before he sold his soul, he still had his name. And that meant something. He had the chance to leave the business. His favorite bar in the Keys could've been his. His retirement fund, he called it, as they hammered out the details. The place wasn't much. But he didn't need much. Just a little tavern, off the beaten path, enough to suit a few regulars and the couple of tourists who'd wander in. With everything that had happened the past few years, he questioned why he backed out.

He chuckled at the thought. It hadn't been him that backed out. Frank

Skinner had gotten involved. Jack had no proof. But Skinner had the means to make things happen. Things like an accidental grease fire that claimed the lives of the owner and his daughter and burned the bar to the ground.

Two more souls Noble would have to account for on his reckoning day.

The only thing Jack backed out of was the life of a beach bum. He let Skinner talk him into returning, then everything went to shit.

And once again, everything had gone to shit, but at least Frank Skinner could no longer reach him. Or so he thought. Sure seemed like the guy was doing a good job from the grave.

Jack hopped off the bed and did fifty pushups, then fifty jump squats. He worked out the crick in his neck and his tight hip.

With his mind clear, he replayed the scene in the field. He hadn't heard them coming. Hadn't noticed Ines creeping up. Hadn't heard the five vans bouncing along the overgrown dirt road.

Instincts took over, as they always did. He could have taken Ines out; dealt with whoever remained. However, a small voice told him to stand down. The net surrounded him. If he got away, he'd be back to living on the run, and the first few days of that life were a bitch. All days were, if he was honest with himself. And he realized, if they wanted him dead, Ines could've pulled the trigger in the parking garage as they stole the BMW. *Her BMW?* He had plenty of questions, and so far, no one had said a word to him other than asking how he liked his steak.

Steak.

In a prison cell.

Maybe they were going to kill him?

Jack stiffened at the soft tones emanating from the keypad on the other side of the door. The electronic latch disengaged. The door crept open, swinging into the hallway. Three feet past the threshold stood an imposing man holding a nightstick. At least one more person would be outside, shielded by the door, and Jack figured someone was waiting out of view to the left.

"Steak again? Medium rare, as usual," Jack said. "Or are you springing for lobster for dinner?"

"Get up." The guy looked to his right, revealing a spiderweb tattoo crawling up his neck and disappearing into his hair. Was the spider up there?

"Taking me out tonight, big guy? I won't put out. At least, not without a hefty amount of bourbon."

"I said, get up."

"Yeah, that can be a problem. Whisky dick is a real thing."

The man nodded at someone Jack couldn't see. A moment later, a shield covered most of the opening as a green gas plumed from underneath and enveloped the room. The stream stopped. The door slammed shut. Jack's head felt light, lifted. Not the most familiar feeling, but one he'd experienced time to time.

It might've been a minute later, or half a day, when the door opened again. He didn't know, he didn't care. The soft tones of the keypad recalled a song from his youth.

The door swung open. The big man looked like an ogre, and Jack told him as much. Seemed the guy fought back a smile. Jack had enough self-awareness to know his sober humor grated on most. But when he was under the influence, he was the funniest guy he knew.

Too bad no one agreed.

The person hiding had no problem entering now. Even if Jack wanted to kill him, his motor skills were so out of tune now, he would've broken his own neck.

"Put these on." She held out a pair of nylon cuffs.

"I barely know you."

She grinned. "After what I'm gonna do to you, it's best you don't."

Jack held out his hands and let her bind his wrist. "You're gonna have to cut up my steak."

"All right, lover boy," the ogre said. "Let's get you down to interrogation."

"My favorite part of the day."

Whatever they had gotten him high with wore off quicker than it hit. Jack went from floating on a cloud to rediscovering how to walk in about two seconds. The ogre chuckled. Presumably, he too had been under the effects of the green dream a time or two. They had to work on their delivery method, though. There was no way some didn't seep out into the hallway.

They traveled through a labyrinth of hallways, each looking like the last. White walls, ceilings, floors. Nothing to break up the whiteness. The effect on his mind was enough that Jack began questioning the last year of his life. Had he killed Skinner? Had he been on the run? Maybe they took him down on that street in France and Skinner had him committed.

"It's the drugs," he muttered.

"What?" the woman asked.

Jack ignored her. He had a reality to rebuild.

"All right, princess," the ogre said. "Here's your next stop."

Jack turned to the woman. "Coming in with me?"

"You wouldn't want that."

"I want lots of things I shouldn't."

"Like what?"

"World peace."

"That's a bad thing?"

"I'd be out of a job."

She glanced at his bound wrists. "I mean, you suck at it anyway."

The ogre shoved Jack into the room and the door clicked shut before he could retort. Now he faced another looming uncertainty. Who caught him and why hadn't they killed him?

The spartan room offered little in the way of clues. Three metal chairs all angled to face each other. Nothing else. Cold air piped in from a vent that ran the length of the room. It was painted white, like everything else he'd seen. It didn't stink. It didn't smell good. It had no odor.

Five minutes passed. Jack paced wall-to-wall, corner-to-corner, around the chairs. As a kid, he'd invent games based on pacing. Now it just helped filter the voices in his head. They'd change based on the direction he walked.

"Take a seat." The voice boomed over a speaker Jack couldn't see. He pointed at a chair. "Yes, that one." The room contained a hidden camera as well.

He tried to pull the closest chair out but found it anchored to the floor. At least they wouldn't beat him with it. He took his seat and waited another five minutes during which time it felt as though the temperature dropped ten degrees.

"I hope the delay is due to the coffee you're brewing for me." He could go for a mug. "And don't bring any of that shit instant Folgers. I need high octane."

The wall opened from a crease he couldn't see and a tall gentleman wearing a suit with no tie entered the room. He had a mug in one hand, and a tablet in the other.

"That for me?" Jack said.

"No."

"The coffee."

"No."

"Can I get a cup?"

"Depends."

"On what?"

"On how you answer my first question."

Jack waited a couple beats for the guy to continue. "Not a mind reader, buddy. You gonna ask it, or…?"

"Your dossier revealed you were a bit of a—"

"Smart ass? Pain in the ass? Asshole? Something with ass, I'm sure."

"Right."

"I can see you're the kind of British dude I don't get along with."

The man smiled at Jack, turned toward what Jack presumed was the camera, and made a gesture. He returned his gaze to his prisoner. "Doesn't matter if we get along, Mr. Noble."

"Mister."

"Mister. Anyway, I just have some questions for you, and based on the answer to those questions, I will determine the best use for you, if any."

"What happens if I don't meet the qualifications?"

"You'll never leave."

CHAPTER 19

Jack's grin lingered longer than it should have for a man who was informed his life might be over. The smile on the British man's face dissipated into a tight-lipped expression somewhere between anger and constipation.

"Perhaps you think I am playing around?"

"Not really."

"Are you sure? You quite appear to think this is a game."

"Listen up, Paul or Robert or whatever the hell your name is. You don't scare me. That ogre out in the hallway doesn't scare me. The woman who put these on me"—he lifted his bound wrists "—actually, she kinda scares me, but in a good way. You know, an exciting way."

"What the bloody hell is your point?"

"My point is death doesn't scare me. I've been close to dying more times than you've stood to piss the past five years. So, if you wanna kill me, then get it the hell over with right now. If you have some use for me, tell me now. But, whatever you do, cut these goddamn bindings off my wrist because the shit is cutting my circulation off, and I'm no good to anyone without my hands."

The man stared stone-faced at Noble for a few more seconds, then glanced at the camera and nodded. The door opened. A stale gust of air wafted past. The woman stepped around the empty chair and stood in front of Jack. She produced a six-inch knife and gestured for him to lift his hands.

"Be gentle," he said.

She made sure to nick his right thumb.

The nylon cuffs fell to the floor. She kicked them out of the way. "Let me see your hand."

"It's OK."

"Let me see it."

He agreed, half-expecting her to put his thumb in her mouth. He was disappointed when she didn't, instead tending to the wound.

"Can we get to the point now?" Jack stared at the woman in front of him.

"My name is Clive," the man said. "I operate a team of highly skilled independent contractors—"

"Mercenaries," Jack said.

"No." Clive pulled his shoulders back and re-focused. "And if you cut me off again, she won't have a simple flesh wound to tend to."

Jack looked up at the woman and noted her smile had grown. She winked before taking a seat next to him.

Clive continued. "My team is all manner of specialists, from tech people, to surveillance, to social media experts. We have field operatives, perhaps you would call them mercenaries, but they are the best of the best from global Special Forces, US Marshals, CIA, MI6, and a couple, what the hell do they call themselves, Dirty Dog detectives, whatever in the name of Tupac that is."

"Are they any good?"

"We caught you," the woman said.

"That we did," Clive said.

"I chose not to run," Jack said.

The woman laughed. "Ines would've shot you."

"No, she wouldn't have."

"Why not?"

"She was too conflicted."

The woman and Clive both laughed.

Funniest guy in the room.

"She would have," Clive said. "She played you well, though. I was impressed you got out of her sight the way you did."

"Did she know?" Noble asked.

"That reinforcements were incoming?"

Jack nodded.

"In a roundabout way. She was on her own, but we had been waiting for tags on the BMW to pop up again, and when they did, we had a team nearby."

"Guess she did play me well."

"Don't feel bad," Clive said. "She's snared tougher game than you."

"Ouch." Noble feigned hurt. "I have a question."

"Go ahead."

"How'd you know to have her in that car? I could've gone out the front door first, missed the bullet, and ran."

Clive smiled as he adjusted his cuffs. "No, you couldn't have."

"Screw you, anything could've happened."

"Walk me through those moments before the journalist died."

The thoughts caught in Jack's head. From what he could tell so far, this man would not ask a question he did not know the answer to. They were there, whether in person or watching through video. They were there the entire time.

"You had eyes on me," Jack said.

Clive neither confirmed nor denied. "Tell me what happened before he was shot."

Jack closed his eyes and replayed the scene after stepping out of the elevator. Some faces remained, others were blurred out now, not worth remembering. He passed through the lobby. There was a small crowd between the front desk and the entrance doors. They had to pass through these people. At the time, he figured this was the best approach. It gave him a little cover, a bit of interference. He was ahead of Schreiber, but then something happened.

It wasn't a full-on body check, but it had been enough to slow him down. His eyes were on the street. The person was only in front of him for a moment. The guy...no, the woman, apologized in German. Had he looked at her? His eyes flicked to the left. The hair dark, her smell lingered. Lemongrass. Was there more? His eyes flicked up from her shoulders. To her face.

"You gotta be kidding me," Jack said. "You knew what was about to happen?"

Clive shook his head. "Wish I could take credit for it. Ines knew of the journalist and his trip to Luxembourg. It was a hunch, nothing more. Ines went and waited. She never told us. We didn't know where she was."

"She let Schreiber walk to his death." Jack stumbled over the words, the thought, and finally, the realization it would've been him who had his head blown off, not the journalist, if not for Ines.

"She saved your life," the woman said.

"Why?" Jack had trouble understanding the subsequent chain of events. "Why didn't she just have you come in then?"

"The city was too hot," Clive said. "And we didn't know what was happening. We only saw it moments after it went down."

"Still, you could've jumped in. What if I had figured out she wasn't who she said? What if I had opened the duffel bag before we left the garage?"

Clive offered nothing more than a shrug. "Then she might've died."

"And you're OK with that."

"It's not that he's OK with it," the woman said.

"Sorry," Jack interrupted. "What's your name?"

"That's not important."

"Why not?"

"Because you'll never see her again," Clive said.

"Something tells me that's a lie," Jack said.

Clive's smile returned. "Look, we can discuss all this in the near future if you accept my offer. Hell, I'll tell you more about yourself and your closest friends than you would ever want to know."

Jack remained silent for the next minute, and no one else spoke. The conversation had reached a point where it could only travel in one direction. Was he ready to hear what was waiting for him? Could he accept whatever they offered? And if he didn't, what came next?

"Not saying I'm accepting anything, but, what's in it for me?"

"Other than living?" Clive said.

"Already told you that doesn't work on me. If I'm dead, I'm dead."

Clive opened his mouth to speak, and Jack cut him off.

"And don't even think about threatening my family. There are systems in place that will rain hellfire down upon you should you come close to any of them."

"I'm not a monster, Mr. Noble."

"We'll see about that."

"Work with me, complete this task, and we'll clear your name. I have a treasure trove of intelligence on Frank Skinner that will show the world you did everyone a favor when you acted upon information that no one, not even your top security officials, has ever seen."

"I do your job; you clear my name."

"Correct."

"Clear my name and give me a fresh new identity so I can drop out of this forever."

"Correct. But, first, I want you to take the night to think it over."

"I think my brain would work better if fueled by steak and lobster and beer. Good beer, too. No damn Pabst. I'm not a hipster."

"Consider it done." Clive turned and the hidden door opened. "Lacy, take him to his new room."

Lacy led him to the hallway. For the first time, Jack noticed she had a slight limp.

Ogre was no longer present. No one was, though Jack knew they were being watched the entire time.

"So, Lacy," Jack said. "Wanna have steak and lobster with me tonight?"

Her hardened exterior broke for a moment and a smile spread across her lips. "I'm vegan."

"I'm OK with you breaking your lifestyle for a night."

"And I'm a lesbian."

He shrugged.

"You really are quite full of yourself, Mr. Jack Noble. Anyone ever tell you that?"

"I got a drawer full of t-shirts with that written on them."

She stopped in front of a door. "This is you."

"Doesn't look like where I was earlier."

"You're part of the team now."

"I haven't accepted anything."

"You will."

"How do you know?"

"I know." She turned and walked away. "See ya tomorrow."

He enjoyed watching her walk away until the latch clicked and the door swung outward, blocking the view. Jack took a deep breath and pulled it open the rest of the way, anxious to see his new digs.

But what he saw ripped that breath right out of him.

"Whole thing's gone to shit now." A can fell and hit the floor. "Should've known this had something to do with you."

Jack stood there, grinning like he was standing in front of his best friend. Because he was.

"Big man, how did you manage to get us such great accommodations?"

Bear rose, steadied himself and welcomed Jack in an embrace.

CHAPTER 20

CLIVE STOOD IN THE MIDDLE OF THE COMMAND CENTER. The buzz of activity reminded him of bumblebees in a cherry tree, the constant drone almost meditative. The room held a different feel than twenty-four hours ago. Then, the activity had risen to a fever pitch, fueled by a race to retrieve Noble and Bear before the other group.

The other group.

The unidentified group had nearly taken Bear out at the hospital. The fact they didn't was a testament to the man's status as a superhuman. The woman, Sasha, had not surfaced, but so far, she had not been found among the dead. The hospital looked like a battlefield, though, and not a medical center.

And thank God Ines had eyes on Noble at the hotel. Had she not bumped into him, stopping him from exiting the building, it would've been his brains being picked out of the concrete, and not the journalist. Letting them run as far as they did posed a major risk to Ines if Jack had uncovered her identity. But moving in too soon for the extraction once they had their location could've tipped off the other group. They had to expand the web. Give themselves time.

Two matters remained. Identifying that group and determining how high up the chain their orders originated. And convincing Noble and Bear to work for Clive.

"It's too quiet in here." Isa startled him with her touch.

He straightened. "Just a lull. You might want to enjoy it."

"Lulls bring out the other voices in my head. The bad ones."

"Maybe you should listen to them for a change."

"Why would I do that?"

"I do."

"Is there a good reason for that?"

"Open yourself to your dark side, and you'll never question anyone's motivation again."

Isa seemed taken aback by the suggestion. The woman was an integral part of the team as their social media and digital tracking expert. If you left anything identifying on the web, Isa would find you. Might take a little time, but she'll find you. She could never be an operative, though. She'd asked to join a team in the field, suggesting she could do her work from the back of a van, that being onsite would allow her more insight because she could see things that their version of Google street view would miss.

But if things went sideways—as they almost always did—she'd be a liability. Everyone loved Isa, even the most jaded operators they had on the team. You can't have those emotions out in the field. Sure, there was a bond between partners, but you signed up for the same thing, and when tracking down hardened criminals, rogue agents, assassins, and everything in between, you knew death could occur.

But not to someone like Isa.

Clive angled his face toward her. "Any—"

"Nothing."

"How do you know what I was going to ask?"

"I've been listening to the *Clive voice* in my head."

Clive chuckled and let his shoulders droop a tick. Not only was Isa an expert in digital tracking, she was the only member of the team that connected with him on a personal level. As a friend. In some ways, he felt like her protector.

"Something will turn up," she said. "No one can remain a ghost forever."

"I'll change your mind one day."

"Oh, really? You, Clive Swift, are going to vanish."

He nodded.

"Just disappear, and you think I won't be able to find you?"

He nodded.

"After this mission is over, why don't you put it to the test?"

"To the test?"

She nodded.

"What do you mean?"

"One week. Book a flight under a false identity I know nothing about."

Clive laughed. "You seriously think you can outfox the fox? Do you remember who taught you how to do all this?"

"Mark Zuckerberg?"

Clive couldn't contain himself over her remark that the founder of Facebook had been more instrumental in Isa's career than himself.

"You've taught me well, Clive. Probably too well. It's the reason I can't hold down a relationship."

"You're too beautiful. These boys you date can't handle it."

She laughed. "No, the crazy voice in my head—"

"Which one?"

She slapped his shoulder. "It alternates, OK? Anyway, once the crazy takes over, I do a little stalking, and BAM, I want nothing to do with these losers."

"You should let me set you up, Isa. I know a guy or two."

"I want nothing to do with the kind of men you know."

Clive shrugged off her words. "Suit yourself. But don't start bringing your future cats with you to work. I'm allergic."

"Figures."

"Doesn't it."

The banter lingered in the air for a few moments like the smell of maple syrup before being wafted away by a few analysts heading out for lunch. They invited Isa and Clive, who declined.

"Seriously, though," Clive began, "we need to nail this down. Noble has been off the grid for some time. No one is particularly missing him, and I think we were far enough away, and he was apprehended in an area without surveillance, so we shouldn't expect any immediate heat on that."

"But Logan," she said.

"Right, Logan." Clive paced to the nearest wall and glanced up at the monitors. All the major news networks. A few surveillance feeds they had tapped into. And the cell where Jack Noble and Bear Logan were getting reacquainted. Smiles. Steak. Beer. He almost wanted to join them.

"What kind of backlash do you think we'll face on this?" Isa asked.

Clive took a deep breath, held it, centered himself as he shifted mental gears. "His location was obvious. They had it for some time, no other explanation on why the two assassination attempts happened so close together."

"Why do you think they massacred so many at the hospital?"

"To make it look like a terrorist attack. Only thing that makes sense. They could have slipped someone inside, a PT or nurse, a bribe and taken Logan out in a way that nobody would have suspected."

"These people are insane."

Clive shook his head. "It is the lack of insanity that makes them dangerous. A crazy person, while unpredictable and unstable, is an easy target. These people, whether driven by money or some other power trip, are our worst nightmare at the present time."

"I've gone over the train station footage dozens of times. No one else was there. We had the platform on lockdown."

"But they might have the footage. Which means they'll have Sadie's face, and a half-dozen of our men."

"Talking about me again?" Sadie slipped into the room like a silent breeze over a still pond. She had her hair pulled back and was dressed down in a pair of jeans and a plain t-shirt.

"Speak of the devil," Clive said.

"And she will appear," Sadie said. "Are we getting backlash for the train station incident?"

"Nothing we can't handle," Clive said.

"Nothing at all, actually," Isa said.

Sadie joined the duo near Isa's workstation. "Have you spoken to Bear?"

Clive gestured toward one of the screens. "Not yet. He's alone with Noble now. We've got someone listening in, but I doubt they've said anything important."

"Knowing those two the way I do—" a grimace crossed her face, "—or the way I did, I should say, they're talking about old times while eating a steak and having a beer."

"You're five minutes late to witness that." Clive studied Sadie as she watched Noble and Logan. The frown faded, and she smiled. He knew they had been teammates at one time. Friends, even. Sadie considered the two men to be big brothers. They'd been in a few jams, and to get out, Sadie learned to trust them with her life.

Sadie drifted toward the screen. "Who ya gonna send in there?"

"I think I built some rapport with Noble a while ago. Lacy had fun with him, but I'm not putting her back in there. Ines might be a good choice, too. She'll rattle him a bit."

"Did Ines bring him in?" Sadie looked surprised and impressed.

Clive nodded. "She's taking after you more every day."

"That's my girl." She grabbed her left elbow and scratched her chin. "I don't know that she's the one to handle this, though."

"Whom do you have in mind?" Isa couldn't contain her grin.

"Oh, gosh." Sadie feigned doubt. "I don't know that I'm capable of making that kind of decision."

"Sure you're not." Clive chuckled at Sadie's attempt to be some sort of Southern Belle who demurred at the thought of taking on the task.

"Well, I mean, if you're begging."

"I'm not."

"And you can't find anyone else."

"I can."

"I guess I can take a crack at it."

"You should."

"I thought you'd never ask."

CHAPTER 21

DEEP BLUE WAVES SLAPPED AGAINST THE ROCKY SHORE. FOAM soared through the air and landed on the blackened shoreline. Tendrils of seaweed, sweet and aromatic while salty and bitter at the same time, draped the water's edge.

Clarissa dragged her bare feet through the sand, creating a line that led back to her entry point. She loved the feeling of cold, wet sand between her toes. It was a pleasure she'd enjoyed since childhood, when her mother would take her to the Outer Banks during late Spring, before the tourists overwhelmed Kittyhawk, North Carolina.

All the good memories of her mother took place there. And it was the final one she held dearest.

Nestled at the tip of a peninsula, the picturesque small town of Medulin, Croatia, looked out over the Adriatic Sea. Several hundred feet behind her, the tourists flocked to the clearer shallows where they wallowed like seals in the water. She might join them tomorrow, after she rested.

Her travels had taken longer than the six and half hours Google suggested. Clarissa aimed to stay off the highways as much as possible while traveling east through Italy. Once she passed the border, she skirted the coastline, stopping here and there to rest, reflect, have a bite to eat, and a drink. Or two. When she finally arrived, her hotel room wasn't ready, so she headed out for a walk.

The bottle of wine she found was local, and pretty good. She thought the bold red would stand up against most of the wines she'd had in the sleepy little town she'd called home, and most certainly when compared to the fancy restaurants Beck used to wine and dine her in.

All part of the stipend!

She doubted that now. The US Treasury Department might literally print money, but they didn't allow members of the Secret Service to blow six hundred euros a night on dinner.

How had she not seen it? Why had she been so blind? And worse, how had her street smarts and instincts been so completely and utterly wrong about the guy?

She stopped and took a few steps closer to the water and waited for the next wave to crash over her, covering her to her knees. The seawater was cool, refreshing, and so thick with salt she felt it enveloping her even after stepping back a few feet.

She wished the undertow could pull her doubts away with the same ease it returned sand to the sea.

"Maybe…"

She couldn't complete the sentence. She couldn't say that maybe Beck wasn't involved. All the evidence pointed to the contrary. And then to top it off, he had pinned it on her.

"Resign, and you'll face no consequences. I'll take care of it, Clarissa."

Lying bastard.

Sort of.

True, she had survived in the little town for months without any problems. The bank accounts remained topped off at a hundred thousand dollars each, which prevented her from needing to access her own numbered accounts. She supposed it was Beck's way, or *someone's* way, of tracking her, and that was why she went to great lengths to make it appear she was drawing the funds from banks in Berlin, and Paris, and London. On the move. Never in one place. If they sent someone, they'd have to peel through millions of people to find her. And, of course, they never would.

So why did she have to run?

She asked herself that many times during her ten hours on the Vespa. Best guess, someone in the town had tipped them off. Beck knew she had a private apartment somewhere along the coast. He could've had an agent, or more likely a private investigator, working his way through the area until fate intervened and placed her indirectly in their sights. Or perhaps she'd slipped up when making a withdrawal or transfer. Failed to activate the VPN to place herself in Berlin, or Paris, or London. She couldn't be sure.

And it didn't matter, anyway.

Life had changed. She had to accept it. For Clarissa, there was no other choice.

She took a seat on the sand and watched the sun fall deep into the horizon, a couple of hours from nestling into the Adriatic. Already, the sea tinged with orange reminiscent of Winslow Homer's *Sunset at Gloucester*.

In between the crashing waves, she embraced the silence. Her thoughts came in and washed away. The nothingness in between is what gave her the fortitude to take on whatever would come next.

For the next two hours, she remained there, meditative, feeling the sea breeze, taking in the laughter of children, the barking dogs, and the songs of the birds. This was all she wanted in life. A place on the beach where nothing could get to her. Where nothing else mattered.

As the pieces of the idealistic image cracked and faded and shattered, she turned her attention to the problems at hand and the steps she needed to take care of first.

Lodging.

Shower.

Food.

Wine.

And not necessarily in that order.

Concrete stairs leading away from the beach were a short walk away. She crossed the packed sand, donned her flats, climbed to the boardwalk. The street vendors had gone. Lights illuminated the narrow street. The crowd had shifted, as locals and tourists alike prepared for an evening out.

Clarissa kept a low profile as she crossed the street and made her way to her hotel. She had reserved a room online using a cell phone she picked up when she had entered Croatia. The hotel's app notified her the room was ready and gave her the option to use her phone as her key. She obliged. The less time she spent in front of people, the better.

Before entering the lobby, she dipped into a small boutique to buy a scarf and a pair of large sunglasses. Big brother wasn't watching the streets here, but he would be present inside the hotel. She would exit the room a completely different person after using the scissors and hair dye she'd picked up at the small store where she purchased the cell phone.

Easy peasy lemon squeezy, Clarissa. Easy. Freaking. Peasy.

CHAPTER 22

"The hell is going on, Jack?" Bear set his fork down, a chunk of steak still stuck to the tines. "One minute I'm rehabbing under an assumed name in Nowhere, France, and the next the hospital's being shot up to hell. Lost Sasha—"

"Those goddamn bastards." Jack regripped his knife as though he were going to run someone through.

"Not like that. I don't think. Haven't seen her, but they say she got out." He shoved the steak in his mouth and washed it down with a swig of beer. "And they've got Mandy set up nice here."

"She's here?"

Bear waved him off. "She's good, man. Made sure of that. Sadie brought me in."

"Holy blast from the past, big man."

"Yeah, right. Thought for a moment she was there to help, showed up outta nowhere, like you did back when I was working with her... Shit, what? A decade ago?"

Jack shook his head.

"Feels longer."

"Right." Jack pushed away from the table and stood. "So, she wasn't there to help, then?"

Bear looked around and swept his hand, gesturing to the room. "You tell me? Look at this place. Better than most of the others we've been holed up in. Even when the government put us up."

"True." Jack paced to the door, checked the handle. Unlocked. "Aside from my first interaction leaving my room, everything has been above board."

"Why is that?"

"They want us to work with them."

"Look at me." Bear dipped his face toward the table. Looked like he was about to go full on bear and chomp down on the steak. He pointed to the scar on his head. "I still can't walk right half the time. What the hell am I gonna do for them? They gave me a shot, said it'll help me recover faster. I doubt it'll work."

"You've always been the brains of the operation, my friend. I'm the brawn."

"You're a puny little rat is what you are, and the surgeons took a chunk of my brain."

Jack laughed. He did so to hide the impact of Bear's words. He knew the big man didn't think of him as a rat. But the tone, there was too much unsaid between them. Bear finished with Noble some time ago. But here they were, forced together, again, and Jack shouldered the blame.

"How'd they get you?" Bear asked.

"I'd really like to see Mandy. Where is she?"

"Tell you in a minute. Answer me."

"Got sloppy, I guess. Two parties found me. One blew the head off a reporter who was going to expose *all* of Skinner's corruption."

Bear leaned back, whistled. "Christ."

"Bullet was meant for me. Someone blocked me, kept me from getting to the door first."

"Guardian angel watching over you."

"They knew my next move would be out the back door. Knew the route I would take after leaving the hotel. Same person was there, waiting in a car, with a different look. Businesswoman inside."

"Party chick outside."

Jack laughed. "Pretty much the mullet of spies." His smile faded. "She got me to a parking garage where she had a car waiting. Fed me a story.

Could've taken me down right then and there, but had to get me outside the city."

"Which city?"

"Luxembourg City."

"Great place. Great beer."

"Right?" That was the cue for both to take a drink. "Anyway, feeds me a story about this duffel bag. I never checked it, was too busy driving. Plus, she's a great actress."

"What's that?" Bear said.

"What?"

"That smile."

"What smile?"

"The one that formed when you said she's a great actress. You crushing on this chic?"

"Please."

Bear tipped his head back and bellowed. By the time he opened his eyes again, tears were streaming down his cheeks.

"Glad you're enjoying my complete emasculation at the hands of a well-trained spy."

"Nah, that ain't it."

"Then what is it?"

"You still can't admit it when you fall for a woman stronger than you."

"Give me a break. Name one time."

"This time."

"Any other?"

"Clarissa."

That struck the most intense nerve Noble had in his body. He tried to hide the grimace, the pain, but it was too much. "About Mandy…"

"What happened to Clarissa?" Bear pushed back in his chair. Thick muscles rippled across his forearms. "Tell me she's dead, and I'll smash your head into that wall."

Jack offered a calming gesture. "She's fine. Was fine last time I saw her. After Skinner, I spent some time with her. Stayed at her getaway for a couple of months." He paused and thought of the time spent with Clarissa wandering around the town, hiking down the mountain to the coast, spending all weekend riding the train to different towns. They had made memories. Again.

"And?"

"Got a call. The heat was on me. They were getting close."

"These guys?"

"Hard to tell, but I am guessing these guys gave me the heads up, and it was the other group getting too close."

"You think we can trust this Clive dude?"

"I can't answer that. But I can say they knew enough to have someone close to that hospital to get you out."

"It was a train station twenty miles away."

"They knew you were down there, just had the attack wrong."

"And they knew about your hit?"

"They narrowed it down. Ines, that's the spy who loved me, she stopped me from taking that bullet."

"But she sacrificed the reporter."

"Guess there wasn't time." Jack bowed his head and thought of the man who had been murdered in his place. "When this is all over, I'll find his family and make things right for them."

"So, what do you think this'll be about?"

"Not sure, but I think we should accept. They've got us. They've got Mandy. They probably have a lead on Sasha. And I wouldn't doubt they know where my brother and Mia are."

Bear struggled out of his seat. He took a moment to catch his breath, then used his hand on the table to steady himself as he took a few steps. He looked down at Jack. "This is what you're taking on. Think you can handle it?"

"I've dragged you home from bars in worse shape than that and we managed to take out five thugs at once. I think we'll be good."

Bear extended his hand. Jack grabbed it. Bear pulled him in.

"Partners. Again." Bear looked him in the eye. "But for the last time. After this, me and Mandy are gone. This is it."

"I agree."

"Let's go see the kid."

CHAPTER 23

THE NEXT MORNING, JACK WAS AWOKEN BY LIGHT TAPPING ON his door. He waited for someone to barge in. Instead, humming emanated in from the hallway. Soft. Light. A familiar song he couldn't place. It stopped. Another knock. He got up and opened the door.

"Hello, Jack." Ines wore a black track suit with neon yellow accents. Her hair was pulled back tight. She looked more like the Tomb Raider than the bohemian drifter he'd met in Luxembourg.

"Ines?"

She nodded and gestured to her right. The woman from the day before appeared. "And you met Lacy already."

Jack noted the two women stood close, closer than two co-workers.

Jack ignored it. "How did you know I'd be in Luxembourg? From what Clive said, they didn't have a clue where I'd turn up. You went off their radar, and by the time they picked up on it, it was too late."

She shrugged and waved him off. "Can't give up all my secrets. Still don't know that I can trust you."

"Simple answer, you can't." He paused. "You're not here to chat, so what's up?"

"Need you to come with us," Lacy said.

"Where?"

"Does it really matter, Jack?" Ines said.

"No. Guess I need to see what this is all about anyway. Give me a second to change."

Ines stuck her foot between the door and frame, preventing it from shutting.

"If you want a show, just ask. No need to be sneaky about it."

Ines rolled her eyes. Lacy laughed again.

Two minutes later they repeated the process with Bear, who put up less of a fight. Ten minutes later, after they had traversed a maze of stark white corridors, they reached what appeared to be a control or command room of sorts.

There were a few dozen workstations, most empty. News feeds and surveillance footage played on monitors mounted throughout the room. Clive sat at a desk that overlooked the operation. Next to him was a younger woman. She spotted them first. Her breath seemed to catch as she tapped Clive's forearm.

Clive stepped down from the platform and approached, and as he did, Ines and Lacy left in the direction they had come from.

"Gentlemen." He waved them over to an open door. A meeting room. A gray table stretched the length of the room. White boards littered with acronyms, pictures, strings, and arrows were on each wall. A projector was mounted to the ceiling.

Jack entered the room, followed by Bear and then Clive.

"Make yourselves comfortable."

"Got a beer?" Jack said.

"A little too early, don't you think?" Clive said.

"For a beer?" Bear said. "The hell country we in?"

Clive grinned as he steepled his fingers in front of his chest. "Nice try, my friend."

"Since when did you and I become friends?"

Clive looked disappointed. "Fair enough. Trust must be earned. It is not given."

"I'll never trust you."

"I took care of Mandy, didn't I?"

"For one night." Bear glanced down at the table. "And I haven't heard anything about Sasha."

Clive's eyebrows rose into his forehead. "Ah, I was just about to mention that."

Bear rose out of his chair. "What?"

"She's back in London. There was a team nearby who extracted her, got her safely out."

As relieved as the big man looked to hear that, there was something bothering him. "That's all we got on her?"

"Of course not. They went back to look for you and the girl. But Sasha was their number one priority, and they got her safely on a private jet at once."

"She knows we're alive?"

Clive nodded once. It didn't instill any confidence.

"Listen up, man—"

Jack cut Bear off. "I think it wouldn't be too much to ask to at least let Mandy speak with Sasha. Right, Clive?"

"That depends." Clive stood, shut the door, cut the lights. He grabbed a remote and turned on the projector. A blue rectangle filled up half the wall.

"Depends on what?" Jack said.

"Whether you agree to help us or not."

"Help you with what?"

"I'm about to tell you, but you must know, it is in your best interest to say yes now. Once I present you with this information, there is a chance you will refuse. And refusal, well, will result in termination, one way or another. I won't say it will be at our hands. And I can't assure you you'll walk out of here alive."

Bear pushed back from the table, almost toppling his chair over in the process. Jack reached out to steady him, but had his hand swatted away.

"Listen up, asshole."

"Bear." Jack did his best to run interference.

"Shut up, Jack. If it wasn't for you going rogue, we wouldn't be in this position." Bear placed his big hands on the table and leaned forward. "I've run out of patience for all of you. Let me take the girl, get us on a plane to London, and get us and Sasha a free pass back to the US. Whatever you need, I'm sure Jack can handle it if you pair him with one of your people.

They are more than capable if they managed to extract both of us safely amid all that damn chaos."

Clive cleared his throat and did his best to mirror Bear. He wouldn't back down. He couldn't, even if it meant ending up in a chokehold that would crush his larynx in less than five seconds.

"I'm afraid I can't let you leave."

Bear straightened up. Jack prepared to stop the fight.

"I promise you," Clive said. "The girl will be well taken care of. We are isolated here. No one knows this place exists. They cannot spot it from the air. It's completely normal above us. We can't be detected down here. We also have two people close to Sasha right now. She will not be in any danger."

Bear took a step back and stumbled. "What good am I to you? I can barely stand. Gonna end up dead. Jack's gonna end up dead. Why do you need us? Just kill us now."

Bear's ragged breath occupied space within the silent void. His features were hard, same as Jack remembered him in the most intense moments they had shared over two decades. All the passion in the big man's body weighed down on each of them.

Clive leaned back in his seat, head against the rest. He held Bear's gaze, though, not sulking away. Not many could do it. The intimidation factor was legit.

"Look," Jack started, "there's merit to what Bear has to say. Whatever you need, it's probably best I tackle it solo, or with one of your people. Ines bested me. Lacy seems tough enough."

"Sadie." Bear eased into his seat. "We already have a working relationship with her."

"That was a while ago," Clive said. "And she's different now. She's a leader."

"She was then." Bear dropped the last few inches. The seat squealed in rebellion.

"It's different now," Clive said. "She won't play second fiddle. Plus, she's already invested in this in a different capacity. And Ines, Lacy, they work two different jobs. Ines needs a break, too. She tracked you down over two months, Noble. It wasn't easy on her."

Frustration mounted in the room as the trio reached an impasse. Jack agreed with everything Bear had said. He also saw Clive's point of view, though he had no idea what the job entailed. What reason would require the two of them to team up? An old associate from the SIS days? From their time on loan to the CIA after enlisting in the Marines? Any of the dozens of jobs they performed as contractors?

"Let's get to the point," Jack said. "Who's the target."

Clive cleared his throat, stood, said, "Wait here a moment," then left the meeting room. The door clicked shut behind him.

"Think that'll open?" Bear asked.

"If not, we can ram your head through it."

"About the only part of my body that works right anymore."

"That's not saying much."

"Screw you. I've always been smarter than you."

"Probably true."

"No probably about it." Bear pushed back from the table and stretched his legs out in front of him. His hands rested on his stomach, which protruded a little further than it had last time Noble saw him.

"What's Sasha been feeding you?"

"All the steak I want."

"And potatoes, by the look of it."

"Just jealous no one wants to cook for you."

Jack laughed, but his smile faded quickly. He did have someone who wanted to cook for him. And he disappeared in the middle of the night. Again. Same woman. Same outcome. Why did she continue to put up with him?

"Stop thinking about her." Bear tossed a napkin at Jack. "The word you are looking for, Mr. Noble, is toxic."

"That's me."

"It sure as hell is." Bear paused a beat. "What do you suppose this is all about?"

Jack shrugged. He still hadn't come close to a solid guess. But he figured he'd try to jog Bear's mind. "There's a few candidates."

"Like who?"

"Remember Reese?"

"Detective? Manhattan?"

"Yeah."

"You ran into her down in Texas, while she was in witness protection."

Jack thought of the days they spent together in that little apartment over the garage. He remembered the old couple, kind enough to take him in when his Wrangler died on him. And he thought of all the trouble he'd brought the people in that Texas town. And the trouble he brought to Reese.

Toxic.

The door opened and Clive stepped in carrying a manila file folder about an inch thick.

"Favorite recipes?" Jack asked.

Clive smiled, but wouldn't meet Noble's gaze. He set the folder down, turned it, straightened it, and lifted the cover. But his arms covered the contents.

"Get to it, man," Bear said.

"Your target will be familiar to you. She's in a lot of danger and faces death or certain jail time, even if we get to her first. But I promise, I'll do my best to get her into the hands of the government who will treat her best."

Clive thumbed through several pages before stopping on some glossies. He pulled a few out, separated them and placed them on the table for Jack and Bear to view.

They spoke at the same time, saying the name like a curse.

"Clarissa."

CHAPTER 24

THE SHEER CURTAINS DANCING IN THE BREEZE AND THE TASTE of the salt air, sounds of children playing in the surf, the chatter from the cafe below all combined to overwhelm Clarissa's senses as she hung in that ether between sleep and wakefulness. The thunderstorm she drifted off to the night before had given way to a clear day. Might be a nice one to get out and explore the area.

She crossed the room and tied off the curtains while taking in the view of the expansive Adriatic. Her gaze drifted to a nearby marina. She wondered what kind of passage she could arrange should she need to leave in a hurry. Might be a nice place to stop off and make a friend.

She glanced at the tied-off bag with hair clippings and leftover coloring in the wastebasket. She caught her reflection in the mirror. For a moment, she didn't recognize the woman staring back, who looked more like Mila Jovovich in The Fifth Element, just with dark hair.

The style fit her face well. It was shorter than she had ever had it, and she'd only dyed it this dark once before. The goth phase had passed her by, something her father was grateful for. The red highlights provided an edgier look, which should keep potential suitors at bay. If anything, they'd call her GI Jane instead of honey or sweetie or yelling out 'I love you' as foreign men often did to American women walking alone.

She ventured down to the lobby, where a small buffet had been set out.

Most of the food had gone cold, but Clarissa's hunger pangs didn't care. She grabbed a half-dozen sausages and wrapped them in a napkin before setting out.

The action along the road consisted of families heading to and from the beach, shoppers in and out of the boutiques, and the general hum of resort-town activity.

Clarissa did her best to fit in with the crowd, popping into a shop here and there, making a few small purchases in cash. She kept her bearings fixed first on the marina, and second where she had left the Vespa. Traveling to the latter would give her an up-close look at the former.

From the road, sighting the layout of the marina had been difficult. It wasn't until she had looked from her hotel window he had spotted the service road entrance.

On her walk, she passed close by and noticed only a single bar extending across the narrow lane. Its release was triggered by a button push. There was no guardhouse. No one watching at all. Nothing to stop her from walking right in.

She snapped a few pics while pretending to talk on her cell phone, then continued on until she reached the packed parking lot where she had left the scooter. There were several in the section designated for motorbikes. After a few moments, she spotted it. She walked past, not stopping, not paying attention, just making sure it did not appear to have been tampered with.

The tripwire shone in the sun, vibrating slightly in the breeze. It ran from the right handle to the seat and was still intact, leaving her to believe no one had attempted to inspect the bike up close.

The best gift Beck had ever given her was a clean, untraceable license plate. The smartest thing she had done during her exit from Italy was swapping the license plate out after she had crossed the border.

She only wished she had another.

Beck could no longer be trusted. Once word got back that she had fled, and it would, he would flip the switch and every license plate reader in Europe would be ready to ping the moment she passed. Fortunately, there were few in Croatia that she knew of, and most were relegated to the few highways that snaked across the country.

She worried about Mrs. Calabase. The original license plate would trigger an alert and would lead back to her dead husband. It was only a matter of time before whoever was behind this, whether Beck or someone else, would know the woman had aided Clarissa.

Would Mrs. Calabase know to get out of town? Clarissa doubted the story about going to her sister's was true.

Clarissa fired up her cell phone while pulling a small notebook from her pocket. In it, she had a few contacts listed. She had developed her own encryption system so that if she or the notebook fell into the wrong hands, they wouldn't be able to decipher it.

The notebook wouldn't give up its secrets. She might, though, and for that reason, she felt vulnerable even having it on her person. In Italy, she had hidden it behind a piece of wall she had carved out. No one would ever spot or find the makeshift safe she had created.

Clarissa located Mrs. Calabase's entry and started to dial the number.

"What are you doing, girl?" she muttered.

If she had wanted to broadcast her location to Beck or anyone else who had a hand in this, there was no better way than calling the woman. She had to find another method to reach out and warn her to leave town for a while.

The ground crunched behind her. She turned to locate the source of the disturbance. A tour van had pulled into the lot. It came to a stop and the doors opened. A stream of foreign conversation followed. She recognized it as Korean.

Several women all wearing white t-shirts with something written in Korean on them entered the lot and gathered twenty feet or so from the van.

Clarissa rubbed her eyes, blinked hard, and worked up a few tears. She approached the women.

"English? Anyone, speak English?"

The first row of ladies stared blankly at her. She repeated her request, adding a please on top of a choked sob. After a few seconds, a hand rose above the group, and a small woman stepped forward.

"I speak English."

"Thank God," Clarissa said. "I was robbed, and all of my stuff was stolen. I have this stupid phone, but it doesn't work. Is there any chance I can borrow yours?"

The women convened in a circle, and after a little back and forth, the lady handed Clarissa her phone.

Clarissa stepped back a few feet and dialed a number she only prayed still worked. It was one of several Jack had given her. The call would route through a private server that changed IP addresses constantly, connecting the next call through a switch in Brazil, or Belize, or Bermuda, or any number of other countries that started with the letter B.

Several button presses and a few moments of dead air later, the phone rang and Mrs. Calabase answered.

"Oh, I'm so glad I reached you," Clarissa said. "You need to get out of town, now."

Mrs. Calabase responded in Italian. Clarissa understood some. "I understand that now and will make arrangements soon, dear. I'm excited to come see the new baby."

"Baby?" Clarissa said, before realizing Mrs. Calabase wasn't alone. "Oh, no. Look, you don't have to keep this up. You can give them my location and they'll leave you alone. I'm in—"

"It's not worth it for you to make the trip, dear. I'll come down as soon as I can."

The line went dead.

And so did Clarissa's hope that Mrs. Calabase would be OK.

CHAPTER 25

THE EIGHT-SEATER TOUCHED DOWN ON A SMALL AIRSTRIP outside of Genoa as the sun crested the mountains. Jack opened his eyes as the brakes locked in and the jet went from a hundred to zero in the matter of a few football fields.

The light coming in from behind Bear's head was blinding and silhouetted the large man, making him look like a wild beast.

"Are we done?" It was the first time Noble had noticed the big man exhale. Bear still had the armrest in a death grip. Of everything that could take the guy's life, it was the safest form of transportation that scared him most. Irrational, yes. But a legitimate fear nonetheless.

"Yeah, we're here," Jack said. "I think. Are we, Sadie?"

Sadie pulled her AirPods out and put them back in their charging case. "Yeah, this is the place."

"Where to from here?"

"One thing at a time, Jack." She unbuckled, shuffled through the cabin, rapped on the cockpit door. It opened, and she leaned her head in and said something in Spanish, then gave Noble and Bear a thumbs up.

The wind was fierce and cool and damp, coming in off the Mediterranean as though a blue norther had set it off. Jack took in the sight of the mountains to his right and the sea to the left. They were south of Genoa, meaning their destination would be further south than where they were now. No point traveling through a city with well over a hundred thousand people.

A black Audi sedan was parked near an unmanned guardhouse. Sadie pulled out her cell phone. Tapped the screen. The vehicle roared to life. Exhaust plumed from the rear and dissipated into the clear sky as the wind got hold of it.

Noble slid onto the backseat and stretched his legs, while Bear took the front passenger seat, and Sadie got in behind the wheel. She messed with her phone for a few moments until their route was set. She eased up to the gate, which opened automatically. A few turns later, they were on a two-lane road heading south, and Jack slid back into the semi-lucid state he considered sleep.

He woke to Sadie's door opening, wiped away the cobwebs, inhaled the air. They were in a village that seemed as though it had been cut from the mountain. The smells were familiar. Too familiar. He'd had a hunch this was where they were going.

After exiting, he gestured to where the road split. One way led out of town. The other to their assumed destination.

"You know the way?" Sadie asked.

Jack nodded. "Walked it a hundred and sixty or seventy times, give or take."

"That's not all we're here to see," she said.

"This is where you went after the Skinner thing?" Bear said.

"Spent a couple of months here. Clarissa would head out for a few days at a time, but for the most part, we were together."

"How'd that feel?"

Jack shrugged. "I don't know, and I don't want to get into it. Not now. Not with everything going on. I can't let emotions get in the way of this."

"In the way of arresting her? You lost your mind?"

Jack waited until Sadie was out of earshot. "Of course not. I'm not down for hurting her. But if Clive is right, and if someone else is after her, we might be her best shot."

"I can't trust that guy."

"He didn't kill us. Not only that, he saved us from those who were trying to kill us. Gotta count for something, yeah?"

Bear waved him off. "We're nothing to him. As soon as this is done, we're dead."

Jack glanced around, spotted a few familiar faces. He did his best to shield himself from them. "I'm working on that."

"A way to bail?"

"Once we have Clarissa."

"They've got Mandy."

"You've got Sasha. She can get Mandy out of there. We just need enough time to make it all happen."

An older man walked up, held up a chess piece, pointed and smiled at Noble. His yellow, crooked teeth told a hell of a story.

"Good to see you, Antonio," Jack said. "I'll come by the cafe a little later for a rematch. I want that championship belt back from you."

The old guy smiled and smoothed down wild wisps of hair as he returned to his path.

"What about Sadie?" Jack said.

"What about her?" Bear said.

"Trust her?"

"She seems different."

"You knew her better than I did. But are you sure it isn't just age? It's been a decade. People change. Now think about people like us. Everything we've seen, done, experienced the past ten years. It had to have hardened her. I mean, what led her to working with Clive?"

"Can't imagine." Bear's gaze followed the woman as she pretended to browse racks of scarves outside a small store. "She's hardly acknowledged me."

"Got your feelings hurt?" Jack poked the bear.

"Actually, yeah."

"They manage to find your feelings when they had your skull peeled back?"

"Fuck you, Jack."

"Fuck you, too, Bear."

An awkward silence lingered a beat too long before Bear broke into laughter loud enough to alert all nearby citizens of the strangers in their midst. Sadie turned and rolled her eyes at them. But a smile formed on her lips for the first time since the trio had been reunited. Bear's hearty laugh had a way of doing that.

The facade had cracked. She was still one of them, and she'd be on their side when it came time to do the right thing.

Sadie strode across the square and met them on a bench shaded by two large fig trees.

"Quiet around here," she said.

"It is," Jack said.

She placed one foot on the bench between them, hiked up her sock. "How long were you here?"

"About as long as you've been."

"Cut the shit, Jack. You dropped off the grid entirely for over six months. I guess there's places you coulda gone for that, but considering where you were, and the footage they had of you executing Skinner—"

"Someone had to play judge and jury."

Sadie continued without missing a beat. "—you couldn't have made it far before being spotted. Getting out on a passport would've been impossible, no matter how good a fake. Your face was your poison."

"Still is," Bear said.

"Big man still has jokes," Jack said.

Sadie put her hands on her hips and tipped her head back. "God, why did you send me these two clowns again? Haven't I had enough already?"

"You got a microphone direct to Clive here? Or…?"

"Jack, just answer my damn question. How long were you here?"

He leaned forward, placed his elbows on his knees, clasped his hands in between them. "Two months. Right after the Skinner incident."

"Spent it all with Clarissa?"

Jack nodded. "When she was here."

"Where else was she?"

"Work, I guess."

Sadie took a step back and folded her arms over her chest. Her eyes narrowed, brows knit together. "What work?"

"Whatever she was doing with that Beck character."

Sadie continued staring at him as though he'd grown a second nose.

"What?" Jack said.

"How much did Clive fill you in?"

"Not a whole lot," Bear said. "Told us it was in everyone's best interest that we find Clarissa before anyone else."

"Jesus Christ." Sadie walked away while pulling out her cell phone.

Noble watched her animated conversation as Bear tried to pull theories out of midair. Jack couldn't entertain them, not now. Not as the reality set in that Clarissa had been lying to him during their time together. He couldn't blame her. It's not like he'd recommend anyone get close to him. There one day, gone the next. No chance of commitment. No chance of this life never catching up to him. It's why his daughter Mia was with his brother Sean. It's why Mia and Sean and Sean's family had to flee and live under assumed identities in Belize or wherever they were now.

But why would Clarissa lie? She could've been direct with him. She always had in the past. What was different this time?

Another townsperson spotted Jack and waved. The young man worked in the hardware store and had been a fixture at the small bar Noble frequented while Clarissa was off on her adventures. The guy strode over and spoke with Jack for a few minutes. Noble played along with the conversation, hoping it would be a distraction. It wasn't. But it passed the time until Sadie hung up.

She stood across the square for a few minutes, speaking to no one at all. Had to be quite the spectacle for the townsfolk.

Anxiety built like bile rising in his throat as Sadie crossed the square again. She shoved her phone into her pocket.

"How are things back at HQ?" Bear asked.

"Shut up," she said.

"The hell did I do?" Bear said.

"Your face is pissing me off," she said.

"What happened to old Sadie?"

"Clive." She sucked in a gulp of air and spat it back out as though it was laced with arsenic. "And I can't believe that son of a bitch didn't tell you what you were getting into."

"He kinda had us by the short and curlies," Bear said.

"That's disgusting," she said.

"Really disgusting," Jack said. "Besides, you like to shave down—"

Sadie threw up her hands. "I don't want this to go any further, you got me?"

Jack nodded, said nothing.

"And I'm gonna kick Clive's ass when I see him again, which better be soon."

"Are you gonna tell us what this is all about?" Jack draped his arms along the back rail. "You left me with a bunch of memories that aren't exactly what I thought they were, and I'm kind of in the middle of an existential crisis."

Sadie dipped her head, shaking it. "You two are going to be the end of me. You know that?"

"Planned on it." Jack rose from the bench and met Sadie toe to toe. "What is going on?"

"You might want to sit your ass back down, Noble. This is gonna suck for you."

CHAPTER 26

THE WIND SHIFTED AWAY FROM THE COAST. DRY, WARM AIR barreled down the mountainside and through the narrow streets until it whipped the debris in the square into a frenzy. Dirt and dust and wrappers and paper coffee cups formed a mini tornado that died moments after it formed.

Then everything fell still, as though the mountain and the sea had reached a stalemate in an ongoing battle for the region.

Jack stared into Sadie's dark eyes. She had pulled her curls back into a loose ponytail. Strands fell about her face, stuck to her cheeks and lips.

"What is it?"

"She stole two hundred million dollars."

"Good for her."

Bear's bellow broke the stillness surrounding them, sending birds invading the shade tree scattering into the air.

"Did you hear me? She committed a major crime while an acting member of the Secret Service stationed here in Italy."

"When?" Jack thought back to his time with Clarissa. She had nothing fancy, no car, no jet to take her anywhere. Her clothes were plain and simple. She didn't wear jewelry or a watch. She preferred basic sandals most days.

"Six months ago."

"Doesn't make sense."

"Why's that?"

"How was she left to be all that time?"

"Details are fuzzy."

"Fuzzy?" Bear stood repositioned next to Sadie. "What the hell is fuzzy about two hundred million dollars. I mean, how the hell does someone even get away with that?"

"OK, they don't know for sure that she took it."

"She didn't," Jack said.

"You can't say that with any certainty," Sadie said.

"Can you say with certainty she did it?" Jack said.

"I just told you I can't."

"Well, I can tell you that two hundred million is no joke, and there's no way she could have continued living here, in this small town, under the watchful eye of whoever would be keeping a watchful eye on this place, if she had actually taken the money."

Sadie closed her eyes and clenched her jaw. " wish someone would tell me what I did to deserve you two in my life. I really do. I had it made, you know. Rising star in the Agency. Until you two botched my job all those years ago. Been downhill since."

"You ain't lying, sister," Bear said.

Sadie gave him a death stare. "Clive thinks there's a coverup going on here. She had a partner, Beck, who negotiated some kind of release. It gave her some time to prove her innocence. She had to come up with concrete proof, though. Because this, well, this goes down a pretty deep rabbit hole."

"How deep?" Bear asked.

"Deeper than I have a shovel for today."

"Yeah, I mean, you gotta dig through all our shit, right." Jack looked away as he digested the intel. He'd been here with Clarissa during part of this. Rather than confide in him, she had kept it a secret. She wasn't going off to work. She was working this case, trying to figure out a way to either get away with it, or bring down whoever was behind it. He leaned toward the latter, but the former had some legs, too.

Two women entered the square with five kids in tow. The ladies took a seat on a nearby bench while the children raced around, kicking a soccer ball. Their laughter filled the gaps in conversation.

"Look, guys," Sadie said. "Either she did it, or she didn't."

"Or she's caught up in something," Bear said. "Which, having known the girl for damn near two decades, I'm more inclined to believe."

"It doesn't matter. Get it? There are people after her. Maybe the same people who were after the two of you."

The words hit Noble like a sack of bricks shot from a cannon. Had this not been about Skinner after all? He'd been with Clarissa for a few months. All it took was one surveillance photo at an inopportune time to place him as a person of interest.

"We can give her a chance. I'll go out on a limb here and say we are her only chance. These other groups, they'll—"

"Kill her," Bear interrupted. "We get it."

"No, Bear," Sadie said. "They won't kill her. Not right away. They'll torture her until she gives up the details. And then they'll kill her."

"What if she doesn't break?" Bear said.

"Let's not let it get that far," Jack said.

"I agree." Sadie sat down next to Jack and put her arm around his shoulders. "So how about you tell me everything you remember while you were here with her. Every villager she interacted with. Every single person you got to know. We need to figure out where she went before anyone else does."

Jack filled her in during the short walk from the square to the apartment. He told her of the villagers he'd met. The bar he frequented. The old men and ladies who made him feel as though he'd grown up in the town. Then he stopped and looked across the street and felt the emotional weight of those months slam down on him.

"That's it right there." They stood at the corner where they were afforded some cover from prying eyes.

"I'll go," Sadie said.

"No," Bear said. "Let me."

Jack put a hand on his shoulder to keep him from moving forward. "What if there's someone waiting?"

Bear gave him a crooked smile. "One shot. That's all I need. Remember?"

Jack scratched a phantom bruised cheek. "Yeah, I remember."

"Here." Sadie pulled a pistol from a holster at the small of her back. She held it up. It smelled freshly oiled. "Still remember how to use one of these?"

"Isn't it enough I get shit from him?" Bear pushed Jack hard enough he backed into the wall.

"I can't be one of the boys now?" Sadie pouted.

"Yeah, prove yourself first."

"Again?"

"All right, you two," Jack said. "Let's break up this little spat." He put his hand on Bear's elbow and pulled him in close. "The door is tricky. It'll feel locked, but you don't need a key. Turn the handle like this—" he pantomimed the motions required "—and then give it a good nudge. Not so hard you could break it off the hinges."

"Baby nudge," Bear said.

"Baby nudge," Sadie repeated.

The big man tucked the pistol in his waistband and crossed the street. He walked uphill and back downhill along the side of the building. He realized the shot they'd given him back at headquarters had worked. He kept on past the front door and circled back around.

The street was empty. The sounds coming from the windows were of afternoon wind-down, not people minding the business of their neighbors.

Bear approached the front door. Jack felt his heart pound in his throat. He slowed his breathing, loosened his focus, let the world blur until it was impossible to tell where street met sky.

He heard the rusted latch. The thud of Bear's knee or hip against the wood. The squeal of hinges that should've been replaced three decades ago.

Bear slid into the darkness and became a ghostly silhouette. Then the door closed. The sound of Jack and Sadie's breathing intensified, ragged and harsh.

"He's gonna be OK," Sadie whispered.

"He better be," Jack replied.

She looked over at him. For a moment, the tough exterior crumbled. Her eyes watered. She'd blame the wind, he knew, but they both were aware of the gravity of the moment.

"I know this is crushing your soul." Sadie shoved a hand in her pocket and stared at the ground. "We never want to believe that someone we trusted so much would betray us."

"Funny, because that's what I'm wondering about you right now." He waited to judge her reaction.

She gave him none.

He pushed the envelope. "Skinner set me up over the course of a decade. Longer, actually. How do I know you didn't do the same?"

"You son of a bitch." There was the fire he sought. "I've given everything to our country."

"And it repaid you so well, here you are, working for the highest bidder."

"You're one to talk, you know. I've followed your *career*, Noble. Know all about your exploits."

"Exploits?" He chuckled at the word. "Everything I did was above board."

It was Sadie's turn to laugh. And she did. Loud enough that someone stepped out on their third-floor balcony to see who was down there making noise.

She nudged Jack in the ribs and pointed the guy out. "Let's tone it down."

"And now we gotta wait a few extra minutes." He diverted his attention across the street to Clarissa's apartment.

"Shit." He dragged his hand down his face.

"What?" Sadie followed his gaze.

"Look." He couldn't take his eyes off the open door.

"Shit."

CHAPTER 27

EVERY MONITOR CLIVE HAD PURCHASED AND INSTALLED IN THE temporary command center was blank. Every television played snow on repeat. The internet had been hijacked. Computers were being wiped at an alarming rate.

He made the decision to pull the plug after the first system failure had been detected. It was ten PCs too late. Their only link now was Isa on her personal MacBook Air, tethered to her iPhone.

Eddie had hacked into the security feed surrounding the location. He, Clive, and Isa gathered around while Ines and Lacy stood guard at the conference room's only point of ingress and egress.

"Does it feel like the temperature's rising?" Isa loosened her collar and wiped sweat from her brow. "Or am I having an incident?"

Clive had already detected the change and assumed the hackers had accessed the building's climate control.

"What are we seeing outside?" Clive asked.

"No one out there," Eddie said. "And I've already cycled through other exterior monitoring devices up to a mile out. No unusual activity detected."

Clive rubbed his cheeks. "So, there's no hit or tech teams disguised as utility crews out there?"

"Definitely not." Eddie flipped through feeds at a rapid pace.

"We could have been hijacked from anywhere in the world."

"Definite possibility."

Isa stepped back from the group and paced the outer edges of the room. This was beyond her comfort level. Social media tracking, sure. Hunting someone on the web, she's your woman. Obvious attack from a group who would be happy to sell everyone in the room to the highest bidder and then watch them be tortured, not something the woman ever imagined when she answered the obscure Craigslist job posting that led her to Clive.

Ines approached from behind Clive. Her breath was hot on his neck. "She gonna be OK?"

"Yes," Clive said. "We all are. Let's just relax and get back control of our comms."

"Boss," Ines lowered her voice. "You don't think—"

"Noble and Logan?" He shook his head. "Not with Sadie."

"How can you be so sure?"

"They have a history. A long one."

"Those guys are killers."

"So is she. It's their bond."

"I hope you're right."

"I do, too."

Isa stopped and stared up at a fuzzy screen. She had her hands on her hips and her head tipped back. Her long, loose hair hung past her waist. She rose up on the tips of her toes. Reached up toward the screen. Pressed a button on the bottom of the frame.

The channel changed.

The fuzz remained the same.

She did it again, and again. Each time, she lowered back down and took a step back so she could take in the entire screen.

"Isa, what are—"

She waved Clive off while reaching up and changing the channel again. This time, the screen morphed.

"Oh, Jesus." Clive staggered forward, mouth open, hand fishing through his pocket for his cell phone. He pulled it out, swiped through his contacts, pressed Sadie's number.

Nothing happened.

"There's no cell signal in here," Ines said. She, too, had her eyes glued to the screen. "I'm gonna head outside." She jogged to the door.

"Stop!" Clive froze, his head turning between the monitor and the door. "Don't go out there." He pointed at Eddie. "We need to lock the facility down, now."

"That's them," Isa said. "That's Noble and Sadie."

"Everyone, pick a screen and start changing channels."

Clive started on the TV next to Isa, flipping through channels until he had the same feed. The angle remained the same.

"I didn't think there was any surveillance footage there?" Isa said.

"They might've hacked into someone's security footage." He pressed the button again and another feed piped in. "Isa, keep yours where it is, everyone else, keep cycling through. We've got different feeds."

Ines hurried past him and began working on the next screen. "Who is doing this?"

"I'm not worried about that now. We need to get all angles in place, and we need a way to get in touch with Sadie."

In all, there were ten different camera angles of the little town. Perhaps whoever had tapped in had gotten lucky, and hadn't been following Sadie, Noble, and Bear. Perhaps they didn't even know the trio was there.

But why, then, would they have taken over this building? These people were pros. The attack at the hospital was evidence of that. Which meant if they wanted everyone inside the building dead, they'd be dead already. Was this a display of power? A *we'll show you what we can do*, kind of thing?

Isa joined him and began pointing out the movements of their makeshift team. "Logan entered the apartment. Sadie and Noble are waiting. He's quite aware, isn't he?"

"That's how he's survived so long," said Ines, who had joined them and stood shoulder to shoulder with Clive. "I thought for sure he had snuffed me out."

"What do you think won him over?"

"Can't say anything did. I think he knew he had to get out of town. He tried to leave me. I wouldn't have it. In that moment, it was easier to appease me by letting me tag along than leave me behind. The picture had been painted; his world had been jostled. It was easy, actually."

"Fortunately for us," Clive said. "It also means it'll be bloody impossible for someone to get the drop on him again."

"You can't be sure of that," Ines said. "He's rusty. No doubt. He's been on the run for months, but part of that time he cozied up in this little village. I'd bet money he lost some of his edge here."

"I think we're gonna find out." Isa had turned to face the other direction. The rest shifted to take in the feed.

"They've got company," Clive said.

CHAPTER 28

THE DOOR SHIFTED A FEW INCHES IN THE BREEZE. NO OTHER movement could be detected from within. Had it been a setup all along? He glanced at Sadie to judge her reaction. Fake or legit? She had always been hard to read, and that was the case today.

Why go to these lengths if the plan was to kill Jack and Bear? They could've done that at the hotel, in the hospital. Instead, they invested time and money and effort into bringing them God-knows-where to work this case because they could reach Clarissa in a way no one else on Clive's team could. Not even Sadie. Clarissa would trust Jack and Bear and nobody else.

"I don't like this." Sadie hiked up her pantleg and retrieved a smaller pistol. She checked the chamber. "Sorry, Jack, this is my backup, and Bear's got the other one."

"All that odds in my favor stuff is overrated."

She smiled, but it was forced. How could it be otherwise right now? "So, what's the layout of this place? You spent time there, right? Once you are in, where do you go?"

Jack imagined entering the apartment after one of his late nights at the bar while Clarissa was off doing whatever she did instead of working. "Stairs on the right, two small couches on the left, perpendicular. Small television under the stairs. Narrow opening leading to the kitchen. Old stovetop. Small fridge. No oven. Microwave. Knife block. Bathroom."

"Back door?"

"No."

"Upstairs?"

"Pretty basic. The stairs open up to a loft type area. No doors other than for a small closet and a wet bath."

"Toilet, shower, and sink all in one?"

"Pretty much all they could fit in the space."

"Any way out?"

"Window to a roof. About an eight-foot drop."

"The roof part of her place?"

"No. Neighbor's."

"Could someone get in that way?"

Jack had never tried, but it seemed possible. "Guess so."

"Shit."

They fell silent, letting their ears observe as much as their eyes.

"One of us has to go in," Jack said.

"We wait here," she said. "Bear would make a noise, call out if something happened."

"Bear's in there. He's not himself. Someone could get the drop on him, take him out, we'd never hear a peep. He could have two guys on top of him right now, choking him out."

"Stand down, Noble."

"Not a chance." He sprinted toward the apartment, leaving Sadie to call out to him to stop. Her words didn't slow him, but the bicycle that came whipping around the corner did when it slammed into Jack and knocked him off his feet.

The impact knocked the wind out of him. His palms, right cheek, chin, burned from grating across coarse asphalt and gravel. He got to a knee and turned his head.

"Jack!"

He caught sight of her running toward him in his peripheral. Her body disappeared, blocked out by the large fist careening toward his face. He closed his eyes, leaned back, felt the wind off the thick knuckles that breezed past his nose.

The man lost his balance and stumbled toward Noble. Jack dipped his right shoulder low, exploded forward, catching the guy on his knee. The man's leg buckled, bending awkwardly, snapping. The man screamed, reached down. Jack grabbed the man's wrist, yanked hard. His shredded knee unable to keep him balanced, the guy toppled over. His head hit the ground with a thud. A pool of crimson spread out on the sidewalk.

Sadie stopped in front of them. She aimed her pistol at his head.

"Don't worry about him," Noble said. "Get inside and find Bear."

Her jacket flapped behind her as she jumped over the limp body of Jack's assailant and trudged up the slope to the front door. She burst past the threshold, pistol out.

Jack pulled his trapped leg from under the unconscious man and pulled himself to his feet. His lower leg hurt like hell. Sprained, likely. Broken, possibly. He didn't care. It wasn't enough to keep him grounded.

He stopped at the door for a moment as memories of the last time he stood there flooded his mind. He watched her, knowing she was pretending to be asleep. He told her where he'd be for part of the next day. She didn't show. She didn't come because they both knew he wasn't coming back.

He shed the guilt and his jacket and went to the stairs.

"Jack," Sadie called out.

"Coming up. Did you clear the kitchen?"

"Yeah, it's good."

"Bear up there?"

"Come see this."

He reached the top of the stairs and saw the window shattered. Shards littered the floor, glinting in the afternoon sun. He followed the trail and saw a lump of a man stretched out.

"Gotta be kidding me." He dropped to a knee next to Bear. "Come on, big man." He turned to Sadie. "Where? Tell me it's not fatal."

She pulled Bear's hair back and revealed the wound to his forehead. Jack grimaced, bit down hard, forced himself to witness a sight he had prepared for long ago but never imagined he'd see.

"Who dropped the Sear's Tower on my head?" Bear's eyes fluttered open. He squinted against the knifing sun.

"Miracle," Sadie said as she pointed up at the wall. "Grazed him."

Jack patted Bear's leg and stood. He inspected the apple-size hole in the wall. For a moment, he felt as though he should crouch, but the realization he had been a sitting duck for the past twenty minutes set in.

"How did they miss?" he wondered aloud.

"I bent down at the last minute. Guess the way I did it put me in the perfect position." Bear reached up and patted his wound. It looked bad, and needed attention, but wouldn't end his life. Not now.

"They knew?" Jack said to Sadie.

She looked toward the window, angling her head, as though she were imagining the bullet's trajectory, coming up with a theory on where it was fired from.

"They might've been waiting," she said. "First person who came in, take them out, get whatever data they could."

"Only problem was us," Noble said. "They didn't count on someone being in the way."

"Literally." She pointed at the cuts on his face. He winced, having forgotten about the accident. And the man. "Shit, the guy outside."

Sadie was already on her feet. "I'll go. You get Bear downstairs."

Jack didn't object and waited until she left the room. "Just hang there for a second." He pulled the dresser away from the wall and felt around until he found what he was looking for. The small handhold allowed him to pull out the seamless cutout section of wall, the contents of which might help him should he manage to break away from Sadie.

A couple bundles of cash and a Glock were the first items he retrieved. Another pass netted a spare magazine with fourteen or fifteen rounds present. He peered inside to see what he was missing.

It took a few moments for the shock of finding nothing else to dissipate. He had left a passport there. He had told Clarissa to keep it safe for him. No matter what, he could return and get it. But she had taken it with her.

She had also taken the spare license plate Beck had made for her.

"Good girl, Clarissa." He had his lead, now he had to find a way to track it.

"About done over there?" Bear said.

Jack reached down, hefted him off the floor and guided him down the stairs. Outside, they found Sadie shaking her head, phone pressed to her ear.

"Are you kidding me?" She glanced around, spotted the duo, held up a finger. "We've got no way out? Two pistols—"

"Three." Jack waved the Glock around.

"*Three* pistols, a half-working man, and a sarcastic asshole. You think I like those odds?"

Jack recoiled in jest. "I know I do."

Sadie tucked her phone into her pocket and pulled out a headset. She threaded it through her clothing and wrapped the earpiece in place. "OK, I'm good. Walk me through it." She waved Jack down and covered the microphone. "We're gonna have to do something with him."

"Bear?"

"Who the hell else am I talking about?"

Jack shrugged and decided now wasn't the best time to test her patience.

"There's a team here. You took that one out." She pointed to the guy on the ground. "At least four more are here."

"How do we know this?"

"I've got Clive and Isa on the phone. They've got eyes on the area."

"There's no CCTV here."

"Someone found a workaround and fed it to them. They hacked the entire facility and broadcast this, I guess."

Jack took a moment to digest this. "They took over Clive's command center to show them what was happening here? This makes no sense. How many damn parties are involved in this?"

Sadie held up a finger. New information coming in. "OK. OK. We'll get in place." She lifted an eyebrow. "Ready to roll, partner?"

CHAPTER 29

Bear remained behind with Sadie's back up piece. The .380 barely fit in his hand. Somehow, he managed to thread his index finger through the trigger guard. If he so much as sneezed, someone was getting a surprise.

Sadie and Jack did their best to blend in as they followed Isa's directions. Neither she nor Clive had told them where they were going, or why. For all Jack knew, this was the plan to separate him and Bear.

That made no sense, though, and he reminded himself that they'd already be dead if that was the plan. Instead, he continued developing a strategy to reach out to the one person who could aide him on his quest to locate Clarissa.

He needed a phone. And some distance from Sadie. The thought crossed his mind he could neutralize her and take her cell. His desperation hadn't reached that point, yet.

"We're almost there," she said.

"Where?"

"There's an older lady who looked after Clarissa. Ring a bell?"

He nodded. He remembered Mrs. Calabase well. The dinners, wine, bread. So much bread. The best bread he had ever had in his life. His mouth watered thinking of the smell. If he had to choose between unlimited wine and that bread, he'd choose the bread.

"She might've helped Clarissa. And these guys might know that."

Jack didn't have to hear the rest. He broke into a run toward the small shop the older woman maintained. Twenty feet away, he heard her cries for help.

He didn't recognize the short guy across the street. Didn't figure out he was a spotter until it was too late. The guy was already on the phone. Jack didn't hesitate to shoot the guy.

The bullet hit true, and the man dropped where he stood, his arms and legs twitching as the final electric currents ran through his body.

The door to Calabase's shop flung open and another short, stocky man stepped out. He barked orders in German, none of which Noble understood. The guy squared up, ready for a fight. Jack figured there were more inside. He adjusted his sights, squeezed off another round, hit the guy dead center.

Noble stepped over the lifeless body and entered the store. It was dim, dank. Heavy dust-filled curtains covered the windows. Rows upon rows of used and new clothing hung from racks jammed together, creating a maze with more dead ends than a Moroccan bazaar.

He made his way to the corner and waited a beat. When nothing stirred, he eased his head over the rack, scanned the room. Empty. Had they left through the back? He lowered a touch and kept his hip to the wall as he moved toward the rear of the store.

The old woman's scream cut through the silence. The sickening thud of a fist smashing against her face came next. Jack's jaw clenched. His pace quickened. He used the clutter to keep his cover, hoping Sadie would soon burst through. She'd draw the attention, sunlight flooding in behind her, drawing every eye toward her. It would give him the cover he needed to rise and take out the next assailant.

It didn't happen, and he began to worry that something had happened to her or Bear. He couldn't think about that. He had to find Mrs. Calabase before they beat her to death.

"I told you, I don't know anything about that girl," the old woman said in Italian. She choked on her sob, then pleaded before another thud. Her groan told Jack she'd had enough. Any more damage and she was going to check out.

"Forget this," he muttered.

He rose and hurried to the back of the store he knew all too well from the dozens of times Clarissa had dragged him in here to try on another sundress. Did she look good? Yeah. Could he have told her that in her apartment? Yeah.

But those boring times had led him to explore the nooks and crannies, and he knew the storeroom area as well as, if not better than the retail section.

He used the barrel of the Glock to push the swinging door open. Pale yellow light spread out in front of him. The bulb hummed, threatening to dim to darkness at any moment.

Mrs. Calabase's soft whimpers reached his ears, as did the low murmur of two distinct male voices.

Jack closed his eyes for a moment, picturing the layout of the storeroom. Where was the best place to tie someone up for interrogation? There were two options. Right was easy. Left hard. And that's the route he chose.

He crept through the storeroom, avoiding the boxes and packaging strewn about. They'd visited the Calabases' home on a few occasions before her husband passed away. It had been pristine. But even before becoming widowed, the woman's store was a mess. Part of the reason Jack wandered through was to straighten up a bit.

A shotgun-blast of popping emanated from under his shoe. He looked down at the deflated packaging bubble. Damn thing must've been four inches thick.

A man said something in German. They'd likely come at Jack from both directions.

Jack stepped back, draped his arms across the rack behind him and gripped the bar. With both feet, he kicked the ten-foot-tall shelving unit in front of him. It toppled forward in slow motion, items careening to the ground starting from the top shelf on down. This had a domino effect when the shelving hit the next row, which also tipped over.

Mrs. Calabase mustered the energy to scream.

The front door crashed open. Sadie called out for Jack.

One of the men yelled in German. Jack looked toward the hall leading to the front of the store. The guy was there. He would take Sadie by surprise.

Jack had the guy dead to rights, but firing would reveal his location to the other guy.

He liked the odds and shot the man in the back. No sooner had he squeezed the trigger, did Jack drop to the floor. He watched for movement from the other side of the room.

A shot rang out.

Not his own. He wasn't prepared. It felt like an icepick penetrated his eardrum.

The other idiot had fired wildly. The bullet lodged into the wall five feet away. Jack had the idiot's location, but no shot available.

"Jack are you back there?" Sadie called from the other end of the corridor.

He couldn't answer. But he saw the last man start moving toward the doorway.

Keep going. Keep going.

Mrs. Calabase spoke in slurred Italian. Jack couldn't understand, but the last guy stopped, bent over, slapped her on the face.

And that was all Noble could take.

He rose from his squatted position, picked his route, and exploded forward. The light was low, but the footholds were obvious. Jack navigated as though running a ladder drill, only this time he had a true incline. It wasn't a silent operation. Couldn't be.

The guy stood tall, looked over his shoulder. His lips separated. His eyes widened. He couldn't square himself up before Noble launched off the last railing.

Sure, it would've been easier to shoot him. But then there's the chance he would've died. This way, Noble could rough him up a bit and then get him to talk.

He collided with the man with the force of a cinder block tossed from the back of a moving F150. The sickening thud of their bones colliding was matched by the terrified scream of Mrs. Calabase as they slammed into her, knocking her chair back and sending her sprawling across the floor.

Jack's momentum carried the two men further, knocking the man off his feet. Jack had his right arm crossed in front of his face, and with the other, he gripped the man's shirt.

At once, they stopped. Noble's head slammed into something hard. He felt the blackness overcome his vision, twinkling lights and fireworks surrounding the edges.

The man underneath him gurgled but didn't move.

"Jack, are you OK?"

He moaned his response.

"Are you hurt?"

He managed a few words. "Calabase. She all right?"

Sadie checked on the woman and returned a moment later. "She's startled, but OK. What about you?"

The cobwebs popped from their anchors one by one. The ache in his head localized and felt like someone had used a sledgehammer to drive a wedge into the right side of his forehead.

"I'll survive," he managed.

"Better than we can say for your friend."

Jack got to his knees and rolled off the guy. He looked into the man's open eyes. Unmoving and lifeless eyes.

"Dammit. That's the whole team."

"And we've got nothing now," Sadie said. "Nothing but Mrs. Calabase here."

And the license plates Clarissa had taken with her.

CHAPTER 30

THE DISTANCE FROM THE LOT TO THE HOTEL WAS A MILE AT most. Clarissa covered it in less than six minutes. Her damp tank top clung to her skin. She pushed phantom hair out of her face while wiping sweat from her eyes. Every gasp of air she pulled in no matter how small seared her lungs.

She stood with her hands wrapped around the back of her head, clasped together to keep them from shaking. She pulled her shoulders back, opening the passageway to allow more oxygen in.

It wasn't the distance. She ran five to ten times farther five days a week, typically at a slower pace, though. Still, she could handle it. The anxiety had taken over and left her nervous system in a lurch.

Someone from the hotel stepped out to check on her.

"Are you OK, miss?"

She nodded and turned away.

"Can we bring you anything? Or help you to your room?"

"I'm good," she said between breaths, even though she wasn't. Instead of cooling off, she was getting hotter.

The man didn't appear to believe her. "Let me show you to your room, Clarissa."

Her entire body clenched. She shook it off, at least in her face, and continued sucking wind. She hadn't checked in under her name. In fact, she hadn't used her name anywhere the past six months. The accounts Beck had set her up with as severance pay were under assumed identities.

Samantha. Jessica. Amelia.

She had rented the room in cash and used a variation, but not one so obvious anyone would catch it.

"Come to think of it," she said. "I could use a few bottles of cold water. I'm having trouble cooling off out here."

He smiled then turned and set off toward the hotel entrance.

Clarissa waited, and once the guy moved out of sight, she scanned the length of the road. There were too many spots that offered cover. Too many locals and tourists about. Anyone could be an enemy. And that meant everyone was an enemy.

She considered the items she had upstairs. Ninety-nine percent of what was up there meant nothing. But there was one thing she needed. She could not leave the envelope behind.

The hotel door stood open and the breeze carried cooled air in her direction. She approached the entrance, careful to keep her gaze unfocused so she could spot any movements around her.

Someone was out there. The employee wouldn't be working alone.

She entered the lobby. Classical music played over the speakers. The vents emanated a floral smell that fit in with the piano arrangement. A young woman maybe twenty years old with the palest blond hair Clarissa had ever seen stood behind the desk. She smiled and called Clarissa by the name she checked in under: Sammie.

The elevator dinged, and the young man stepped out. He aimed a finger at her, then waved her toward him. In his other hand hung a water bottle he grasped under the cap. Even at a distance, she could see the condensation on the outside.

"Ms. Tahini," he said. "I got this for you, but I put a case of nice cold water in your room. Please, let me escort you."

She studied him as she approached, careful not to give her suspicions away. Doubt crowded out other thoughts, leading to irrational thinking. She began to replay the scene outside. She heard his thick accent saying the words, slowly at first, then increasing the pace.

"*...show you to your room, Clarissa.*"

That's what he had said, right? She'd heard it, right?

Or had she?

The rushing blood dominated everything. It pulsed in her vision. The *whomp-whomp* of her heartbeat was louder than the passing traffic, sound of the sea, children laughing as they played on the sidewalk.

He led her to the elevator, held the door until she had boarded. The mirrored glass had a golden hue to it. They both looked tan, as though they were returning from the beach.

He smiled when she looked into the reflection of his eyes. The guy was no hardened criminal. He was soft. Baby fat cheeks. Manicured hands. Nicely pressed uniform.

The anxiety melted away, and for the first time since she took off from the parking lot, she caught her breath. She uncapped the water bottle, feeling the seal tear, and took a drink. Half the bottle slid down her throat in a matter of three seconds.

"What did you call me outside?" she asked.

His brow furrowed as he glanced toward the ceiling. "I don't think I did?"

"You said you'd take me to my room and said a name."

He smiled and the tension left his face. "Let me show you to your room to rest."

She parroted his words and his accent. "To rest-ah." A laugh escaped her throat. "Sounded like you said the name of an old friend of mine."

The elevator halted, dinged, opened. He stretched out his arm again, and with a sweeping gesture, waited for Clarissa to exit.

She smiled, glanced at his uniform again. The perfect white shirt. Black pants. And a paisley vest with the hotel's name embroidered on it.

Two steps later, she felt a tug at the strings of her awareness.

This isn't right.

The young woman at the front desk, what did she have on? She was covered from the mid-torso down. Her shirt was a white button up. Her vest, paisley, too. But something looked different.

Clarissa had practiced the walk from the elevator to her room multiple times the previous night. She knew how many steps she had taken. And how many were left. Seven more until she reached her door.

She glanced over her shoulder, not focusing on any one thing behind her. Rather, she took the sight of the man in as a whole and let her mind process the differences between him and the lady downstairs.

He narrowed his eyes. His right hand, which had hung loose at his side, swung behind his back.

She began scanning his uniform.

Three steps to go.

His arm started to come back around.

Two steps to go.

He's not wearing a name tag.

One step to go.

"Let me show you to your room, Clarissa."

Her hand reached for the knob.

His hand reappeared holding a long silver pistol.

She turned the handle. The door whipped open, pulled free from her grasp by the suction tunnel created by the wind. She lurched forward, forced the door shut, stepped to the side. Her hand fumbled across the dresser top looking for something, anything, she could use in a fight.

The guy didn't bother trying the knob. It sounded as though he used a sledgehammer and had attacked the frame. The door smashed inward and splintered at the latch and broke free without the need for a second kick.

Clarissa crouched, knowing the man would sweep the room at eye level first and she would be out of his line of sight long enough for her attack.

The barrel poked through two feet above her head. He followed. It all happened in a second. He spotted her and stepped back while trying to shorten his arms and readjust his wrists.

Clarissa exploded upward, the sharp end of the thick nail file driving out and up. She had figured the attack would strike the groin, doing enough damage to make the guy drop his gun, if not send him collapsing to ground in agonizing pain.

However, his evasive maneuvering to realign his shot had taken him out of harm's way.

Clarissa's momentum carried her to her feet. The file's path would slice into his throat, and she could seat the blade deep, dig it around, and cut the carotid.

He saw it, though, and dropped his head back while arching his back.

Clarissa's balance shifted, and she turned into him. As soon as he regained his composure, he'd have her in a headlock, and could easily render her unconscious with a couple of pistol butt smashes.

The sunlight streaming through the side window shone on the handgun. The glint caught her eye. Her right arm, already lifted above her head with the file, came down hard on the crook of his elbow, driving the blade through skin and muscle.

The gun went off.

The world bellowed and swerved and pain clawed from one side of her brain and then back.

The man had fared no better against the sound. They were far too close, and not ready.

Clarissa released the file and brought the knifed edge of her fist down on the base of the guy's thumb. In his disoriented state, that was all it took for him to release his grip on the pistol. It clattered against the tile floor. She kicked it to the side, then brought the same leg up and delivered a knee strike to his groin.

He bowed over in front of her. She clenched both hands high, drove them down at the base of his neck. He flopped to the ground and made a squealing sound as all the air in his lungs escaped at once.

She searched the room and located the pistol.

"Who are you?" she yelled, the firearm aimed at the mass of man on the floor.

He groaned but managed no words.

"Tell me!"

He wouldn't, or couldn't, reply.

She moved toward him. There was noise in the hallway. How could there not be? It sounded like a bomb had gone off in the room a few seconds prior.

His hands and legs twitched. His face was turning from blue to purple. She tried to kick him over, but he didn't budge. His body had already turned lifeless.

One final gasp emanated from his mouth and then his expression went as slack as his body.

She knelt and felt for a pulse. Not present. She rummaged through his pockets and found a folding knife, a wallet, two cell phones, and a crumpled piece of paper.

A man started barking orders at her. She looked up at the guy and lifted the pistol in his direction. He stumbled backward, tripping on the lady behind him and colliding with the wall. He grabbed his shoulder as he slunk to the floor, muttering something over and over. She didn't need a translator to know the man begged for his life.

Gotta get going, girl.

She took one last look at the room and remembered why she had made the trip up to begin with. She pulled open the dresser drawer and grabbed the envelope.

Now all she had to do was get out of the hotel alive.

Most people would've welcomed the sirens that cascaded like the sound of a waterfall throughout the hotel.

For Clarissa, it meant one more obstacle.

CHAPTER 31

Jack and Sadie found Bear seated atop a three-step walkup. His legs were spread wide. His head buried in his hands with his wild hair hung over them.

"What happened?" Jack asked.

Bear looked up. Blood dripped down one side of his face. "He got up. Had to put him down. Feel bad."

Jack approached Bear, placing his hand on the big man's shoulders when he was a couple feet away. "He shouldn't have come here. They shouldn't have roughed up the old lady."

Bear chuckled, then recoiled at the blood that had worked its way into his mouth. He spat off to the side. "Don't give two shits about the dead guy, man. Physically, I feel bad." He threw out his arm. "Help my weak ass up."

Jack pulled him to his feet and assisted him down the steps.

Sadie stood off to the side, phone against her ear. Every answer was affirmative. Clive and his people had watched it all.

"You think—" Bear started.

"I'm not gonna try to guess anymore," Jack said. "If he wants us dead, why send us out here?"

"Fetish?"

Jack couldn't help but laugh at the off-the-wall joke.

Sadie tucked her phone away and walked up to the guys. "Well, they were completely blindsided."

"Didn't have eyes on the place?" Bear asked.

"There were none. At least, Clive didn't think so."

"What happened?" Bear let go of Jack's arm and stood on his own.

"Hacked. The entire command center shut down, basically."

"How could that happen?" Jack asked.

"There's some smart people out there, guys. Better question is, how do you two keep outlasting them?"

"Bear could've been a Harvard guy."

"Told you never to tell anyone that."

"Focus." Sadie snapped her fingers and waved her fist in front of them. "Everything was offline. Even the TVs had no reception. Isa gets an idea to start changing the channel. Guess what?" She paused a beat, but neither man spoke up. "Someone had accessed the private cameras throughout the town and were feeding them back on different channels."

"How?" Jack asked.

"Do I look like a cable guy?" Sadie said. "So, they watched this bit play out."

"Figured all cell phones were routed through the internet in there," Bear said. "If they were down, how'd he call you now?"

Jack added a finger wag for emphasis. "What he said."

Sadie rolled her eyes at Noble and took a deep breath to recenter herself. "Everything came back online right after."

Jack strode out to the middle of the street and stopped there. He peeled back his shirt and yelled out, "Here's your chance. Take your shot. Do it. Now."

Nothing happened.

"What are you doing you damn fool?" Sadie tried to grab his ear, but he ducked at the last second. Her nails caught hold of his hair and a few strands ripped free.

"They're toying with us," Jack said. "They're gonna send us to the next place, and the next, and they'll always be a step ahead."

"Who?" Sadie said. "Because if you can answer that, we can put this all to bed right now."

He shook his head, his chin dipping to his chest. A bead of sweat trickled down the length of his nose. "Can't answer that. So many people want me dead."

"But who else hates you enough to torture you like this?" Bear asked.

"Grab a pen and notebook, because that answer will take a while." He looked up at Sadie. "Answer me honestly, you know the man better than I do. Could—"

"No." She put her hand on his chest like she was going to shove him back. Instead, she grabbed his shirt and pulled him closer. He caught a whiff of lavender. "I've been around Clive for the past ten years on and off. Does he like money? Sure. We all do, right?" She glanced over at Bear. "I've seen the man turn down a big payday because the terms weren't moral. He'd kill you in a heartbeat, Jack. *If* you deserved it. But he'd never touch Mia."

Jack narrowed his eyes. "How do you know about Mia?"

"I know everything about you, Jack. I was forced to keep tabs on you two knuckleheads."

"By Clive?"

She shook her head. "That's not important. Clarissa is. She's in real danger. They knew enough to attack the old lady, and I'm gonna go talk to her in a minute to see what she knows, but that means we've got a bit of a chance. About thirty minutes worth of a chance to track Clarissa down." Sadie tossed her keys to Jack. As she headed back to the store, she added, "Get that big oaf in the car and meet me up here."

Jack wrapped his arm around Bear and helped him down the sloping sidewalk until they reached the car. After a quick check for signs of tampering, he helped Bear into the passenger seat. They drove the few blocks to the store and idled half a block past.

The AC dried any remaining sweat and cooled his body temperature.

"Hell of a mess, huh, partner?"

Bear groaned.

"Didn't think we'd be doing battle together again, did you?"

Bear groaned again.

"Bet you never knew about that time I hooked up with your cousin."

"What?" The big man had a hand on Noble's throat in record time.

Jack's smile stretched ear to ear. "Just making sure you're not over there hemorrhaging into your skull."

"Asshole."

"Present and accounted for."

Bear adjusted his vents and leaned in closer. The steady stream of air made his hair dance. He closed his eyes and shook his face side-to-side. "This is a disaster, man."

"Ain't gotta tell me."

"These people know our every move. Going back to the hospital. And you in Luxembourg. Who in the hell would ever look for you there?"

"Everything was backchannel, taken from one hand and delivered to the other. There was nothing digital, nothing to be intercepted. The response came back with the same courier. Someone you know and trust, by the way."

"Who?"

"You know that's not a good idea."

"Kamel?"

"Shit no."

"Larry?"

They both yelled "Larry" in unison and then broke into laughter.

"It's always like not a day has passed with you." Jack slapped the steering wheel and gripped it tighter than before. "These moments, man, they're effortless."

Bear nodded as his gaze dropped to his knees. "Lots of days are gonna have to pass, Jack. I can't do this anymore." He held up his hand and shoved it open-palmed to Noble's face. "And I know I've said that plenty the past decade. But look at me." He turned to face his friend. "I can't do this anymore. Arms don't work right. Legs don't work right. I wanna say shit and I say piss. I wanna say piss and I say giraffe. I wanna say giraffe and I say shit."

"Circle of life."

This time Bear did put his hand in Jack's face, forcing his skull to the window. "Ain't funny. This is serious."

"There's physical therapy, right? Takes time."

Bear let his hand drop. He took a deep breath, sighed it out. "My progress was stunted following the procedure."

"Stunted? So, you mean, slowed down, right?"

"As in not happening. They say it sometimes takes a while, but, this one doctor, he said this might be as good as it gets." Bear made a sweeping gesture from his neck to his knees.

Jack couldn't look Bear in the eye. For men like them, an unworking body was their death sentence.

"And I think I can manage this if, you know, I'm an insurance salesman, or whatever."

"You don't ever have to worry about money."

"I know, man. I control half the accounts. We're set and all. But I'm not gonna be able to *sit* there all damn day."

"So, travel, then."

"Ain't getting on a plane again unless I'm forced to."

"In an RV."

Bear snickered. That was low. Even for Jack. "Screw you and your damn RVs."

Jack joined in the laughter. It ended when he saw Sadie step out of the store, her face drawn tight.

She opened the rear passenger door and hopped in. Realizing the lack of legroom, she slid across the seat. Her hands gripped Jack's seat and pulled him back an inch.

"What'd she say?" Jack asked.

"I got two words out of her." She closed her eyes, shook her head. "'I'm sorry'."

"For?" Jack said.

"Didn't you hear me say two words? I swear, it's like dealing with a toddler. Anyway, it doesn't matter about what. All those men are dead and with them, any secrets Calabase told them."

"So, what's the problem?" Jack turned in his seat and they were eye to eye.

"There was a shooting at a little resort town in Croatia."

CHAPTER 32

Clarissa waited at the loading dock for what felt like hours but, spanned fewer than sixty seconds. The sirens rose and fell and dissipated entirely as they switched off one at a time. The silence that overtook her left a hum in her ears and a pit in her stomach.

How did they know her exact location?

She eased into the gap between the thick plastic drapes that served as doors wide enough and tall enough to allow a box truck to back up.

A truck had been idling on the other side for five minutes. The driver, she presumed, had ventured around the corner of the building to check out what was happening out front.

Clarissa lowered herself and slid underneath the exterior flap and eased down to the ground, unable to prevent the loading dock from scraping her back. She grimaced against the pain, which was soon forgotten.

The driver had been so preoccupied with the situation that he had forgotten to secure the lift gate. Clarissa opened it wide enough to slide under, then, before lowering it down, jammed a wood shim into the locking mechanism to keep it from latching.

She waited for several minutes. The space grew hotter. The tiny sliver of light that had penetrated when she first closed the gate now felt like knives sent directly from the sun to penetrate her soul. But she had to look. She had to watch for shadows. She had to be ready to pull the hand cannon she had taken from the man and use it on whoever confronted her.

The cabin door opening and closing reverberated throughout the cargo area. Clarissa flinched at each echo. But relief took anxiety's place, at least momentarily, as the driver shifted into gear and the idle turned into a low rumble and the truck eased away from the loading dock.

Her body rolled with the movements.

He turned left.

Good. That took them toward the coast.

One more left.

They came to a stop, and she prayed he was going left again. The driver had an exchange she couldn't follow even if she knew the language. The barrier between the cabin and her was too thick.

The door opened. Closed. Reverberated. Echoed. Anxiety overtook relief.

She reached behind her and retrieved the pistol from the small of her back. Eleven shots. She had dropped the magazine and checked. Ten in the magazine, one in the chamber. If she needed more than eleven rounds, she deserved to die.

The floor beneath her vibrated as someone pounded on the side of the cargo area. They walked around, talking the entire time, rapping on the exterior. With a hand? A baton? A baseball bat?

She pictured the driver and cop moving around the truck until they stopped behind her.

The men had a back-and-forth exchange. One spoke better than the other. The conversation dipped into English for a moment.

"Nothing. I brought the produce. Now I am going home. Here's my manifest."

Two other men spoke in their native tongue. The driver cursed in English.

Then several seconds of silence. It washed over her in waves that never retreated, each piling onto the last, suffocating Clarissa with panic.

Footsteps faded. The front door opened and closed. The driver shifted back into gear. Idling turned into a low grumble. The truck inched forward, then turned right. It picked up speed quickly enough for Clarissa to know the driver meant to go this way.

She had to act. Fast. But they were still within sight of the hotel. She got to a crouching position and reached for the door. The truck dipped and bucked and knocked her back on her butt. It sent a jolt up her spine. She clung to the pistol. Thank God, the thing could've gone off and who knows where the bullet would have come to rest.

By the time she realized what had happened, the cargo area went dark. The wood shim had dislodged. The gate had shut. The lock had latched.

Clarissa rose to her hands and knees and crawled forward. She bumped into the door and felt along the floor to the right. There was nothing to grab hold of. She moved to the left, inch-by-inch, fingers grating along the shredded sheet metal. She reached the corner.

"Where is it?" She heard the panic in her voice. "Phone. Flashlight." She recalled the phones she had taken off the man in her room. Pulled one out. It was dead. She grabbed the other and flipped it open. A dull blue screen welcomed her. She shone it outward and could barely make out the door. But she went back to the right and then left again. The shim was nowhere.

Defeated, she dropped back and draped her arms over her knees. She'd have to wait until the guy stopped, and even then, there were no guarantees she could escape until his next destination if he opened the gate.

What had he said? Fresh produce.

Couldn't be that far, then. She clawed at the base of the door, found the handle and tugged. It gave only enough for light to filter inside. She grabbed the handle and yanked it up, pushed it down until it freed.

Fifteen seconds later she hit the asphalt hard and rolled in the street after jumping out of the back of the moving truck. She scrambled to avoid an oncoming car, feeling a gust of wind as it missed her head by two inches.

Her arms were covered in scrapes. She felt the road rash down her side from her chest to her knees. Blood trickled across her skin like baby snakes. She ignored the searing pain and staggered to the sidewalk. A few people came up to her offering help. They backed off, one turning to run, after seeing the large pistol in her hand.

Clarissa took a moment and let the sea breeze wash over her, inhaling the salty air, centering herself. Focus and determination won out, and a plan formed. She had to get to the parking lot, back to the Vespa. Could her legs carry her there?

The path to the marina hadn't changed, but it would be a tougher run than earlier. More people. More obstacles. More cops. Damn, the cops were everywhere. How did this little town support so many cops?

She relaxed her gaze, turned in a half-circle. Something had to exist in this location to help her.

And it appeared in the form of a bicycle. Two sizes too small, but unlocked, resting against the war-torn facade of a building.

She limped across the street. The pain in her bones had subsided while the scrapes had intensified. Every gust of wind felt like added salt and lemon to her wounds.

The owner of the bicycle was nowhere to be found. She took one last glance, spotting a few onlookers who still watched her. One had a cell phone to his head. Probably calling the cops. Were there more who could respond? There wasn't time to wait and find out.

Biting down hard, she rushed forward, grabbed the handlebars, and jumped on the bicycle. The route would be looping, but the destination was set.

The marina.

But she had to make one stop first.

CHAPTER 33

THE JET TOUCHED DOWN AT A PRIVATE AIRSTRIP OUTSIDE OF Pula, Croatia. What would have been a seven-hour drive took a mere seventy minutes. Going direct over the Adriatic helped.

They were an hour and a half removed from the shooting. Close enough that the corpse might still be warm. The cops would be all over the site collecting evidence that could lead them to who was behind this. None of that mattered to Jack. Only Clarissa.

Their intel indicated she had escaped, but the last footage of her was from inside the hotel. She hadn't been found by local law enforcement or the hotel staff even though the place had been on lockdown since the shot was fired.

Clive's team worked to get access to any and all CCTV available, but so far, cooperation had been nonexistent.

They had to be careful on the ground. They would stand out, no doubt. Sadie offered to do the bulk of the heavy lifting. There was less concern over her being detained since she had nothing of note against her in Croatia. Jack and Bear painted a different picture. The government might use them as pawns to get something in return. And they wouldn't care who made the highest offer. And if the highest bidder happened to be the US government, they wouldn't throw the kind of welcome home party Noble would find entertaining.

They crammed into a smaller sedan and sped toward the resort town. Sitting in the back seat, Jack pulled out his cell phone and connected to a private server he hadn't had the audacity to use in months.

He sent a message, using codewords for the request.

If anyone could perform the operation without others noticing, it was Brandon. The tech God had never let Noble down, though Jack had failed Brandon plenty.

He redirected his attention to the conversation in the front seat. The witty banter between two old friends eased his mind and allowed him to rest for the remainder of the drive. Nothing he could do at this moment, no point in stressing about it.

It took twenty minutes to reach Medulin. The contrast between older war-torn buildings with large bullet holes riddling their facade and newer developments meant to lure the tourists in was striking and a harsh reminder of the civil war that pulled the region apart for years.

He imagined the resort town operated at a slower pace and always felt tranquil. Not today. Police cars cruised the roads in pairs, with officers paired up inside. The entire block surrounding the hotel was barricaded and taped off.

They pulled into a nearby parking lot and waited for Clive to feed them the latest intel. He piped in a couple minutes later.

"You're not alone," he said.

"Who else is here?" Sadie asked.

"Can't tell you that, but there's plenty of chatter. I will assume it is whoever sent the hitman."

"Can you confirm his status?"

"Dead."

Sadie looked at the guys, her features relaxed, an audible sigh escaped her lips. They all felt it.

"Any chance we can get in there?" Sadie asked.

"None," Clive said. "The hotel is on lockdown. We have no friendlies anywhere in this area. Not exactly a hotbed of espionage."

"We might need to split up," Jack said.

"It is best you three stay together. We're working on CCTV feeds, and, in fact, Isa just told me she's got three, and one is near the hotel."

"Where are the other two?" Sadie asked.

"Hold on." Clive's voice became muffled as he called out to his team. He came back on the line. "One is at the far end of town. Another about a mile away, looks to be overlooking a marina."

Jack tried to ignore the tingle traveling down his spine.

"Hold on again," Clive murmured.

A few more minutes passed, and the trio grew antsy.

"Don't like this," Bear said. "What's going on?"

Jack mirrored the big man's sentiment. He judged each person who passed or stopped nearby, every car, every passenger. He wanted out. They were wasting time now. Every minute that passed, Clarissa could be further away, or closer to being caught by the other team.

"We've got a location for you," Clive said.

"Clarissa?" Bear asked.

"No, whoever is looking for her." He said something off mic again, then returned. "West from your location, past the hotel, about half a mile, so almost exactly in-between that marina and the hotel. You'll need to drive around back to get there."

"Already on it." Sadie slipped the transmission into gear and worked her way through a side street and alleyway until they were on another larger road. She pulled to the curb and cut the engine. "This'll do."

"There's at least three of them," Clive said. "I'm sending you images, pretty detailed, so you'll pick them out, I hope, before they realize who you are."

Sadie held her phone out and navigated to their private app. The photos downloaded. Nondescript faces Noble had seen thousands of times. These guys were all the same to him now. If they needed to die, he felt no guilt over expediting the end of their lives.

"We need to go dark now," Clive said. "Check in when you can."

"You guys ready?" Sadie opened her door before either man replied.

They joined her on the sidewalk and wound their way back to the coast, past the other team's location. Stopping at the corner where a building concealed them, Jack pulled his phone out and checked the server for a response from Brandon.

Nothing had come through, not even a confirmation.

"What's that?" Bear looked down at the phone.

"Tell you soon."

Bear chuckled. "I'm sure you will."

Sadie was on her phone, too. She tucked it away. "I'm going first."

"Not a good idea," Bear said.

"Chances are these guys are more aware of you than they are me." She reached behind her back and felt for her pistol, seemingly relieved when her hand grazed the butt. "And I'm a great shot. I'll get at least two before I'm hit."

Neither man returned her smile.

"Lighten up, guys." She laughed as she rounded the corner.

Jack took a moment to watch her. She didn't go far before stepping inside the building.

"Trust her," Bear said. "She ain't led us astray yet."

Jack paced the length of the building. His mind raced, anticipating gunshots at any moment. Approaching the team was the wrong way to go about it. They had numbers. One person could watch, and the obvious choice was Bear. The big man would be against it, but the reality of the situation was he was the biggest liability in the group.

Jack made his way back to Bear, who tried to engage him in conversation. Jack ignored him. He couldn't focus on a single word the man was saying. Not after the phone buzzed in his pocket.

The other end of the building couldn't be reached any quicker. He glanced over his shoulder at Bear, who stood there with one arm against the facade like he was holding the entire town up.

Jack fished the phone out and fumbled with the unlock screen. "Easy, man," he muttered as he punched in the code incorrectly. His heart was in his throat as he connected to the server, passing each security check. He could only error once. Then his IP address would be locked forever, or at least until Brandon fixed it.

"*On it.*"

The best two words Noble had heard all day. Followed by the worst four.

"We gotta go now!"

CHAPTER 34

BEAR LOOKED LIKE THE ATHLETE HE WAS, GOING FROM ZERO TO semi-sprint in a matter of seconds. Adrenaline had lit the big man on fire. He grunted as he took off, leaving behind an open space for Jack to stare at blankly.

The elation over his first communication with Brandon in months had been replaced with anxiety knifing through his chest. He pushed forward, his gaze on the widening slice of the street. Every face was a potential enemy. Any commotion caused could lead any of the dozens of cops a half mile away to their location.

He had his hand on the pistol grip before he turned the corner. What would he find? There had been no gunshots, no shouting. No one had come running this way.

He eased past the safety the building provided and stepped into the open. A block down, a large group of people gathered. Bear was pulling them apart, discarding them like they were paper dolls.

Jack surveyed the situation as he picked up his pace. He never broke into a run but came close. The commotion was everything. Not missing a thing became critical.

Halfway there, the sound of sirens bounced off the building. Brakes locked and tires squealed. People backed off. Bear knelt over a body. Sadie's body. The cops exited.

"Not good," he muttered, as a wave of people moved toward him. He resumed moving forward, pushing people out of his way as they collided. The crowed thinned enough that a view of Bear emerged. He had his hand behind Sadie's back. She was upright.

"The hell happened, big man?"

Bear was too far away to have heard him, but he turned and looked at Jack anyway and shook his head. Not a sign of what had happened there, rather a warning. Back off.

Noble had already heeded it. He backtracked, checking every few steps to see how the police were handling the situation. The cops were helping Sadie to her feet. She was animated, waving them off. Law enforcement had enough going on. She might succeed at getting them to leave her alone. Bear was shaking his head. Jack could hear Bear's words, "Just came up on her and found her on the ground. Never seen her before."

A car braked ahead at the same spot Jack had been pacing. A white Genesis. Three people inside. Looked a lot like the ones in the photos. They'd pick him out just as easily.

He took another glance toward Bear and Sadie. Bear was walking back, limping badly enough Jack figured he was embellishing to keep the cops from following. Sadie was less animated. She must've succeeded. One of the cops was back in his car, waving the others to join him.

The Genesis peeled onto the main road and settled in between a couple other cars traveling in the opposite direction. Jack didn't want to lose them, they might have a lead on Clarissa.

He turned toward Bear again, held out his arms, hiked his thumb over his shoulder. Bear nodded. The connection, the bond, the brotherhood they shared, still existed.

Jack took off on foot, running, pistol in hand so it wouldn't fall out and accidentally discharge.

Pedestrians crossing the street kept traffic in a stop-start-stop pattern, allowing him to maintain minimal separation with the Genesis. He had a couple hundred yards before they started to pull away. He picked up his pace, so zoned in he didn't hear the car pull up next to him.

"Get in."

He looked over and saw Bear leaning his head out the window of the sedan. Sadie was in the driver's seat.

"White Genesis," he said, sliding into the back seat. "The hell happened back there?"

"The people in the white Genesis, I'm guessing," Sadie said. "Came up behind me. One rushed past, the other tased me. The third was about to shoot me, but the crowd was too much."

"Cops didn't follow up on that?" Jack asked.

"Told them I got knocked over. Nothing else. Bear told everyone to shut up if they knew what was good for them. Maybe someone'll talk, but we'll be long gone by then."

"Check it out." Bear pointed ahead. The Genesis had stopped. A door opened. Someone hopped out.

"That's my cue." Jack didn't wait for Sadie to stop before opening the door and putting his foot on the ground. "Stay with them."

Momentum carried him across the sidewalk to the railing separating beach from concrete. He grabbed hold and leapt over. The packed sand offered little cushion; felt like lightning bolts running up his legs when he landed.

The guy was about a hundred feet ahead, moving at a steady clip toward the marina. And within a few minutes, that was the obvious destination.

BEAR DRUMMED HIS THICK FINGERTIPS ON THE DASH, LEAVING behind a white film that dissipated within a second. He watched the two remaining men in the Genesis. He planned which he'd kill first.

"Still don't get why he didn't shoot or stab me," Sadie said. "They knew who I was."

"Don't overcomplicate it."

"What's that mean?"

"Someone told them not to. But they wanted you incapacitated."

"They don't know you two are with me."

"That's too much of an assumption. I'd lean toward them knowing everything and being pleasantly surprised when we find out they didn't know about us."

"They're slowing down." Sadie switched lanes and settled in one car behind. "What's up there?"

"Looks like a parking lot. And they're turning into it."

Sadie slowed.

"No," Bear said. "Go a little further past and pull over. Gonna put some theories to the test. Make sure you pop the trunk for me."

They rolled to a stop and the trunk popped open with a clunk. Bear hopped out and went to the back. He pulled up the mat and lifted the spare tire. The crowbar felt heavy, solid, and capable of bashing a skull in. He let it weigh his arm down, holding it so it was out of sight. The little .380 brushed against his thigh. He reached in his pocket and threaded his finger through the trigger.

The front doors of the white Genesis were open. The men were looking at the scooters in the parking lot. They barked orders in German at a family passing by. The little girl started crying. Her father scooped her in his arms and carried her away. One of the men laughed.

Bear didn't have to decide any longer. That man was dead.

Even with the limp, he moved light on his feet. The ground hardly crunched under his size fifteens. The men sure as hell didn't notice him. Not even at twenty feet away.

Twenty feet that Bear covered in a couple seconds. He brought the crowbar up like a warrior ready to take a scalp. He brought it down hard and fast. The guy had no chance, never knew what hit him. The crack and stifled scream were nothing compared to the bloody mess left behind.

The other guy turned, mouth agape. He froze in place. All but his eyes. They drifted past Bear.

Sadie.

He heard the car door open. He saw the guy grin. He felt the concussive force long before he felt the searing pain in his back.

Security was non-existent at the marina. Jack followed the guy right to the docks.

Boats rolled gently in the calm sea. A cascade of creaking vessels and singing birds and chatter from the outdoor restaurant filled the air.

The guy stopped.

Jack slowed.

The guy reached under his shirt. Pulled out a black handgun.

Jack scanned ahead.

He saw her. The hair was short and dark, but the rest was unmistakable.

Clarissa.

The guy lifted the pistol, took aim.

He cupped his hands over his mouth and yelled loud enough for half the town to hear. "Clarissa!"

She turned. She spotted the would-be assassin. She looked past the guy. Looked Noble right in the eye.

The guy fired a wild shot. People screamed. Plates crashed.

The overabundance of law enforcement in the town would soon mobilize to take on the second shooter of the day.

Clarissa sprinted down the closest dock, dropping all but one bag. Styrofoam food containers spilled out. Soup spread in a puddle. Noodles formed a pile. At the end of the line of boats, a man stood working the lines and waved her toward him.

The gunman was looking back at Jack. He fired another round that slammed into the wall next to Noble. The guy didn't fire another shot, switching his focus instead to Clarissa. He sprinted forward, firing again and again.

Did he think it would make her stop?

It didn't, but whatever was in her path that tripped her did.

Jack was sprinting toward the shooter. He was on top of Clarissa. He didn't want to kill her, that much was clear. But he reared back and smacked the pistol against the side of her head. She went limp. For a moment. The guy eased up, thinking he had her down. She lashed out, catching him in the throat. He fell back. She wriggled out from under him. Her boat was only a few steps away.

The gunman got his footing. Steadied his shaking arm. This time he aimed to kill.

Noble slammed into him as though the shooter were a tackling dummy. They hit the ground hard, near the edge of the dock. He felt the rough wood splinter into his forearm.

Clarissa called out. "Jack!"

He wanted to say, *hold please*, but the hand in his face trying to separate his head from his neck made it a little tricky.

The boat's engine shifted from purring to roaring. The captain maneuvered it to the side.

Jack's opponent landed a groin shot and took the opportunity to get up and kick him. The shots landed on his ribs, then diaphragm. Knocked the wind out of him. The pistol lay a couple feet away. The man reached down for it.

The boat was still close to the dock, and if the guy tried, he could probably jump on board.

It appeared that was his plan.

Jack scrambled to his knees, his feet, bent over, he sprinted and dove at the guy, knocking him into the water, his momentum carrying him in, too.

They struggled under the surface. But this is where Noble wanted the shooter. Sure, the guy could stand there and kick Jack after racking him in the nuts. But up close, he'd never escape Noble's grasp. And this guy had no chance as Jack worked the man's back, wrapped his right arm around the guy's neck, and pinned it there with his other arm.

He only fought back for thirty seconds before going limp. Jack let him go and floated to the surface.

The boat named *Abandonment* had cleared the others and was drifting away. Clarissa stood at the back. She wiped tears from her cheeks. She held one finger up until Jack did the same.

The same gesture Clarissa had made a few times while they were together.

PART 3

CHAPTER 35

OLIVE TREES DOTTED THE TRANQUIL PROPERTY LIKE guardians. The thick trunks latched into the dusty earth like weathered pilings. Pale leaves looked white in the noon sun; danced when the breeze came through. Overhead, a few wispy clouds floated past. Jack attached his rampant thoughts onto each cloud until a single one remained.

Clarissa.

It had been a week since they lost her to the sea. Finding the boat had been a challenge. Once the slip number had been noted, it took less than an hour to get transponder information. But the boat went dark until it resurfaced after the trip across the Adriatic. A makeshift team was put in place, ready to move in. But when the vessel reached shore in southern Italy, Clarissa was gone.

The man said she had jumped when they were within a mile of the coast, but they had traveled a good twenty mile stretch at that distance from shore. If she had jumped, she had a head start on them.

But if she saw Jack on that dock. She'd find a way to make contact.

Noble had spent the last two days under the same shade tree, in the same chair, with the same laptop opened to the same screensaver. He had requested and received the laptop, new phones, and a passport. Clive told him up front, he could track Jack's every move with the devices, and the passport could be called in at a moment's notice.

"Try to fly, and you'll die."

Sadie was en route, at last. Bear was left out of commission. A baseball bat to the back had done some damage, and when combined with his reduced physical abilities, they all agreed he was a liability. He and Mandy had been moved to a secure location. Contact had been made with Sasha. Soon they'd be reunited to be the family Bear wanted.

As long as Jack could finish the task.

The door to the small farmhouse opened. Clive stepped out, shielded from the sun by the overhang. Five remaining beers from a six-pack dangled perilously close to the ground as he crossed the sparse landscaping to join Noble.

"Any news?" Jack asked.

Clive pulled back the tab on a can and handed it to Jack after the head retreated. "Nothing." He took a long pull from his own beer. "Any thoughts on where she might go?"

"Gonna say dinner with Mrs. Calabase is out of the question."

Clive forced a laugh but didn't look up from his drink.

"Who did it?" Jack asked. "Who shut you down and left that clue for you?"

Clive appeared to measure his words. "I don't know, and I don't like that I don't know. It would take a team of top hackers just to infiltrate one of our systems. Whoever did this took us down entirely, and, for fun, left a way for us to see what they were doing."

"You think it's them, then. Whoever hacked you was responsible for what happened in town? Every one of them seemed to have German accents."

"Does that tell us anything other than where they've been recruiting?"

Jack shrugged. "You're the brains, man."

"I've thought about it, too, and there are some connections we can reach out to. Ask who's been nosing around. But you know as well as I do whoever it is has been smart enough to leave no traces. I am aware of my own vetting process. There's ten steps before you ever reach me. I'd wager they are operating the same. We may uncover a step or two in the process, but getting to the top, that's another matter."

Jack finished his beer and reached for another. Clive obliged, opening another can.

"Who hired you to bring me in?" Noble asked.

Clive looked up, smiled, scratched the stubble on his chin as though it made his face the most uncomfortable it had ever felt. "I'm bound by confidentiality."

"Would that confidentiality extend if I had you hanging over a saw blade by a thin rope?"

"Do what you want with me, Jack. You'll suffer a worse fate."

And Noble knew it. If he made a move now, a guy positioned in the upstairs bedroom would send a .308 Win round through his skull.

"I'm still alive," Jack said. "Bear, too, as far as I know. I imagine Sadie can confirm when she gets here."

"I'll do you one better." Clive set his beer down and stood. He smoothed out his pants, then reached into his pocket, producing his phone a moment later. After a few taps on the screen, he flipped the phone and showed Jack the video stream of Bear and Mandy playing chess at a kitchen table. Behind them, an armed guard stood watch at the door. "He's there to protect them," Clive said, presumably noting the concern on Jack's face.

"Why're you doing this? From what I can tell, the entire operation has been a fiasco. Someone got the drop on you, over me, Bear, and now Clarissa. You don't strike me as a guy who's hurting for money."

"As one who has reviewed your financial documents, at least the ones I can access, you're not hurting, either. So why have you continued to do what you do?"

"A mix of bad luck and needing to right my negative karma."

"Maybe I'm the same." Clive tapped Jack's beer can with his own.

"Wouldn't it have been easier to have Ines kill me? Get it over with?"

Clive cleared his throat. "I'm hesitant to speak on this, as what I say may upset you."

"As long as you didn't sleep with my mom..." Jack aimed his finger at Clive's face.

Clive didn't respond to the joke. "If we had found you in the first month, we'd have brought you in, but if you fought back, tried to run, you'd have been wounded, perhaps fatally."

"Bear, too?"

Clive shook his head. "He was not an original target. Once it became clear the route we had to take, Logan became a necessity."

"A necessity? What, so I'd agree?"

"It was him or your daughter, and I know how that would've gone."

"It wouldn't have. I'd have pinned your ass to that table in your secret laboratory and killed you and anyone who tried to save you."

"I know." Clive tipped his head back and stared up at the dull green canopy. "It's a fiasco."

"What happened? You wanted to kill me, then you were determined to bring me in, then you were racing against a hit squad who was not after just me, but also Bear. And they wanted him so bad, they slaughtered dozens of people in a hospital. What gives?"

Clive glanced around as though there might be a clandestine unit listening in on them. He cleared his throat. Shifted in his seat.

"In the thirty-six hours following Frank Skinner's death, there were three parties who reached out to contract with us to deal with you. The options ranged from bringing you in and turning you over, to outright terminating you in broad daylight, execution style, similar to Skinner's own death."

"He had it coming."

"I don't judge you one bit."

"You must judge me a little bit. You agreed to an offer."

"The most intriguing offer, though." Clive paused a beat, perhaps judging how to handle the rest of the conversation.

"Spit it out, man. You're not the first person who was willing to take me out for money."

Clive held his hand up. "It's not about the money."

"Yeah, it never is."

"There's a sense of duty, as well. And we felt that this party had the most sensible reason for contracting with us."

"Which was…?"

"They weren't sure what to do with you yet. Everyone else wanted you dead."

Jack eased back, fighting off the smile eager to spread across his face. Who the hell would care enough they wanted to talk to him first? Not the

CIA. Not any person or organization within or associated with the US government. Who did that leave at this juncture in his life?

"Drawing a blank?" Clive asked.

Jack nodded.

"Too bad, could've used your input."

"You really don't know?"

"Shadows, my good man. We're all just shadows in this world."

"How would you have handed me over?" He shook his head. "Stupid question."

"I disregarded it the moment you asked it." Clive laughed.

"Who'd you work for? MI5?"

Clive shrugged and dismissed the question. "Don't think that matters."

"It might." Jack angled his body toward Clive to look him in the eye. "I've met a lot of people the past twenty years. What are the chances this person or group knows both of us, and that's why they contracted with you?"

"I don't play what-if games, Jack. They are an exercise in futility, and one that I simply do not have the time or patience for."

"There's something here. I feel it." Jack set his beer on the table between them. "Were you in the field?"

"Briefly."

"Out of country?"

"At times."

"Ever killed a man."

"Yes."

"Enjoy it?"

"Yes."

"Ever gone against orders to do what's right?"

"Yes."

"And what's wrong?"

"Yes."

"We're not so different, Clive." He extended his beer in a momentary toast. "You're smarter, taller, more handsome, and have that whole British vibe going on, but other than that, we might be the same person."

Laughter from behind caught them both off guard.

"That's the funniest thing I've heard all month." Sadie laughed again as she walked around Jack and found a seat. She had on jeans, a t-shirt, and hiking boots. Her hair was back in a messy ponytail. She had no makeup on. Didn't need it.

"Thought you were a few hours out," Clive said.

"You know I like keeping you guessing." She shifted to Jack. "How're you feeling?"

"A little bruised, mostly in the ego department."

"She got away again. Might be time to stop chasing her."

"You're probably right." Jack stretched his arms out and folded them behind his head. "How's Bear?"

Sadie shook her head. "That guy."

CHAPTER 36

THE GIRL IN FRONT OF HIM LOOKED MORE LIKE A WOMAN THAN a child. When did that happen? He didn't get all the moments with her a typical father would. Didn't change her diapers, read her stories, try and fail to put her hair in braids. They never took daddy-daughter trips. Never attended a father-daughter Valentine dance.

But she was his daughter. From the moment he met her, took her in, swore to be her protector. The bond was there and would never be broken. Not even death would keep him from unleashing a fury few had ever witnessed should someone hurt Mandy.

"Why are you staring at me like that, weirdo?" She tucked a stray strand of dirty blond hair behind her ear. Her knit eyebrows shaded her hazel gold eyes.

"What?"

Mandy leaned forward, those same eyebrows arching into her forehead. "Is that… are you crying? Oh my God, you big baby."

"Shut up." The girl had inherited one trait from her time with Noble, or Mr. Jack, as she called him. Her jokes were laced with enough sarcasm it could make a hardened criminal feel like swallowing themselves until they were nothing but a ball to shield themselves from her cutdowns.

"I worry about you, Bear." She giggled as she made her next move. It was a good one. She now had control of the center. "I'll have you checkmated in four moves." She loved counting down like that to get inside Bear's head. For a thirteen-year-old, she was surprisingly good at it.

"I worry about what we're all teaching you."

"You don't teach me anything anymore, dude. It's all Sasha." She had picked up calling him dude from Sasha. The rest was Sasha molding the girl into her personal intel assistant. "Have you talked to her yet?"

Bear made his next move. "I'll have you checkmated in three moves."

"No, you won't." Mandy cut her timetable down. "Check."

Bear cursed under his breath and contemplated his plan of attack. "No, I haven't heard from her, but I think that's just a temporary glitch. No reason we can't get to England and move on with our lives."

Mandy had eased back in her chair. Her gaze drifted over Bear. He worried for her. Worried about PTSD. Any person in that hospital should have it. This girl in front of him might be affected the rest of her life from the attack, let alone everything else that had happened to her.

"You with me, kiddo?" He slid his Queen across the board and mocked pushing her King off the board.

"Better knock that off, or I'm gonna call you loser all night after I beat you." Her smile was forced, but Bear obliged it and laughed. It seemed to relax Mandy.

"Why don't I see if they'll get us some hamburgers for dinner?"

"OK, but first—" she made her next move, beamed a smile at him as she knocked his King over. "Check mate, loser."

Bear waved her off as he stood and went to find one of the guards stationed at the house. He located the man in the next room and inquired about dinner. The guard placed a call, presumably to someone in a car parked outside, and said dinner would be there within thirty minutes.

Back in the kitchen, Mandy was setting the board up for another match. "Ready for round two?"

"Think I'll pass. Need a few minutes." He opened the cabinet and rummaged through the liquor selection, settling on a Scotch he'd never heard of. He poured three normal fingers worth into a glass and returned to the table.

Mandy had already resorted to occupying herself with the iPad they had provided for her.

Bear sighed. "And she's gone."

"And I'm still listening."

"And that's too bad." He let loose a belch that might've shaken the house on its foundation.

Mandy laughed, the same as she always had when he burped, ever since she was a little girl. A stupid thing, but sharing in the immature moment was one of the lighter ways they bonded.

They played another match. Mandy pulled off another win. Bear pulled down another bottle. They sat at the table talking while waiting on dinner. The words were effortless, and both meaningless and meaningful. The sense of levity that filled Bear told him the mission in Croatia had been his last.

A beaming smile formed on Mandy's lips.

"What are you smiling at?" Bear asked.

From behind him, a woman said, "Someone order some hamburgers for delivery?"

Bear twisted in his seat, a smile of his own forming, and winked at Sasha. She rushed to him, knocking him back in his chair, tossing the two bags of food on the table. He pulled her onto his lap and kissed her.

Sasha pulled back after ten seconds. "In front of Mandy, really?" So proper. So British.

"I don't care," the girl said.

"Well, if you don't care." Sasha snaked her fingers through Bear's thick mane and pulled him closer. She overemphasized the kissing sounds, and they all three burst into laughter.

"Didn't know if I was gonna get to see you anytime soon," Bear said.

"One of the most highly frustrating experiences I've had." She hopped off his lap and began distributing food around the table. "After we were separated, I got a contact on the phone, someone with a fancier version of Google Earth, so to speak. We had you located, then, *poof.* You vanished."

Bear shoved half a burger in his mouth and swallowed it down. "You saw us at the train station?"

"Was on my way there."

"Didn't see the team that took us?"

"You stepped inside, and nothing happened. Boring footage. By the time we got there, witnesses explained you had been detained."

Bear nodded, realizing Clive had tapped into the satellite and looped the transmission Sasha's contact had been monitoring.

"Who are these people?" she asked. "Why all the destruction at the hospital to then apprehend you? And why would you go down without a fight?"

Bear's gaze flitted to Mandy for a moment. He locked in on Sasha's eyes. "They were different groups. The choice between A and B was pretty obvious."

"Who was behind it?"

Bear glanced away before shaking his head. "I don't—"

"I know you're lying to me."

He couldn't look at her. "I can't say."

"Why?" She released her grip on his shoulder. "You were almost killed."

"Kidney bruise from a baseball bat. I've had worse."

"You were clearly incapable of serving in any type of agency capacity. Why were they forcing you to be out there?"

Bear wiggled his leg to shift Sasha and get some feeling back to his foot. The pins and needles eased. "Things had to be done, Sasha. That's all I can say."

"Why are you protecting them?" She stood and huffed as she walked to the refrigerator. Bottles clanked as she searched through the mess of milk, water, and beer. She settled on a Belgian Trappist beer.

Bear scarfed down the remaining chunk of burger. He wiped his mouth with the back of his hand. Sasha rolled her eyes. She tossed a roll of paper towels at him.

"This is all you're going to tell me, then? You'd rather protect whoever abducted you than fill me in here so we can actually help someone?"

"I'm not protecting them." Bear's voice rose to a level that caused Mandy to straighten up.

"I think I should go," Mandy said, knocking the chess pieces off the board so she could flip it over and store them inside.

"No, stay right here," Bear said. "I want you to hear this. There's no greater trait than loyalty. It might get you beat up, knocked down, even killed at some point. But when you're brothers with someone, you're always brothers."

"It's Noble."

Bear clenched his teeth, biting down on his tongue in the process. His pursed lips hid the pain as he looked down, away from Sasha.

"Is there more?" Sasha crouched and angled her head so she could look Bear in the eye.

He stared back at her, nostrils flaring, feeling the burn in his cheeks and ears.

"Oh my God." Sasha rocked back on her heels and almost lost her balance. She reached up and grabbed the table to steady herself. "You found her."

"Who?" An exercise in futility. He knew Sasha had figured it out.

"You found Clarissa."

Before Bear could answer, the front door crashed open and an armed guard stormed in. "We've got to move everyone. Now."

Stunned, Bear rose and ushered Mandy forward. The guard met them at the kitchen entrance.

"Not here," he said. "Through the back."

"The hell is going on?" One hand was on Mandy's back. The other grasping Sasha's hand.

"We don't have time," the guard said. "Let's go."

CHAPTER 37

THE SUN HOVERED OVER THE ADRIATIC, THE LAST SLIVER OF deep red fighting for its final breath before succumbing to the tranquil sea. The sky remained a mix of pink and purple for the next several minutes until the dark blues of night eroded the peaceful facade and nothing remained.

The earbud's cord snaked down Clarissa's tank top to the iPhone in her pocket. It had no cellular service and only a few hundred songs. John Mayer's ironic lyrics about gravity reflected the whirlwind that had been the past few days.

She continued down the narrow path stretching the length of the small town situated along the coast. The area had been one of her favorite places to sneak off to.

Across the street, the door to a used clothing shop stood open. The breeze carried the smell of mothballs which reminded her of Mrs. Calabase. She had to get back and thank the woman for her troubles and repay her for the Vespa the old lady would never reclaim.

The men that had arrived must've known about Clarissa because of the scooter. She'd triggered a license plate reader somewhere. Or a cop had run the plates while the Vespa sat in the lot. Whatever had happened, she knew who to blame.

And before she checked on Mrs. Calabase, before she made good with the man who took her away from Croatia and placed her on the vessel that carried her the rest of the way to Italy, Clarissa had to deal with the turncoat.

Up to this point, she had done everything he asked. But the past seventy-two hours had eroded his All-American Boy facade to the point she didn't think she would recognize Beck if he were standing in front of her.

Not the Beck she knew and had at one point loved. *Maybe.*

Love was a stretch, and she knew it. He had said it first. She went along with it. Their romance was brief, and not that intense, if she was honest about it. But he was a good man and he wanted to take care of her. Clarissa didn't need that. But she appreciated the gesture, and decided he deserved a shot.

The relationship, their friendship, and their partnership went downhill from there.

The weeks spent tracking those behind the theft had placed a strain on the two of them. Long hours were put in. Sometimes together. Often apart. The latter Beck's doing.

Clarissa believed she had hampered the investigation, and that was his reason for pushing her away. The way things went down after that, well, she believed he was setting her up to take the fall.

But it didn't end that way. She got to leave with a clear name and a new identity she could use if she chose. Her bank accounts under additional aliases would always be full. Of course, she knew that could go away at any time, and probably would.

She stepped off the path and hiked down a rocky hill. From here she could see her rental cottage and its one entrance and three windows. Soft light shone through all, illuminating the sandy ground outside.

Clarissa remained in the shadows, watching for movement in and around the structure. A slight breeze blew in off the water. The air felt cool on her damp skin. Tall grasses growing out of the rock and sand danced in the pale moonlight.

The lull felt meditative. Tranquil. Serene. And everything in between.

Satisfied the cottage remained unoccupied, Clarissa covered the distance swiftly and entered. She checked her traps: a strand of hair, a clothespin, and candy wrapper. None were disturbed.

Earlier that day she had picked up fresh-caught sea bass and left it marinating in lemon juice and herbs. She preheated the oven, set a thirty-minute timer, and placed the fish inside. Afterward, she grabbed the largest glass in the cabinet and filled it to the brim with a Pinot Noir she had purchased earlier. With everything prepared, she took the wine out onto the beach.

Wise?

Probably not. True, the alcohol would ease her mind, lessen her worries, reduce her anxiety. It would also dull her awareness, lessen her reaction time, and reduce her ability to defend herself.

"Just chill," she muttered as she lifted the glass to her lips. The Pinot was fruity, light, sweet in the front and nothing in the back. She could drink the entire bottle.

She stretched her legs out in the sand, crossing them at the ankles. One hand reached behind to support her as she leaned back and stared up at thousands of tiny holes in the sky. Her eyes drifted from familiar constellations to the stars she had grown accustomed to seeing on clear nights in Italy. Probably the same ones back home, but how often was she in a place where light pollution was so minimal?

She savored every minute she sat there, aware the opportunity might not arise again for quite some time. After this, she had to set things straight. She had to get to the evidence that would clear her name.

Would it implicate someone else?

Probably.

And she didn't care.

CHAPTER 38

THE VAN'S MIDDLE ROW WAS CRAMPED, WITH SASHA AND BEAR bookending Mandy. The girl fought to get her elbows to her side. Bear pressed his head against the glass. Sasha worked her cell phone, despite the two men in the front seat telling her to put it away. Bear agreed with their assessment someone was likely tracking her. Who? Anyone's guess was as good as Bear's. Apparently, the whole bloody world was watching now.

"Where are we going?" Sasha asked.

There was no answer.

"Do you know who I'm with?" she said.

"Do you know where we are?" Bear said.

She shot daggers at him.

Bear feigned retreat. "I'm being serious. I don't even know what country we're in."

Her laugh cut the tension for a few moments. "You really don't know you're in France?"

He shook his head. "What happened to Sadie? No one's told me anything. She make it out OK?"

Sasha hesitated before answering. "She's OK."

Bear adjusted in his seat so his back leaned against the door. He eased into it, allowing the tension in his shoulders to dissipate like a fizzy tablet in water. His head felt light, his heart a little less clenched.

"What is this smile?" Sasha said, a playful grin on her lips. "You still have a crush on Sadie?"

Mandy giggled.

"Who said anything about a crush?" Bear combed his fingers through his beard. "I practically raised that woman."

Sasha giggled this time. "I'll be sure to tell her that. I'm pretty sure I know what her reaction will be."

"Me too," Mandy said. "Gonna put a foot up his ass."

"Dude," Bear said, nudging her shoulder.

Mandy rolled her eyes, opened her mouth, but the situation changed, and they all directed their attention forward at the cacophony of strobing blue lights.

"What's going on?" Bear asked.

The driver said nothing. The passenger, who had escorted them out of the kitchen, held up a finger as he punched the screen of his cell phone.

"Yessir," he said, then paused. "Right, can't tell what's up ahead. Traffic stretches over a hill, but you can see the emergency lights bouncing off the sky. Any chance we can get some eyes on it? Mhmm. Mhmm. OK, I see." He set the phone on the dash.

"What is it?" Bear asked.

"Probably nothing, but we'll—"

The first round shattered the side window and obliterated the driver's face. Blood and chunks of bone and flesh sprayed through the car, the majority of it settling on the other guard.

The air was sucked out of the car. Mandy screamed. Bear pulled her close to him.

The glass on the other side of the guard imploded. His head exploded. His body went limp.

Sasha reached for her door handle. It was locked. She searched for the button, smacking her open hand everywhere.

"Bear!" Mandy grabbed him tight. He pulled her in even closer. They could riddle his body with bullets and he'd never let go.

Sasha looked at him, her face bathed in blue light. "Can you open your —" Her eyes widened. Bear didn't hear the round punch through the vehicle's door. Not at first. But as the red bloom spread across Sasha's chest, he heard the impact echo throughout his head.

He reached out for her, bracing for impact, and welcoming it. End it now. He couldn't go through this again.

"Sasha." He almost crushed Mandy as he reached for her. By the time he had a hand on her, she had gone limp.

Bear unleashed a yell few had ever heard, and none would ever want to witness. Mandy joined in, presumably a mix of fear and rage, too.

He cocked his right arm across his chest and drove his elbow through the window. Ignoring the searing pain, he scraped the glass away with his bare flesh and then hoisted Mandy through the opening.

"Get low and run."

"What?" She looked at him from outside, her face bathed in similar light as Sasha's.

"Go, girl, now! Run to the cops."

She took off and slid out of sight at about the same moment he felt the impact on the side of his head, whipping it hard to the right through the opening where the window had been.

He blinked against the dark encroaching the edge of his vision and turned back to see the body slumped against the opposite door.

"Sasha." But it sounded more like mush coming out of his mouth. Pain rifled through the left side of his face. He brought his hand up. Found his jaw shifted about an inch to the right. Fighting through the agony, he reached out for the woman he loved.

A projectile slammed into his left shoulder. His entire arm went numb. His momentum kept him going and he fell onto the seat, onto Sasha's legs. Bear worked his right arm up to hers and felt for a pulse. Any lingering hope faded at that moment.

He looked up to find the source of the voices. German. Three men, maybe four. They had him surrounded. The door whipped open. Sasha slid out, her head hitting the concrete and the rest of her body following like a snake slithering through the weeds. Bear tried to reach for her. His arm wouldn't comply.

"Get her out of the way." A man said in a thick German accent. He followed it up with a command in his native tongue, then stepped back. Bear thought he made out part of the exchange.

It's him.

The next guy appeared with a firearm extended. Bear tried to plead with the guy. He just needed them to free him from the vehicle. Then he'd kill every last one of them.

They'd never give him that opportunity.

The sound when the guy pulled the trigger wasn't what Bear had expected. Nor was the penetrating feeling of a needle in his neck. He brought his right hand up, fingered the back end of the dart.

He felt high, lost sensation in his extremities. The fear and anxiety faded, as did his desire to kill. The pain in his shoulder and face dissipated. The ache in his heart intensified.

A larger man reached in and dragged Bear out, letting him fall on top of Sasha. One of them laughed. Bear stared into her lifeless eyes. Those sweet eyes where warmth once radiated.

"Get him off of her."

The laughing ended. Bear was hoisted to his feet by two men. He spotted the awaiting van on the other side of the concrete barrier. They pushed him over, letting him crash to the ground again. Bear mustered every ounce of strength he had and got his good hand down first, stopping his fall. Someone tried to kick it out. He grabbed hold of their foot, yanked, twisted, brought the guy down hard on his face. And then Bear jumped on him. He didn't have much he could do, but he could bash the guy's head in with his own.

And he did until they knocked him off. Bear smiled at his handiwork as one of the men aided his bloodied companion. They stood Bear up.

"That was stupid, my friend." The scar on the man's cheek dug into his smile.

Bear spit at the guy, but due to the state of his jaw, it just dribbled down his chest.

The man laughed.

Bear mouthed something at him.

The man leaned in. "I couldn't hear you."

"I'm gonna fucking kill you."

The man leaned back, laughed harder, and then smacked Bear upside the face with a club, rendering him unconscious.

CHAPTER 39

THE TRAIN PULLED INTO THE SMALL STATION, WHIPPING DUST and debris and a few loose pieces of paper around in coordinated chaos. The hot air smelled of trash and thankfully settled down within a few moments.

An announcement came over the speakers. A few people filed in from the benches outside. The doors to each train car opened. No one got off, but they had to wait before boarding. Once they were allowed, Clarissa paused until the others were on, then she climbed aboard.

She was still walking through the cars when the train started moving. She wanted quiet. She wanted to be able to see around her. Best place to be was in the back of the last car. She continued until she reached it and took a seat in an empty row.

The morning sun shone across the table. She reveled in the warmth on her outstretched hands. After a few moments, the scenery shifted, trees blocked the sun, and she turned her attention to the phone on her table.

Powering it up would send a signal out, revealing her location. She had been told to only do this if she truly needed help. It would get back to one man. The only man she could trust. When she last saw him, they each held their index finger up, a sign of solidarity between them.

And maybe more.

But she couldn't think about that. Not today, not tomorrow. Not ever.

She hoped he understood after this was over. After everything was over.

She set the phone on the table and spun it with her index finger. It circled around and around, as though the motion of the train kept it in perpetual orbit.

The door to the car opened. Clarissa tensed. She slid the phone off the table and stuck it in her shorts. Conveniently, she had a knife stolen from the cottage in the same pocket.

The conductor walked through the sparsely populated car and checked tickets. Clarissa held her paper printout for him to see. He stared at it, then her, then back at the ticket before handing it back to her without a word.

After he left, she settled into her seat, deciding that the time to turn on the phone had not yet arrived.

Soon. It would be time soon.

CHAPTER 40

Jack sat in the same chair, drinking the same beer as he had the day before. Only this time, he was alone. Clive and Sadie saw the pain in his eyes. Felt his grief. They told him to take what time he needed; they'd leave him be.

So, he came back out and stared at the olive trees and the sky and inhaled the dusty air and felt as pale green as the leaves reflecting the sun.

Sasha had been a part of his life for long enough that he'd miss her. They worked closely together for a spell. He thought there might be something between them at one point, but that faded quickly, and he knew that she and Bear were the right match, even though that would never play out.

A familiar feeling surfaced.

Guilt.

It ate at him, the way it always did when he knew someone had passed due to his recklessness. If he hadn't dragged Bear into the mess with Katrine Ahlberg, a botched hit he messed up and had to correct, this wouldn't have happened. He should've done it on his own. The outcome could have been the same, him taking out Skinner the way he did. Or maybe Skinner would be alive, and Noble would be dead.

Either way, a positive result depending on who you asked.

The target on Bear's back would've been a lot smaller. And it wouldn't have extended to Sasha.

When he'd gone in for another beer, Sadie filled him in on the details, adding a few more. Mandy hadn't been found. There was no word on Bear other than from a few eyewitness accounts who said the attack team loaded him into a van, but not before he put one of them into a coma.

If Bear didn't finish the rest off himself, Noble was going to make sure every last one of them suffered a death far more horrible than Sasha's passing.

The beer did little for his anger and grief. He dumped the remaining alcohol in the can, crumpled it, tossed it into the fire ring. He shoved his hands in his pockets and went back to staring at the thickest olive tree in the orchard.

The screen door slammed, and Sadie stepped onto the porch. The wind whipped her loose curls about. She stepped down and approached Jack.

"Wanna talk?"

He shook his head. "Nothing to say."

"That's all right. We can talk about nothing, like the old days."

"We talked about all kinds of things."

"Did we though, Jack? I mean, Bear and I had lots of conversations. You, however, kept your distance from me."

"Did I?"

She nodded while pouting her lips. "Got the feeling you didn't like me." She looked at a bare patch of dirt between her feet. "Still get that feeling."

He felt his shell retreat. "Look, Sadie, I never had any problems with you. I've always tried not to get close to people in this business. Lost too many friends. This thing with Sasha, Christ, I just can't put into words."

"You blame yourself?"

He didn't answer.

"How'd you two meet?"

He told her about the little restaurant. Great steak. Even better beer. The old man running the place, and his daughter helping out. Sasha.

They talked and even laughed for a few, and when things went silent, Sadie excused herself for a few moments. Jack watched her cross the barren lawn to the house, her sundress rippling in the wind, rising, showing off the backs of her thighs. He brushed off the thoughts that arose. It would be a nice distraction from his current feelings, but then it would create an entirely new problem. One he had no time for.

She returned a few minutes later, carrying a bottle of whiskey and two rocks glasses.

"Seemed like the beer wasn't doing the trick, so thought this might help." She stood in front of him, uncorked the bottle, filled a glass halfway. She took a sip, smiled, handed it to him. Before sitting down, she poured her own. He inhaled the honey and oak scent. They sipped together. Jack grimaced as the whiskey made its way down. Sadie did not.

"Thanks for this."

"Sure. It's a pretty good rye."

"Not the drink." He smiled. "The distraction."

"We all need one at times, right?"

"Suppose so." He took another sip, then set the glass down. "Where's Clive?"

"Working from his mobile command center." She looked over her shoulder at the house. "I swear, the guy never sleeps. He is always working, always figuring something out, making connections between the letter A and the number thirteen."

Jack chuckled. He found the guy impressive in his ability to relate. He figured Clive's background helped him to do so. A lot of guys that smart had trouble finding common ground with the grunts who did the dirty work. He supposed that's why Clive had so much success. His team believed in him. Trusted him. Even when everything went sideways, they weren't bailing. They were working to find the solution.

"What's your feeling on him, Jack?"

He mulled it over for a moment. "I'm sitting here, aren't I?"

"You didn't have much choice."

"I could've left at any time. He's not watching me."

"He trusts you."

"Why?"

She shrugged. "I told him not to."

Shaking his head, Jack lifted his glass and offered a cheers to Sadie. "Dick."

She laughed and said it back to him. After swallowing her whiskey, she continued, "He knows you're a good man who made some bad choices that led you down the wrong path. And that you've spent the time since atoning for those mistakes. And in doing so, you made a possible error in judgment when you righted the worst wrong of all, Frank Skinner."

"If you knew the things the guy had been doing for the past decade or longer, Sadie." His right hand clenched in a fist. "The guy was selling the country out, and worse than that, his own agents, both in the SIS and the CIA. He fed all the intelligence he could get paid for to the highest bidder."

"Why didn't you call it in, deliver on the evidence?"

"Who're they gonna believe? Me? Or him?"

She shrugged. "That's a pretty bad tossup, gotta admit."

"Dick," he said again.

She said it back again.

"We would've made a great team," he said.

"We did. Don't you remember?"

"That was the three of us. You and Bear worked alone, not us."

"Well, for what it's worth, I agree with you. And you didn't hear this from me, but we might be working together for the next few days at least."

Jack waited a beat as a gust of wind danced across the property. He inhaled deep, his throat grating against the mouthful of dust he swallowed. After the wind died down, he cleared his throat. "What aren't you telling me?"

"Got a lead on that van."

"The one that took Bear?"

Smiling, she nodded. "Dumb bastards took the highway. Clive had a few people combing feeds in the area. Narrowed it down to a few possible vehicles. Long story short, we've got a name that flagged in the database, and it's tied to the license plate."

"Could be a dead end."

"Might not be."

"When do we leave?"

"Not even curious where it traces back to?"

"I don't need to know. Don't want to, actually. Just get me there, arm me, and stay the hell out of my way." He fired an imaginary weapon into the distance.

She refilled their glasses, set the bottle down, excused herself. He watched her jog back to the house, her sundress lifting again with every bounce.

"Stop thinking it, man." He shook his head, smiled to himself. The buzzing against his left thigh wiped the smile off his face. He glanced back toward the house. Sadie was out of sight. He pulled out the phone and tapped on the screen.

One message waiting.

He opened the secure app where he had a notice from Br@nd0n. Jack had once asked him why he spelled it like that. Brandon just laughed and said Noble would never get it.

Jack swallowed hard, looked over his shoulder again, then opened the message. It read:

"you getting the band back together, man? not only do I see Bear online, Clarissa just pinged in."

CHAPTER 41

Jack powered the phone off and shoved it back into his pants pocket as Sadie stepped through the door onto the porch. She'd pulled her hair back into a messy bun and slipped a thin white button-up shirt on over her dress. The sun was high and hot and the extra layer would give her a little protection from its harsh rays.

A Florida boy at heart, Noble didn't care.

She smiled as she sat down, crossing her legs in a way that her dress scooted up her thighs toward her waist as she eased back into the chair. Her shirt smelled of faded perfume. She angled her head, softened her look. "You OK?"

He didn't answer right away. He couldn't say yes, and for some reason, he found himself unable to answer her with a lie.

"Jack, what's going on? Look like you saw a ghost." She grimaced right after saying it. "I'm sorry, that was the wrong choice of words."

He reached out and put his hand on her arm. "It's OK. Look, I need a minute. Do you mind?"

She shook her head as she took a drink.

He walked off into the orchard and paced through the rows of trees, repeating the message from Brandon in his mind. How was Bear online? Unless he had managed to take out the attack team who apprehended him and killed Sasha, there was no way he had *that* phone online. Maybe the assault team found it and powered it up, but they should be too smart for that, realizing it would lead anyone looking for Bear right to him. So, what was the answer?

He pulled his phone out, checking on Sadie while waiting for it to power up. She sat in the same seat, her head tipped back, face toward the sun.

Noble fired off a quick message to Brandon.

"Bear's in custody, can't be online. What's the 20?"

A few seconds later, he got a reply, but it didn't include a location.

"Will send details after switching us to a better encrypted server. Stand by."

Jack typed up a quick message about Clarissa but didn't bother sending it. The change Brandon was making could take five minutes, or five hours. Noble had no way of knowing, so he waited. He walked back to Sadie and left the phone on so he'd know the moment the message arrived. There were a handful of excuses useful for getting away for a few moments.

"Everything OK?" She leaned forward, drink in hand, revealing a little bit of cleavage when Jack walked up.

"Yeah. All good." He sat down next to her. "Think we should be drinking like this? Sounds like Clive might have us on the move soon, yeah?"

She shrugged. "We've got strong coffee, Jack. Your favorite, right?"

"Depends on the brewer."

"Of course it does." Sadie's smile lingered a few seconds longer than normal. Effects of the relaxing environment. Or the alcohol. Maybe both. Her lips thinned as she leaned closer. "Look, I know what you're going through. I'm there, too, but in our line of work, these things happen. You know that, Jack."

He stared off as far as his eyes would focus, rendering the world in between points A and B into a blurred mural.

"What details do we have?"

She frowned. "Nothing, yet."

"Yet. It's always yet." A new message arrived, sending a jolt of excitement through him. A feeling that had to be stifled. Sadie was a master at reading emotions. She would pick up on the change in demeanor.

"What is it?"

Apparently, he had failed.

Fortunately, he had a lie ready.

"A million memories racing through my brain, just happened upon a good one."

The front door opened. Clive didn't appear, but he called for Sadie. She excused herself and trotted back to the porch, more mindful of her dress this time. That was one distraction Jack had looked forward to.

He waited until the pair were out of sight and then retrieved the message from Brandon.

"NW France. still triangulating. Clarissa's position is updated rapidly. best guess, train. ran some data on the coords. if she's looking for a big city…"

"Milan? Genoa?" Jack whispered. The three dots danced as he waited for confirmation in Brandon's next relay.

"Genoa is on the route. Milan could be possible. and moving along the coast also possible."

What had Clarissa mentioned about their time in Genoa and Milan? He thought back to their time together at the little apartment. The quiet moments. The dinners. The walks. The exploration. They talked about anything and everything. Never had the two of them been so open and honest. Clarissa joked that Noble's maturity level had finally caught up to hers. Not quite.

The connection failed to materialize. It would in time. That's how things worked. The brain chewed on a mystery in the background until it was solved.

Jack replied to Brandon.

"Keep me posted on both developments. Doubt that's Bear on the other end, and I'd love to meet the person with his phone."

"hahahahaha I bet you would. aight dood. hit u back l8r"

Jack stood, pocketed the phone, grabbed both glasses, headed toward the house. Sadie had been gone a while now. Something was brewing.

The door opened and she stepped out, dressed in jeans and a t-shirt. She was tucking her pistol into the holster at the small of her back. The airiness to her had vanished. All-business Sadie stood in front of him.

"Guess I'm gonna need that coffee after all?"

CHAPTER 42

LEAVES AND TWIGS DANCED IN HARMONY WITH THE CONSTANT *whomp-whomp-whomp* of the helicopter's rotors. Dust clouds filled the sky, a hazy orange reminder of the aftermath of recent events. The hot air moved too quickly to breathe. The dirt choked their eyes, noses, and throats.

The co-pilot opened the side door and waved them forward. Clive went first, stopping to yell something in the man's ear. The rotor noise was too great for anyone else to make out what was said.

They squeezed onto the small bench seat, with Sadie in the middle, and strapped in. The helicopter rose and the tranquil olive orchard was left behind, a memory that would go the way of most others Jack held. Faded into oblivion.

Only Clive had a headset, and he appeared to communicate regularly with the pilots while checking his phone. Jack couldn't hear anything Clive said, and the mic interfered with his ability to read Clive's lips.

After leveling off a few thousand feet in the air, they took a westerly course. Where were they, exactly? The terrain, the olives, the heat, and humidity indicated southern Italy, but Clive and Sadie hadn't revealed the precise location. He figured they could be in a range spanning five hundred miles, north to south. What he knew for sure was they were on the coast of the Adriatic. Beyond that, logical guesses.

The coffee had been hot and seared his tongue. He told Sadie she'd never make another cup of coffee for him. After, she had to spit on the ground and throw salt over her shoulder. He told her that looked like voodoo. She told him to go do something to himself they hadn't the time for.

He traced the roof of his mouth with the tip of his burnt tongue. Felt weird. Alien-like.

Clive had handed him two pills before they walked out to the rendezvous point. He took one, saved the other. Might come in handy later. It rested in the pocket opposite his phone. The phone which had buzzed seven times, at least, while airborne. Could it have been the rattling cockpit? Sure. His mind raced at the possible contents of the messages Brandon had fired off in rapid succession.

The helicopter rose higher to clear an upcoming mountain. Why not go around, he wanted to ask, but no one would hear him. As they passed over, the pilot tipped to each side for a couple of seconds, giving them a view of the crater of a dormant volcano. His mind peered into the matrix of grass and trees that had taken hold among the jagged rock and saw Clarissa looking up at him for a moment. Jack imagined the fire and fury that once existed there. Would it ever again?

Their course adjusted northwest. According to the atlas in Noble's head, this was going to one of two places, and he knew exactly why. Bear wasn't their concern now. Sasha's death meant nothing in the grand scheme of things. This was about the target. And they were going to her last known place of employment.

Settling in for the remainder of the ride, Jack closed his eyes and snagged an hour of much-needed sleep.

The landing jarred him awake. He rubbed the sleep from his eyes and blinked hard. As the world came into focus, he recognized the terrain being near Naples. He had spent time in the region years ago. Were his old haunts still around?

A cup of coffee greeted him in the van waiting next to the airfield. They took a roundabout way to their destination, maybe to throw Noble off. They weren't aware of his knowledge of the area. He knew exactly where they were. He knew how to get away, too.

Curiosity over the destination lingered in the air. Presumably, Sadie knew, though she hadn't said. She had been inside the house with Clive for an extended period of time.

The phone buzzed again. Noble reflexively reached for it. He glanced left. Sadie glanced right, making eye contact. Her gaze slid downward. She felt the message come in, too.

Noble considered his odds against four people in the confined space. Giving up the phone was not an option. If she went for it, she'd pay, same as Clive, and the two goons in the front seat.

Sadie said nothing, though, and the remainder of the thirty-minute drive passed without incident.

They never made it to town, which both relieved Jack and filled him with anxiety. Naples had eyes everywhere. The countryside held secrets no ears ever heard.

The house sat alone in a clearing, with a snaking driveway that curved left before straightening in front of the two-story home. An open garage door offered little insight as to the purpose of the visit. A few bikes on one side. Workbench with tools on the other. No sign of cars. No drop cloth on the floor. A positive sign.

The man on the porch stood and greeted them with a wave. Beck. Noble had never met the guy, but Clarissa had shown him photos.

After greeting the trio, Beck led them inside. The place had hardwood floors the color of honey. White walls and ceilings stood in stark contrast to the weathered wooden beams intersecting to make large squares.

They seated themselves around a bar-height table. Beck sat across from Jack, and it was tense. The men knew of each other through Clarissa. As far as stories went, Clarissa had more on Jack simply due to how long they had known each other. Some were good. Plenty were bad. The look Beck shot Noble indicated he had heard all the bad ones.

"Let's get started," Clive said, switching on a tablet. He swiped through a couple of apps and settled on a map of the country. "We know she escaped Croatia on this boat." He fiddled with the tablet again and pulled up the *Abandonment*. "What we're not sure of is whether she remained with the captain for the entire trip."

"My guess would be she didn't," Beck said. "She's too smart for that."

"Or too untrusting," Jack said.

"You would know," Beck said.

"That doesn't matter," Sadie said. "What does is that she wound up in Italy."

"That's known for sure?" Beck tapped his index finger on the table.

Clive cleared his throat as he navigated his device. "Pulled from CCTV. Caught her entering and exiting a boutique store."

"She loves her boutiques," Beck said.

Jack didn't offer anything. He stared at the image. At first, when he saw her in Croatia, he didn't believe it was her. The short, dark hair looked all wrong. No denying this image, though.

"A few more glimpses tracked her to a cottage rental on the beach. Rented for six days, it was empty on the second morning. Nothing but a couple empty wine bottles."

"She loves her wine," Noble said, staring at Beck, who nodded once and said nothing in return.

"That's where it ends." Beck set his tablet down and clapped his hands over the top. "We had eyes on Clarissa for a long time. A simpler task, Beck, when she worked with you."

Noble hid his surprise. Why had they been tracking her more than six months ago? Wouldn't they have found him if they had eyes on her then?

"Quickly, she dropped out of sight. She would surface here and there, but for the most part, she was a ghost."

Beck nodded, clasped his hands together, and leaned forward. His elbows slid out a few inches. "That's my experience as well following her departure from the Service."

"What was the reason for her leaving?" Sadie asked.

"Wasn't cut out for it. Didn't like rules. Well, she didn't like following them. Breaking them was another story." He stared Jack down. "She picked that up from you, right, Noble?"

"Taught her how to live, man. I see I failed. How else you explain her winding up with you?"

"Guys." Sadie slapped the table. They all stiffened as though their mother had threatened them with a wooden spoon. "You need to have a dick measuring contest, you do it after we figure this thing out. Got it?"

Jack held back his smart-ass remark, nodding his approval.

Sadie continued. "You're the last two to have had close contact with her. Did she ever mention contingency plans? A secret apartment? Anywhere she planned to go if things went sideways?"

"Look, I want to know where she is as much as the next guy," Beck said. "She's lucky she managed to get out of here when she did. You want to talk about sideways? She threw this whole case ninety degrees to the left."

Jack glanced at Sadie, who averted her eyes.

"I covered as best I could for her, you know." Beck pulled away from the table and crossed his arms over his chest. His short sleeves peeled back, revealing a special forces tattoo on his right arm. "Two hundred million's a lot of dough. People ask questions. People wonder why she disappeared. They all look to me for answers, and I don't have a damn one. So, believe me, if I knew where she was, I wouldn't be telling you, I'd be hauling her in."

Noble felt he now had fifty pieces of a thousand-piece puzzle. But that might be enough to get an idea of what had happened until he could talk to Clarissa again. She held all the other pieces. Her version of the story was missing. Hell, any version of the story was missing. All anyone spoke of was the money.

The conversation went nowhere fast. Clive excused himself, leaving Sadie, Noble, and Beck to stare at one another for a few minutes. When he returned, he said there were developments and they had to leave.

Noble wasn't there for that part. He was in the bathroom, catching up on Brandon's messages.

CHAPTER 43

THE AIR PIPING IN FROM ABOVE SMELLED LIKE FRITOS AND FELT like the broken air conditioning in Bear's 1970 Mustang, his first car. The ceiling headliner fell apart months into ownership, hanging down like a divider between the front and rear seats. He had people hold it up while driving so they could talk. Eventually a girl with the face of an angel whose name he could no longer remember sewed it up for him.

Simple fix.

As most things were.

This time, an easy way eluded him.

Aches and pains exacerbated his suffering over Sasha's death. The guilt that she remained behind, lifeless, a speed bump in the road, ate at his gut. Fear that Mandy had not run far enough fast enough gnawed at his brain.

The thought that both would remain gone forever pierced his heart.

Over the last twenty-four hours, the guy with the graying beard had tried unsuccessfully to break Bear. He didn't even listen to the questions, remaining in the meditative state he learned to escape to years ago. All the abuse they heaped upon him wouldn't bring him down. And death? He laughed to himself at the thought. *Bring it on, baby. Bring it on.* He'd take someone to the grave with him.

The familiar buzz preceded a heavy door thunking open. Footsteps. The door closed, crashing shut. The man approached, his thick-soled boots slapping the cold concrete like a paddle on flesh in a fetish club.

Bear shifted his legs so his feet stuck out over the edge of the cot. Rolling right and left climbed his shoulders up a few inches and put him in position to use the wall for support. He braced himself, sat up, prepared for the man.

Nothing different happened when his door opened. No extra light flooding the dim, dank cell. No music piping in. No team of assailants ready to whale on him.

Only the man. The wiry, five-foot-eight, hundred-and-nothing, graying, bearded man.

"Your injuries look worse today," he said, his accent thick. He lifted his club and poked Bear's face with it. They hadn't set his jaw, and it hurt like hell.

Bear willed himself to ignore the pain. To not fail this test. Up to this point, all of their attacks had been at a distance or with multiple people in attendance. His despondency had perhaps lulled them into a false sense of security that this man could handle Bear on his own.

But his refusal to give the man what he wanted—a spectacle of pain and suffering—pissed the guy off.

The man laughed to himself, looking down, head swinging side to side in rhythm with the club dancing from his hand. "My friend." That was all he said. He whipped the club faster than Jose Canseco swinging a bat. The collision with Bear's face sent his head reeling back. The base of his skull thudded against the wall. Warm blood slid down the back of his neck like a slug sliming his way across a surface.

A brief grimace was the only thing Bear's attacker could take as victory.

"I heard you were tough," he said. "But not stupid. Why do you do this?" He poked Bear in the chest. Tapped his chin. He drew his arm high, preparing to smash the club over the top of Bear's head.

An opening.

Bear's eyes fell shut, sending the world into almost darkness. The guy's silhouette stood stark amid the fuzzy green-black surrounding it.

When Bear had positioned himself on the bed, he hooked his right foot under the frame so his Achilles was on the metal. His heel hooked behind it.

His knee hugged the mattress tight. His other leg lay loose, foot ready to hit the ground.

He tightened his right hamstring and quad. A jolt of energy raced from his hip to his big toe. Using his elbows, he pushed his torso forward while his leg pressed into the mattress so his foot could lock in, providing maximum torque. The opposite foot hit the concrete. The pitted surface offered solid traction.

It didn't matter what the guy did with the club; there was no stopping this train. Two hundred and ninety pounds of gristle launched forward and slammed into the thin man, steamrolling him like a boulder over a tricycle.

Bear grabbed the back of the guy's thighs, lifted him into the air, drove him straight down so that Bear's right shoulder landed directly on top of the man's sternum. The crack of the bone snapping was louder than the club slamming into Bear's face a few moments earlier.

Bear had one hand on the floor, the other on the guy's neck. He forced his chest up, drew his knee closer. The man's eyes were wide, his mouth open, a soft hiss gurgling from what little space was left in his windpipe. Bear didn't intend for there to be any. He latched on with his other hand and pushed his own body further in the air like he was performing a pushup so that all his weight drove down on the man's neck.

The guy's face turned blue, then purple. His eyes bulged like a whack-a-mole that was permanently stuck out no matter how many times you beat on it.

It didn't matter that he stopped struggling.

It didn't matter that he stopped breathing.

It didn't matter that Bear had a grip on the guy so tight his head might pop off.

He wanted it to. He wanted the guy to die a thousand times. He wanted his soul to feel the wrath Bear had prepared his entire life to enact at this very moment.

A minute later, with no signs of life remaining, Bear let up. The smell of the man's emptied bowls overtook the room. Bear covered his nose, touching his face in the process. Fire spread across. He tried not to bite down. A futile attempt at best.

The door burst open and the man with the scar on his cheek from his mouth to his eye rushed in. The man's smile quickly faded when he saw the scene. He reached for his side, but not before Bear sprang into action.

It took less than a second for Bear to cover the distance. He slammed his shoulder into the guy's midsection, and they crashed into the door. The guy grunted. Bear grabbed his right arm and twisted it in the wrong direction. The sounds of bones snapping were drowned out by the guy's screams. Bear worked his hand up until he found the man's neck. It wasn't enough to strangle him. Bear wanted the man to feel pain. He worked his fingers around his larynx and crushed it like an empty box of raisins.

The man's eyes bugged out as he struggled to get his hands around Bear's wrist. The fear in the guy's eyes brought a smile to Bear's face. He was sure he looked like a madman, and that's what he wanted. He hoisted the guy up and began slamming him into the wall. A red spot grew on the block with every repetition.

The man went limp. Bear dropped him to the ground. The sound of the man trying to breath rattled from his chest. Time to end him. Bear put his foot on the guy's neck and pressed down with all his weight until it was over.

He dropped to his knees and searched the man's pockets, finding a laminated card, a wallet, and a cell phone. On the guy's right hip was a concealed holster. In it was a H&K 9mm. He peeled back the slide, saw a round in the chamber. Dropped the magazine. It was full. Sixteen shots at his disposal. He hoped to use them all.

Because that's how many bastards had to die today to make him feel at least a little bit OK.

CHAPTER 44

WHEN CLIVE TOLD SADIE AND JACK HIS TEAM HAD A POTENTIAL location on Bear, Noble felt his stomach drop. Had they been tracking his messages to Brandon this whole time? How would that even be possible? Brandon probably built all the systems they used.

Then he remembered: the license plate. Someone with a cell phone camera caught the van racing away from the scene. They uploaded it to Twitter. Isa found it under the hashtag #WTFjustHappenedHere. It didn't take long to trace the van back to a dry cleaner owned by a Montague Sanderson. Odd name, yes. Also, an alias for Sanders Montague, a European "activist" known to use far right and left ideology to whip crowds into frenzies that turned into riots which served as backdrops for various crimes and assassinations.

For all their planning to make these events happen, they failed to do the one thing to keep them from being tracked. License plate readers along the highways left a breadcrumb trail for Clive's team to follow. Once it stopped, they had an area to search. MI6 wasted no time providing highly-detailed and real-time satellite imagery. Sasha was one of their own. Legoland offered their full support to the team.

It took Clive's gurus all of ten minutes to identify three possible locations. Another five minutes of zooming and panning and changing angles led them to the van.

They had their destination.

Now, back at the same airstrip, a jet en route, Clive, Sadie, and Noble hovered around Clive's laptop and iPad, both connected to a high-speed satellite network run by MI6, watching a live feed of the operation.

Ines and her team were already in the area, having followed the LPR data. It took them less than an hour to liaise with MI6 operatives. Together, they had a force of over a dozen, armed to the teeth, ready to burn the place down.

After they retrieved Bear.

Jack was aware of the general area where the building was located. And it was a hundred miles from the ping Brandon had locked in on. Clarissa's had gone dead. Vanished. But Noble had an idea where to head to find her.

First, Bear had to be saved.

Then Noble had to break free from Clive's grasp.

Clive had Ines on speaker as they watched footage from her body cam.

"We're in position and ready to move in. Good cover until we hit the parking lot. We'll slam into the building if we have to. Nothing nice and easy about this one. Everyone got it? Maximum carnage. They need to pay for this."

Clive muted the line and turned to Sadie. "Still can't figure out what they want with Bear and Noble. These guys, this isn't their thing."

"Who are they working for?" Jack said. "That's the question."

"I agree with you, Jack, however, even that deviates from everything they do. They use political disruption to achieve criminal goals, but rarely is any one person's or group's ideology or desire the basis of their crimes. They take what they want to take and kill who they want to kill for themselves."

"Then I must've really done something to piss them off."

Sadie's laughter melted the tension. "That could be anyone, and I mean anyone."

"Everyone needs a talent. Mine is being a jackass."

Ines saying the word "go" refocused their attention on the op. On one screen, they had satellite footage of the vans' approach. There had to be cameras on the route to warn the group of incoming traffic. Nothing much else was on the road, and it dead ended at the building. Everyone knew it.

The team raced in at full speed, one van in each of the two narrow lanes between parked cars. Hitting the brakes at the last minute, the vehicles stopped feet from the building's entrance. Frag grenades exploded near the front doors. A haze lifted into the air, obscuring the view.

Jack turned his attention to the laptop, Ines's body cam. She was the only one that spoke, barking orders to the team. Two small groups provided perimeter support as the remainder breeched the building. The first shots rang out, followed by several more.

The smoke cleared and the footage became easier to discern after they cleared the entrance. Anyone who popped out of a room or raced down a hallway was mowed down.

No questions asked.

No mercy shown.

Payback for the hospital massacre that kicked this whole thing off.

Isa piped in from the temporary headquarters. "From what we can tell, the back side of the building is where the most heat signatures are located."

"How the hell do they know that?" Jack asked.

"Spy craft has come a long way," Clive said. "You can't get away with bashing your head into a wall anymore."

"Wanna bet?"

"Everyone's luck runs out, my friend. Remember that." He lifted an eyebrow while pointing at Noble.

"Mine did a long time ago. Living on borrowed time now."

Isa continued. "There is a group moving, Ines. If you continue down the current corridor, there is an intersection. Go to the right and they'll appear at the next intersection in less than thirty seconds."

Ines asked, "How many?"

Isa replied, "Four to six. Some of the signatures are blurring."

"How many others in the building?"

"Can't say exactly, but I'll let you know what else is coming your way. Teams outside, be prepared, too. You'll have the advantage, but this group could split off and exit on the north side."

Ines led her team to the intersection. Jack didn't recognize the man with the angled camera allowing them to see what waited on the other side.

"All clear," she said.

The team moved as one, checking rooms as they went.

"You got five seconds," Isa said.

Ines gave a signal. The team dropped into position. The men coming had no chance as dozens of rounds exploded from HK MP7s in rapid three-burst shots. They dropped almost as a collective unit, bodies flinching and twitching on the ground, puddles melting into one lake of blood. Ines held steady for a few moments, waiting for any hidden attackers.

Isa said, "You're clear, but proceed with caution, there's one signature at the end of the hall, could be two people."

Ines replied, "Shouldn't be a problem." She glanced down, leaned over, looked the dead man in the eyes.

Two men advanced forward, ignoring the bodies in the way. They stood in the opening with their weapons aimed down the hall. They barked orders.

Ines rushed forward.

Jack felt his chest, neck, abdomen constrict.

"C'mon," Clive said.

One of the men fired off two three-burst shots. The other did, too.

Ines rounded the corner and a large figure on the floor came into view. His outstretched hand clawed at the tile.

"No," Sadie said. "Jesus Christ, no."

Jack had the computer in his hands. The words coming from his mouth were indecipherable. The tears threatening to burst from his eyes stung his sinuses.

Then they broke free.

Not from sadness.

But because of the big man coming into focus from the other end of the hallway, looking down at the body on the floor as he staggered past, yelling, "Yo, this my rescue party? Or I gotta kill y'all, too?"

CHAPTER 45

THEY TOUCHED DOWN OUTSIDE OF STRASBOURG, FRANCE, LATE evening. Situated on the German border, and not far from Switzerland, the town offered plenty to visitors with its central location and attractions, including an Astronomical clock dating back to the fourteenth century, located in the towering Cathédrale Notre-Dame of Strasbourg.

The mess Noble faced started a hundred miles from here, in Luxembourg. His thoughts drifted to the reporter. The guy suggested a secure meeting online. Safer for all parties. No, someone could track him if he did that, was Noble's response.

I'll make it right. I swear.

He added it to the long list of things to make right, which now included Sasha's murder. Chances were good the op team took the shooter out. They had not left a single soul alive at the facility where Bear had been detained. But if not, Noble vowed to hunt them down one by one until all were dead.

He was anxious to see Bear, but he had been moved to a U.S. medical facility in Stuttgart for emergency surgery. Clive had connections there, and assured Jack they would have several guards protecting him while he recovered. The moment Bear was cleared to move, Clive would take care of it, and get him to safety.

A new life.

Noble's request for his best friend. Get him back to the States and let him forge a different path.

Sadie convinced Clive to let her take Jack out for dinner. They caught a local train into town and wandered around until they found a small place that sold American style hot dogs and cheap Budweisers.

"Doesn't get much more perfect than this while in France, eh Jack?" Sadie pulled the door open without waiting for his input. The perfect smell of a baseball stadium in late spring greeted them.

He followed her in and told her what to order him, then stepped down the hallway to the restroom. It looked like something out of the late eighties. Posters for Guns N' Roses, Metallica, and The Beastie Boys were plastered on the walls and stall door. His face scrunched. Smelled like it was last cleaned in the eighties, too.

He returned to the dining area and found a cold can of Bud Light waiting for him. He picked it up and offered a cheers to Sadie, who smashed her can against his, causing a mixture of their beers to spill over on the table.

"Only the best." She winked.

He took a sip. Felt the burn of bubbles encircling his tongue and washing down his throat. "Only the best." He exhaled as he set the can down and looked toward the kitchen. "What'd you order?"

"A dozen dogs."

"A dozen?"

She shrugged and pouted while blinking her eyes. "Don't judge me."

He leaned back in his seat, stretching his right arm over the back. "Oh, I'm not. Kind of impressed, actually."

"I figured you'd eat eight or nine."

"Probably figured right."

"I know my guys."

"I'm your guy now?"

"Close enough." Her smile lingered for a few extra moments. Her eyes were bright tonight. Hints of gold flecks amid the dark brown. Her loose curls draped over her shoulders, blending well with the caramel leather jacket she wore.

"Anyway," Jack said, pointing to the counter. "They're plating up a bunch of dogs over there."

She lifted the can to her lips and took a long pull. Sighing, she said, "Another?"

"At least."

She winked as she rose and turned toward the counter. He couldn't help but notice how her jeans hugged her curves. He had never allowed himself to go there with Sadie due to her close relationship with Bear. And Jack didn't do the boyfriend thing well. He didn't do the side piece thing well, either. Serious, casual, it never worked. If there were multiple connections, he stayed away.

Well, mostly. There were exceptions.

But Sadie wouldn't be one. Not a decade ago. And not tonight.

She came back with two beers and set them on the table. A few seconds later, she returned again with a tray filled with hot dogs and two large baskets of fries.

"We're gonna be worthless tomorrow. You know that, right?"

"What do we gotta do tomorrow?" She laughed while shoving a hot dog in her mouth, chomping down on a third of it in one bite.

"There's the whole Clarissa thing."

Sadie rolled her eyes. "I am so tired of this woman, Jack. I don't know her. Never met her. But damn if I didn't get tired of hearing about her a decade ago. And I'm tired of hearing about her now. Swear to God, if she really did this, I'm gonna put her away myself."

"Tell me how you really feel."

She smiled and covered her face sheepishly after a piece of bread fell to her plate. "Look at me, Jack. I'm a hot mess. You see why I'm single, right?"

"I thought it was because of your pantsuits."

She aimed a finger at him. "Better watch your mouth, young man. You can't say things like that anymore."

"I only insult the people I love."

"People that say that usually do so to hide what they're really feeling."

"Wait a minute, I thought we came here for dinner, not a therapy session."

"You need both, so eat up and answer my questions."

"Don't think I like where this is going."

She shoved another quarter-dog into her mouth and shook her head, covering her smile. After swallowing, she said, "I think you're a good man."

"Thanks. Most disagree, but I appreciate your input."

"Ugh." She rolled her eyes again as she grabbed a napkin to wipe off her hands before pulling out her ringing cell phone. "It's Clive. This'll take a minute. Grab us a couple beers, OK?"

She slipped through the open front door and walked left a few steps, spun on her heel, and came back the other way. Her free hand animated the conversation. She looked through the glass and smiled, shook her head, kept going.

His own phone buzzed against his thigh. He checked the message.

"got the location of Bear's phone. coords incoming"

Noble looked over his shoulder. Sadie continued further. Scanning the street, he spotted an alley on the opposite side not fifty feet away. Did it cross over? It would be worth the risk to find out.

He dropped forty euros on the table, finished both beers, and grabbed two hotdogs, wrapping them in the paper lining from the red woven basket they sat in. Bruce Springsteen played in the background. No hungry hearts here, but Jack did step through the door and never looked back.

CHAPTER 46

THE NEXT MOVE WOULD BE AMONG THE RISKIEST OF JACK Noble's life, but his proximity to Switzerland afforded him an opportunity he hadn't been willing to take since Skinner's death.

Throughout his years of service and contract work, he had set up several numbered accounts, and had safe boxes at a few banks in Geneva, a place he could not go.

But Bern, Switzerland provided some anonymity. Not the numbers of people in Geneva, but not as many prying eyes, either. And the account he could access there was one nobody, not even Bear, knew about. His *oh shit* identity. One that could get him anywhere in the world, at least once. He wasn't crazy about burning it to get to the other side of France. But if it worked, and he did it fast enough, he could reach the coordinates of Bear's phone safely, too.

The guy Noble hitched a ride with smoked a lot and talked a little. He offered Jack a cigarette each time he lit one, which happened to be every ten minutes. Jack almost gave in, having inhaled half-a-packs' worth of second-hand smoke the first two hours of the ride.

The box truck hummed along the four-hour drive, avoiding the highway and skirting small towns. Noble had the driver stop so he could run into a pharmacy. He grabbed the driver's hat. It took a moment to locate the items he needed, which he paid cash for. The family restroom offered privacy. He took his purchase in, locked the door, wet his head. The next part was the hardest thing he'd ever done. Using the scissors, he cut his hair as short as he could, rinsed it again. Did the same to his beard.

The shaving cream lathered up nicely in his hands, and he coated his head and face with it. The pack of five-blade razors was plenty, and he changed blades after getting the thick patches off his face, and again after smoothing it out. It took three more blades to finish the job.

Noble stared at his bare reflection for a few minutes. Shaking his head, he said, "You look like a dick, Jack." It made him chuckle, though, and no one would ever recognize the docile-looking man as Jack Noble.

The driver got a kick out of Noble's new look and offered him another cigarette. Jack didn't bother declining. He leaned his hairless face against the window and reveled in the cool feeling against his skin. Then he slept for the next ninety minutes, when the truck came to a stop.

The soft red glow of the traffic light filled the cab. The driver looked like a demon, smoke pouring out of his nose. He said something in chunky German as he pointed at a building ahead.

Jack shook his head, shrugged his shoulders.

"Hostel. There." The man's finger bounced. "Good place for guy like you."

Jack opened the door and slid down to the street. Before shutting it, he asked for the driver's hat. The man shook his head no, but said, "Wait." He reached behind his seat and grabbed a bright orange hat that said *Being a Princess is Exhausting*. "Take this."

He caught it mid-air, tucked the bill into the waistband of his jeans. He strode toward the hostel with no intention of entering. The traffic light turned green. The box truck rolled forward. Jack ducked into an alley and navigated from memory across town to the bank, where he found a stoop to wait until morning light.

THE SUN CRESTED THE BUILDING ACROSS THE WIDE STREET. Warmth spread across his arms, chest, chin, part of his cheeks. The hat blocked the rest of his face. He considered not wearing it. It stood out, which made him stand out. But it also made him look more like a homeless person, and that worked to his benefit. He'd made it through the night with no one bothering him.

Not the best night of sleep ever.

But not the worst.

He powered on the phone. The battery was low at thirteen percent, and he had to conserve. There were ten new messages. The coordinates. An adjustment to the coordinates. Not much, but a little. Then a series of concerning messages.

"bro, what happened tonight? just heard about Bear. HMU"

"where you at? what's the deal with Logan. can't get anything from my channels."

"finally heard. JAYESUS! what a mess. sounds like he'll be OK."

"hearing they're hooking your boy up!"

"whoa, what did you do man?"

"you're hot right now. REALLY HOT. i'm switching servers again, hold tight."

"back. you need assistance? interference? let me know."

If he could have one friend and one friend only right now, he was glad it was Brandon. Jack carefully typed out a message detailing his situation. Then sent one more.

"Bank opens at 8. Make sure something is happening to pull every law enforcement official away from here."

He left the phone on and hid it inside his boot. Uncomfortable? Yes. His only lifeline should something happen? Also yes.

CHAPTER 47

Jack ditched the blaze orange hat and opted for a pair of sunglasses he found on the ground. The frames were large, but black, and less likely to draw attention. He did his best to clean them, wiping off the dirt and grime. They had a purposeful life of a minute, at most. The time it would take to walk into the bank and walk down the corridor with the glass ceiling. He'd reach the security panel, punch in his twelve-digit code, and access his box, which required another code made entirely of twelve words.

The scene played out several times. He visualized each step in detail so they would appear natural enough no one would pay attention.

He walked around the block a couple of times, sticking to the shadows and dipping his head when encountering a possible camera. After resolving this situation, he planned on having a long talk with Clive and Clive's best digital forensics experts. He needed tips. Couldn't take five steps without it being recorded anymore.

After the second lap, Jack returned to the bank where an open door welcomed him in. A burst of air drove down from above the threshold. The temperature balance had been perfected in the lobby, matching the brisk morning.

Jack tucked his chin to his chest and turned left after pushing through a thick bulletproof glass door. Sharp rays of sunlight penetrated the glass ceiling. Rainbows were cast throughout the hall. It was warmer here. Sweat formed on Noble's forehead.

He reached the second security panel. The green light above the door meant the room was available. He punched in his twelve-digit code and counted the seven locks unlatching separately. The cell phone buzzed in his boot as the door opened. He ignored it. Pushed aside the thought Brandon was warning him of danger. Plenty of time after he emptied his deposit box to face whatever situation presented itself.

Then he remembered he had powered the phone down. All he felt were phantom alerts.

"Get it together," he muttered.

The door shut on its own, sucking a little air out of the room. After a few seconds of working his jaw, the pressure in Noble's ear stabilized. A green button next to the door would need to be pushed to unlock it when it came time to exit.

He grabbed the device on the table and located his box. A cord dangled from the device. He inserted it into the USB slot on his box. A series of numbers and letters in random order appeared on the screen. He went through his twelve-word passcode, retelling himself the story he had created from them.

The small square door unlatched and opened an inch. He unplugged the device and set it back on the table before retrieving the shoebox like container holding his belongings. The Glock 19 would only be useful for the trip from the bank to the airport. Since he didn't count on being in Bern again, he decided to take it with him.

He set the pistol aside and retrieved the documents. The Canadian passport, driver's license, and government employee ID were cleaner than a newborn's birth certificate. Never been used. Mint in the box. There was enough cash in Euro, GPB, USD, and CAD to last him up to a week. He could always get more with the included ATM card and banking info. Forged family photos inside the wallet and on the iPhone, along with a list of contacts, completed the legend.

He pocketed everything, including the Glock, and returned the container to the box. After closing it up, he pushed the green button next to the steel door and waited for it to pop open an inch. The rush of air through the crack washed over the room and filled it with the smell of pastries.

A woman wearing blue pants and white top waited in the hallway, holding a plate. She smiled as Jack stepped past her on his way to the front door. He felt her eyes bore into him; resisted the urge to look back. Every step took ten times longer than it should have until the vault door clicked and opened and fell shut again.

He exhaled and picked up his pace. The bank was livelier now, patrons roaming about the lobby waiting for tellers and bankers to service them. One obstacle stood in the way of a clean exit. A security guard old enough to be Jack's father. That didn't matter, though. He knew plenty of old men who could whoop his ass.

Noble remained steady, nodded at the man, exited the bank into sharp sunlight. The view obscured, he wasn't sure what waited across the street. Traffic buzzed past. People walked in herds. He shuffled into the middle of a group and went back the way he had come.

"Sir," a woman called out from behind him.

Jack paid it no mind. There were plenty of sirs around. No need to draw unwanted attention. He pushed on while keeping distance from the person in front of him.

"Sir." Same woman. Closer. A hand on his shoulder. He turned his head and saw her, the woman from the bank. "You left this." She held up a stack of Canadian dollars.

"Might have trouble getting coffee when I land in Montreal, eh?" His lips twitched into his most disarming smile. Reserved for mothers of women he'd dated. It worked out here in the wild, too.

She returned the smile, handed him the money, hurried back to the bank.

Jack stood off on the side and watched her go. The crowd had thinned. Less cover available. He moved to reenter the stream when the security guard caught his eye. He stopped the woman, presumably to ask her what had happened. Was this protocol? Someone with a safe deposit box tied to a numbered account leaves a little cash so they have to investigate it?

The security guard had his phone to his face and his eyes on Jack. Not good.

Noble pushed through the crowd and stepped out in front of an approaching vehicle. He jogged forward, but not before the driver honked. An alley stood a short distance ahead. Where would it lead? It hadn't been on any of the routes he had walked earlier.

Sirens piped in and grew louder with every passing second. Every single footstep. The alley cut through to the next street, but the cops would be there soon. He needed another route. And he spotted it.

After making the turn, he sprinted to the ladder that extended four stories to the rooftop. It banged against the wall with every rung he climbed. The sirens stopped maybe a half-block away. The security guard would be talking to the cops. Giving a description. Telling them Noble turned down the alley. They'd race over, block the exit with their patrol car.

The door on the nearest balcony was wide open. Jazz streamed into the air. A sign? Perhaps, but there was still six feet of distance from the ladder to the patio. Noble climbed about that much higher and repositioned himself so his right hip pressed against the ladder.

The sirens blared. The cruiser gunned its engine.

Noble leapt.

The landing made more noise than the ladder slamming against the building. The patio shook; felt like it might pull away from the building. An older man wearing a towel and holding a bowl of fruit in one hand and a banana in the other stood with his mouth open, staring at the intruder outside of his apartment.

Jack stepped inside. "Sorry, I'll be out of your hair in a moment."

The man started going off. He dropped his fruit, and his towel. Held onto the banana. Jack held up a hand to block the view as he walked past. The other guy got aggressive and reached out for Noble. Jack's shirt tugged away from his body. He couldn't move forward.

Noble had no intention of hurting this man, but the older guy threatened to punch. Jack had his hand ready to deflect should the man try something so stupid.

"You're gonna need to let me go."

"Get outta my apartment."

"Brother, I'm trying."

The man tried to pull him close. Jack gave up the nice guy act and pulled the Glock from his pants. His shirt freed immediately. His host backed away, hands up.

Jack reached down and tossed the guy the towel. "Cover yourself up. The cops might be coming over."

He exited to the hallway. The unit was smack dab in the middle of a building with no elevator, not that he'd use it. Heading right would lead to a stairwell exiting out to the same street he had been on. Left would get him one block over. His plan to climb the ladder made less sense than when he hovered twenty feet above ground. But he had an idea.

He sprinted left, busted through the door, and took the stairs up two flights until he reached the rooftop. The building across the alley blocked his view of the bank. The building on the opposite side was four stories higher. Noble realized how horrible the plan was. Making things worse, he had trapped himself atop the roof of the building of the apartment he had broken into.

The door was open...

He powered on his phone and was disappointed to see that Brandon hadn't replied that he had set up a diversion. Jack sent a message to Brandon; told him to make a flight reservation from the nearest airport to the location of Bear's phone. He shut the phone down and it hit him. After he'd gotten the guy off him, the man's hair looked off. It had moved. The guy wore a wig.

Jack sprinted back down the stairs and paused at the doorway. He listened for sounds of activity in the hallway. Quiet. He eased the door open and checked. Clear.

Ten seconds later he was back in the man's apartment, Glock out, telling him to turn over his wig. The guy had underwear on now. His large belly hung over and covered most of his groin.

It took a little convincing in the form of two thousand euros to get the guy to part with his hair, a pair of reading glasses, and a beige cardigan sweater. The man told Noble they looked like brothers after he donned the disguise. Jack disagreed. Turned out to be a nice guy. Gave Noble a cup of coffee in a to-go cup. Even offered to call Jack a cab. Noble declined. He had already disconnected the guy's phone and hid the cord.

He did however accept a phone charger with hopes he could use it on his flight across France.

CHAPTER 48

THE DISGUISE GOT NOBLE PAST POLICE ON THE STREET. HIS CAB driver thought he was an old guy. Jack shed it in a bathroom at the airport. He checked in and printed his boarding pass at a kiosk. Security was a breeze. Even if they had footage of him, it wouldn't be quality, not with the way he shielded his face. And once he was in the air, chances of repercussions were slim.

And it wasn't as though he'd done something wrong. The situation arose from his own paranoia more than anything else. Perhaps the security guard didn't like the way he looked. The bank could have a policy to question anyone who leaves something behind. The cops a coincidence. Could've been Brandon's doing. No one knew him there. He had only visited one time in recent years to update the passport.

The plane landed in Lille, France, five minutes past two o'clock. The afternoon sun stood high. The blacktop roasted with the heat rising off and distorting the view beyond.

Jack made his way through the airport. Each step pinched another nerve. Every face carried a hint of danger. He'd made it this close to finding the phone. To be stopped here would be the proverbial dagger in the heart.

The last ping had been from a small village forty miles to the south. He had coordinates; needed something to punch them into. Using the credit card registered to his alias, he purchased a new SIM card for the iPhone. It connected to the network after the device restarted.

He downloaded a GPS app and put in the coordinates. The motorway would carry him most of the trip. What would the signal be like farther from town? He screenshot the location, then punched it into the map's app while waiting in line at the car rental kiosk.

An Audi A6 wagon was available. It fit him perfectly and provided the kind of camouflage he needed. Stick to the speed limit, and he'd make it down with little trouble.

Twenty minutes later, he pulled off the highway and powered on the other cell phone for the first time since Switzerland. A power outlet had been available on the plane. The phone now had a full battery. Five messages rolled in.

"on the move again"

"Bear's phone. Clarissa's is still offline. working another method to find it"

"still moving"

"stopped. stand by"

"this might be it"

Jack sighed after reading the last message. In some ways, he felt relieved. The phone being stuck for so long in a remote location led him to fear he might find a body, one he wouldn't want to discover, at the location. Not that it being on the move meant she was OK.

He started typing out a message when the three-dot indicator starting bouncing. Brandon had something new.

"nice move on the A6"

Jack replied, *"Thanks,"* then, *"What's the update?"*

Brandon sent new coordinates. Jack punched them into the GPS app on his phone, got an address, put that into the iPhone.

"Want this new number?" He paused before hitting send. If someone or some organization watched over Brandon, Jack would broadcast his location to all of them the moment Brandon reached out. He held his finger over the delete button. Hit send instead.

"not necessary. yet. keep powering the other one on every five minutes for updates"

Back on the highway, he noted his new route would take twenty minutes longer. She hadn't gone far. Could be a good sign. Or a bad one. He was fine either way. There'd be no way to procure a handgun along the route, though. He felt naked. If the situation dictated the use of force, he'd have to get close, and if the other person was prepared, it would get ugly.

He moved into the right lane and activated the adaptive cruise control before powering on the phone. There were two new messages.

"had someone check on your boy...your large man friend habahabaha. successful surgery. watching him like a hawk. no one knows who my guy is but he's in a position no one will question him being around"

Following that was, *"we are still good on the location so keep rolling on bro"*

He powered it off again and checked the iPhone Messages app. Why? No one had the number, so if something showed up, he would know to alter plans. Brandon didn't often get cozy and cordial in his transmissions. Not through that channel. Perhaps he missed Noble that much he had to throw some gossip in?

Jack continued to check for new messages at five-minute intervals. Temptation to leave the phone on hit hard. Wrong choice, and he knew it. That would set a continuous beacon anyone could follow. He'd learned to never doubt Clive and his team. Hell, he half-expected Sadie to be holding Bear's phone when he found it. And it wasn't only them he had to worry about. Someone had bested Clive at his own game. Multiple times.

His thoughts drifted back to Sadie. Noble did not look forward to the fury he would face when she caught up with him. She'd understand. Eventually. If he was lucky. Hell, she could whip his ass and leave him for dead, and he'd consider himself lucky because that meant he survived this leg of the journey.

He still had one more stop to go but couldn't risk even telling Brandon his hunch.

As he closed in on the location, Jack exited the highway and pulled into a gas station. He filled up, went inside, found the automotive section. The shelves were stocked with all manner of items. He grabbed a utility knife. Best he could do without going into a big box store that would have cameras everywhere.

Clive's team had abilities beyond what most people had seen in any movie or TV show. Rumors. And shaved head or not, Clive had enough footage of Jack he could map his face and upload it to software running an algorithm that scanned CCTV footage around the world, looking to match Noble's face with one on a camera. Could there be false positives? Sure. And they'd determine that with a manual review. He had to avoid that manual review.

Thinking about it made his head hurt. So, he stopped worrying.

He slid into the Audi. Turned up the AC. Turned up the music. Rolling Stones.

Five miles to go. Five miles to find her. He closed his eyes, listened to the lyrics.

"You're right, Mic." He hummed the tune to "You Can't Always Get What You Want," and smiled. "I always get what I need."

CHAPTER 49

BEFORE CUTTING THE ENGINE AND HALTING THE STEADY stream of cool air hitting him in the face, Noble checked the phone one last time for messages. Brandon hadn't sent anything new. They were in business.

The GPS app showed the phone a half-mile down the road, a quarter-mile off it. He stuck to the street for part of the trip, then opted for the cover of the woods.

The neon green canopy of fresh leaves afforded protection from the sun. The temperature dropped ten degrees under their cover. It felt cool, refreshing.

The clearing came into view along with the exterior of the wooden house set in the middle of it. A minivan parked in front of a detached garage. A swing set off to the side. Blinds all drawn. Nothing moved, not even the tall decorative grasses lining the driveway.

Noble stopped short of the wood's edge and watched for movement. The scene reminded him of a time recently with Bear, right before the incident with Skinner. This place looked nicer, though, like an actual family lived here.

He powered on the phone and sent one message.

"Am I in the right place?"

Seconds stretched into minutes as he waited. Leaving the phone on for longer than it took to send and receive messages was a bad idea. Brandon had drilled that into his head over the years. When the phone finally buzzed in his hand, Jack nearly dropped it.

"fifty feet from each other"

All he needed. He crossed the yard and went straight for the door, unfolding the boxcutter as he walked. He hurried across the porch, grabbed the knob, drove his shoulder into the door as he pushed.

A woman standing ten feet away shrieked and dropped her drink. The glass shattered on the floor. Ice skittered across the room. A puddle of vodka and soda spread out. She covered her face and pleaded for him not to hurt her.

Her husband, presumably, entered carrying a set of tongs held up as though he were a samurai ready to do battle. He started to charge Noble. Must've thought better of it because he stopped in his tracks. Unable to hold eye contact, he looked at the mess on the floor.

"What the hell is happening?" He adjusted his thick-rimmed glasses that made his eyes look two sizes too small and his accent sound even more British.

"Where's the girl?"

"Y—y-you can't have her. You can't hurt her." The guy's resolve steeled. He straightened, held those tongs out again. Ready to do battle.

Noble smiled. The man, while not a threat, had balls. So, Jack held his hands up and delivered a simple message. "Tell her Mr. Jack is here."

"Jack!" Her voice shrieked in a way that made her sound like she was six years old again. When Mandy appeared, he saw her as the little girl he rescued on a street in Manhattan, not the young woman she was now. She slammed into him with the force of a bullet, slipping on the vodka soda remnants along the way. He wrapped his arms around her, lifted her up, kissed her cheeks. She did the same, her arms wrapped in a death grip around his neck.

"Oh, girl, what happened? How'd you get here?"

She tried to answer. Emotion got the best of her. She sobbed heavily; her tears coated his cheek, neck, shoulder. He held her tight, fearing if he let her go, they'd both die.

The couple looked on, holding each other. They brought awareness back to Jack.

"You folks have to leave," he instructed.

"What? This is our home. We can't leave."

"You're not safe here." He looked at Mandy. "Do they know?" He assumed they did. Her nod confirmed. "These people, they'll find this place, and they'll kill anyone here. I need you to go, now. I'm gonna give you a number to call." He set Mandy down and found a piece of paper. The wife told him where to get a pen. He scribbled down a name and number and handed it to her. "Get out of here, now."

"Yeah, yeah, OK." The man started for the stairs.

"What are you doing?" Jack said.

"I have to get stuff."

"No, don't you get it? You don't have time to get stuff. Get the hell out of here."

The couple grabbed each other and stumbled to the front door.

"Wait." Jack grabbed the man's shoulder. "Do you have anything I can use as a weapon here?"

He nodded. "Come with me."

Upstairs, in the bedroom, he unlocked a dresser drawer and pulled out an old revolver and a box of ammo. Jack held the weapon up and inspected it. Didn't look like it had been shot, or cleaned, in years. But it would have to do.

The house felt too quiet after the couple left, too still. Jack tapped away at his cell phone while Mandy remained close. She kept a hand on his back as he paced, doing her best to keep up.

"You're gonna have to give me a sec, kid. Gotta get this message out, then we need to bounce. Trouble's not far behind us. Can feel it."

She nodded and sulked over to the blue velvet corner chair. It consumed her. She drew her knees to her chest and hugged them.

Jack finished his message. *"Need you to reach out to Sadie for me. Tell her I've located Mandy. Need a safe place for her."* He finished it off with Sadie's number. Then added, *"Before you do that, I know this is gonna kill our comms for a while... Anything new on Clarissa?"*

The reply came back within thirty seconds. *"nothing new…I got a connection not far from you…take her there then I'll contact Sadie. safer for u"*

Jack's iPhone buzzed. He glanced at it and saw a contact downloading.

Another message arrived. *"just sent you the deets, he's good ppl will take care of her, and yeah, I know about your other phone, don't worry I secured it for you"*

"All right, kid, let's get moving."

The long stretch of road blended with the gray sky. Thick clouds bundled together like sheep in a small corral. Rumbles of thunder shook the car as the storm enveloped the area. A sign of what had happened, or what was to come?

Before driving away from the house, he had given Mandy a lesson with the revolver. She took to it fast, nailing her target dead center with her final three rounds. The man taking her in had been vetted by Brandon, but Noble had nothing on him, leaving Jack feeling more than uneasy.

In the final miles before the exit, he felt a chill. Not one to give into premonitions, Noble had to pull over. He exited the car and paced the shoulder for a few minutes. Something was off, didn't feel right. But this was Brandon. The man had virtually been by Noble's side for years and had gotten him out of many jams. If he had a trusted source, Jack needed to let go of control and take Brandon at his word.

He took a deep breath, headed back to the car. Mandy watched in her mirror. She smiled. As Jack slid behind the wheel, he received a text on his iPhone.

"killed the server. this is too hot. my guy is dead or detained don't know which yet. GTFO of there and get rid of this phone."

"Shit," he said.

"What is it?" Mandy asked.

"Looks like you're sticking with me for a while, kid."

"I was hoping I would."

CHAPTER 50

A SINGLE FINGER HELD UP BY ONE PERSON FOR ANOTHER TO see. For some, a gesture of solidarity. Or a symbol that they'd see each other again, one more time. Another couple might use it to suggest the one thing that means more to them than anything else on earth.

For Jack and Clarissa, there had never been any of that. He saved her, possibly, from the hit team, and ended up in the water as she drifted away on the boat named *Abandonment*. It felt natural to return the gesture as she stood at the stern with her index finger in the air.

He dwelled on the possible meanings and settled on something she had told him during their few months together following Skinner's death.

"There's one place you'll find me if things go wrong, Jack."

She wouldn't tell him when he pressed.

"You know the answer already, bud. You'll figure it out when the time comes."

He cycled through his memories. The location had to be in there. She'd revealed her plans to him months, or maybe even years ago. The internal data file was huge, time limited. Losing access to Brandon posed a problem. The guy was Noble's last confidant, but Jack was on his own now with a thirteen-year-old girl to worry about. Presumably, Brandon was working to fix things, but now Noble had no means to make contact.

The iPhone. Gone now, but Brandon had made contact on it.

Then it hit him.

Noble swerved between two semis and slammed on the brakes as he entered the curving off ramp. The tires chirped until the speed dropped enough Mandy wasn't pressed against him.

"Jack." She swatted his arm. "The hell are you doing?"

He looked at her and burst into laughter.

"What?"

"Sound just like Bear."

"Like father like daughter."

Warmth spread through Noble as his mission solidified. It wasn't enough to solve the Clarissa mystery. He had to get Mandy to Bear. Had to turn her over himself.

The grocery store wasn't an ideal place to stop, but he knew he could get what he needed from there. The Audi slid in between two vans. Noble told Mandy to stick close to him and smile at anyone who made eye contact. He kept his face hidden as they entered. She did the same. He grabbed a hat off the rack and put it on. She laughed at his choice and repeated the slogan *j'aime les bananes*.

They picked up a few snacks and some water. A deck of cards and some dice. Deli meats and cheese. And a cheap phone with prepaid service that he activated as soon as they stepped outside, paid for with the credit card under his alias. He now realized that Brandon had that alias flagged because Brandon had created the identity. There was no more solid legend available than the one he was using.

By the time they reached the wagon, the phone was activated and had received a text message. Noble smiled at Brandon's *"praise Jesus"* note and string of emojis.

He typed up a message and hit send. *"Keeping Mandy close, not taking chances. Going back to Italy, need to know how hot I am there."*

Lingering in the parking lot was begging for trouble. They got back on the highway for five minutes, then pulled off again, this time avoiding places with cameras. He had a new message waiting.

"still hot, but not scalding. reached out to Clive through a backchannel. full support there. Sadie will meet you anywhere. by herself. take all that with the grain of salt you keep up your ass you crotchety bastard"

Jack laughed. Brandon had an odd sense of humor and no sense of timing when it came to delivering his jokes. Another message came through with instructions on how to contact Sadie.

"Everything OK?" Mandy leaned against the door; her left foot tucked under her right leg. The kid held up well despite everything that had happened. That wouldn't always be the case. She'd have plenty to unpack in her twenties.

"I think so," Jack said. "Sometimes you just gotta have faith that the people around you have your best interests in mind."

"Bear always has for me." She lowered her watery gaze. "Sasha for him."

Jack reached out and Mandy leaned into him. They hugged over the center console. Her tears wet his neck. Her sobs pained his heart. The people behind Sasha's murder would pay. Didn't matter they slaughtered the entire building where Bear was being held hostage. Someone was behind this. And Noble didn't plan on resting until he had their head on a stake, no matter how high up the chain of command it ran.

"I have to stop being weak." Mandy pulled away, wiping her tears with the backs of her hands. "There's no time for crying."

"You're not weak, kid. Far from it. What you've seen, been involved in, had happen, all since running into me… You probably would've been better off if I'd gotten in that car and left you standing there calling for your mother."

"Maybe," she said. "But you wouldn't have been better off."

"How's that?"

"I saved your life."

"Is that right?"

"Bear said more than once I'm your guardian angel."

"He did, did he?"

She nodded. "Mmhmm. I told him you were lucky he was around because he saved your ass so much."

"How old were you when this conversation happened?"

"Nine or ten, I suppose."

"And you said 'ass'?"

Mandy giggled the way she did when she was a little girl. Probably the only part of that child left.

"Well," Jack said, "let me tell you that Bear was right. You did save my life. I never would have redeemed myself if it hadn't been for you interfering. Probably be dead now. Or in jail. Or, worse, working for some agency full time."

"Yuck to all three, man."

Jack laughed. "Gotta get you a better mentor than Bear."

Mandy's broad smile faded. She pursed her lips, took a deep breath, then asked a dreaded question. "Any updates on him?"

All Jack could do was shake his head. He didn't want to go into too much detail, and it had been hours since he heard anything new.

"I'm sure he's OK. So tough." Mandy flexed the way Bear would after completing any mundane task like pulling a box of cereal off the top shelf or picking up a pair of socks off the floor.

Nodding, Jack pulled out the phone and fired off another message requesting an update. It came within a few seconds. Jack read it aloud. "Recovering well. Gonna be moved soon. Should reunite them within a couple of days."

Mandy's demeanor changed as the shadow of death dissipated, banished from the vehicle.

Jack sent one more message. A time and location for Sadie to meet.

"One more stop, then we're back on the road."

CHAPTER 51

THE LITTLE APARTMENT LOCATED AT THE EASTERN END OF Nice's Promenade des Anglaise had an amazing view of the Mediterranean, Castle Hill, and the constant stream of 737s, A220s, and every other model of plane made by Boeing and Airbus landing on the other side of Nice. A steady stream of cars and people passed by, even at three in the morning. Jack knew because he crashed hard when they reached the apartment midday so he could stand watch all night.

The view of the Nice LOVE sign afforded him the ability to monitor the rendezvous point without standing out. He wasn't watching for any one person. Rather, a *type* of person. What he had seen since sunset had been of no concern. If Sadie, or a third party, had sent someone to scout ahead, they did their job well.

He hung it up around four-thirty when the stream had turned into a drip and turned in for the night. Sleep was fast and fleeting. The sun pierced a crack in the curtains and knifed across the bed, slicing through his closed eyes, sending a pain through his head with the intensity of a migraine.

Jack rolled over, pulled on his pants, stepped into his flip flops, and wandered up to the kitchen. Mandy sat at the counter, a bowl of Cocoa Puffs in front of her. She slurped the milk from her spoon before sucking in the cereal contents. Repeatedly. Jack counted down from a hundred while waiting for water to heat. He had six packs of instant coffee and planned on drinking half of them before ten.

The kettle clicked off. Hot water blended with the dry coffee and created a decent-smelling brew. He held it to his face; inhaled the warmth; felt it spread from his chest outward. He carried the mug to the porch, stopping along the way to don the blue ball cap with the ridiculous slogan, sunglasses, and the fake mustache.

The Promenade was full of early morning walkers, bicyclists, people on roller skates. Sunworshippers flocked to the smooth stone beach, each step made gingerly so as not to stub a toe or sprain an ankle.

He set up at the patio table and pretended to play with his phone as he perked up with his first cup. His eyes scanned the crowd, picking out possible suspects. The LOVE sign never changed, but those surrounding it did. A line formed, people in groups of two, four, and more. They took turns taking several pictures. A few minutes later, an entire new group of people waited their turn.

Mandy joined him for his second cup. She had on her blue wig, sunglasses, and sundress. She'd already powdered her face to make it paler. Was it too much? Would it draw the kind of attention he didn't want? Perhaps. And it worked because of that. So many eyes would be on Mandy that should something go down, the other party couldn't overreact. Too many witnesses.

After Noble's third cup, they set out on foot into the old town behind their apartment. The narrow alleyways offered a glimpse into life in Nice throughout the last four centuries. The hardships those people faced existed in history books. But the legacy left behind in the hundred-years-old buildings, the imprint of all those lives, could be felt with every step, every inhalation of the stifling air.

Mandy stopped for a picture under the colorful flags strewn across an alleyway in front of an Indian restaurant. She tried to drag Noble into a vegan restaurant. The attractive host did her best, too. Jack couldn't be lured. Any other time? Sure. But not today. He pulled Mandy along until they found a little place that offered the kind of breakfast he could eat: eggs and a pork product. It cost as much as a burger in Manhattan but hit the spot. After a few bites, Mandy agreed the little restaurant was the best choice, even though she wished she could watch Noble choke on alfalfa sprouts.

They continued through the winding maze of small streets until they located a small grocery store that offered prepaid phones. It would've been quicker had they gone two blocks to the west, where they'd be on a main road. But old town afforded protection from prying eyes.

He purchased a prepaid card and basic phone for Mandy using the same credit card as before. He held his breath as the clerk swiped it, fearing it had been flagged by a system outside of Brandon's control. They'd track his location, and the moment the decline went through, a strike team would be on him. But none of that happened. The transaction processed. He set service up outside, and texted Brandon immediately, letting him know Mandy would have the phone throughout the day. Told him to watch it non-stop.

They went back to the apartment and relaxed for the next few hours, reconvening at the patio table for afternoon coffee.

"Will I be able to text you?" Mandy spun the phone on the patio table's glass surface.

"Probably not."

"Call you?"

"Nope."

"Message you on Facebook?"

He laughed. "You think I'm on there?"

"You might want to be with your fake identities and stuff."

"Why would I do that?"

"Everyone is on Facebook, Jack. *Not* being on there makes you look guilty."

"Or it makes me look like a normal human being."

"No." She rolled her eyes and clicked her tongue. "That is abnormal. These days, everyone is on some sort of social media. Don't want Facebook? Do Instagram. Or TikTok."

"That thing where people dance and make fools of themselves?"

"Exactly. You have to appear normal. And you, Jack, are not normal at all."

He set his mug down and stared at her through the steam dissolving before his eyes. "When did you grow up?"

"Life with you and Bear did it to me."

"I'm sorry."

"Don't be. I'm OK. I'm going to be OK. Better than OK. You and Bear made me strong."

"God help the world when you turn eighteen."

She puffed up. "God help the world now, because I'm ready to take it on."

He thought of his own daughter, Mia. Wondered where she and his brother Sean's family were now. He had to find her. Had to make up for the lost years. Had to make sure she grew up to be as strong and amazing as the girl…young woman sitting in front of him.

Mandy looked at her phone and frowned.

"What is it?" Jack asked.

"Better drink up." She jutted her chin toward the LOVE sign. "About time to do this."

Mandy hiked to the top of Castle Hill. Two-hundred-thirteen steps up. And it would be two-hundred-thirteen steps down. She counted each. It allowed the threads in her head to process everything going on around her. Whether an incoming person was a threat. Whether the crying child needed help or was simply being a brat.

From the top of the hill, she walked the path and stopped to look out over the sea. The view was serene, filling, uplifting. A whole world awaited her someday. Out there. She would be out there, making her own way. One day.

She continued on the path around a sharp bend; made her way to the edge. Huge yachts lined the inlet next to a marina. These were the kind of boats she imagined existed in films, created by CGI. One was gold. All gold. *Solid freaking gold.* Who lived that life? What did they worry about? How could they worry about anything?

After imagining a world in which she dined with billionaires, movie stars, and her favorite musicians, she returned to her perch overlooking the Mediterranean. This time, though, she didn't imagine what life beyond the great wide blue would be like. She homed in on the shifting crowd at the colorful Nice LOVE sign. Her right index finger tapped the railing at one-hundred-ten beats per minute, like the deep house music she enjoyed listening to. The beats, like the steps, occupied the threads in her brain that liked to drag her into an endless loop of pain and anxiety and ADHD-like bouncing.

It put her in a trance. One she could control at any time.

Bear had taught her these lessons over the years. Sasha had helped her see their true power. Two very different people. Two people who loved each other with great intensity. Two people who loved her with all their hearts.

One remained on earth.

The other would be with her the remainder of her days, even if those days expired on this one.

Ten minutes passed. Several curtain calls at the Nice LOVE sign. But two actors remained. Sadie was disguised from the images Mandy had seen. She had no idea who the man was, but if he was with Sadie, he was good people. That's what Jack had said.

She scanned the street for him. A futile exercise. She would never find him. He even told her so. Still, she looked. She wanted to see that stupid hat and ridiculous shirt and silly mustache one more time.

They had walked along the alley behind the apartment until they reached the spot where it curved. Continue on, and you find the Promenade. Cross to the other side, and you reached the first of two-hundred-thirteen steps that led to the top of Castle Hill.

He had told her this might be the last time they would ever see each other. That's what she loved about these men who had adopted her. They treated her like an adult. They didn't sugar coat anything. They recognized Mandy was wise beyond her thirteen years. Noble believed in her, that she could do this task. He'd be watching, he had said. And she believed in him.

Her phone buzzed. She pulled it out to check the message. *"It's time."* She took a deep breath, from her navel to the top of her head. She held it until she felt slightly euphoric, then slowly released the air from her lungs.

Two-hundred-thirteen deliberate steps down. She reached the bottom, adjusted her backpack so it covered the revolver's handle. The steel felt cool against her sweaty back.

"Can you pull the trigger if you have to?"

"I have enough to piss me off, Jack. I can do it."

He had squeezed her shoulders, hugged her, and set off across the Promenade.

Now standing near that same spot, she looked around, but couldn't locate him. The crowds moved in rhythm with the sea, in and out, crashing, colliding, separating, over and over. She crossed the main road and joined a group on their way to the LOVE sign. When they got in line, Mandy wandered a bit in the alcove. She passed the man she didn't know who had now been standing there for twenty minutes. He paid no attention to her. She went to the railing, climbed up a rung, leaned over as though she were going to dive onto the same rocks the sea slammed against. Mists rose as each wave hit, enveloping her, cooling her, soothing her. She breathed the salt air deep into her lungs, so deep that it hurt when she exhaled. Then she turned and went up to the beautiful woman with the caramel curls.

"Hello, Sadie. I'm Mandy. Please take me to see my dad."

CHAPTER 52

THE SIGH OF RELIEF JACK FELT WHEN SADIE EMBRACED MANDY had no comparison to any other moment in his life.

It could have gone sideways. It should have gone sideways.

It didn't.

He lingered too long, watching the scene unfold. The man with Sadie went first; cleared the path. The guy had experience on a security detail, that much was certain. He communicated through an earpiece. Noble had not identified additional team members among the crowds. They could be on the beach, top of the hill, or looking out from the six-story apartment building where Matisse had once lived behind their rental. Did it matter? Not once the SUV pulled up and Sadie and Mandy climbed in.

He cut through old town Nice to the lot where he'd stashed the Audi and turned his focus to the next step.

The next destination.

He notified Brandon when he went dark; typed up a simple message. Brandon would piece it together in time, preferably after Noble had made contact with Clarissa and set her on the right path. Only then could he avenge Sasha's death.

The route hugged the coast. Noble stopped a few times, places he'd been where memories spanning two decades were stored. Most, though, were spots he and Clarissa had visited during those two months together.

The final detour happened after crossing into Italy. A rocky beach with a steep hike down a cliff face. The further you went down the coast, the beach disappeared, and the Mediterranean collided with the jagged stone.

He found the little cafe where they ate and drank wine and laughed while talking about an impossible future. One where they were together. An exercise in futility was what he had told her. As much as she lured him into a sense of belief that he could settle down, it would never work in practice. She had crossed her arms and hiked her shoulders an inch, eyes looking diagonally upward, her lips slightly pouty. She killed him with that look.

Every. Time.

Noble ordered the same meal. Sat at the same table. Drank the same wine. Imagined Clarissa in that pose as though his brain were stuck on repeat.

Maybe someday. Maybe...

Back on the road with around two hours left in the drive, Noble settled into a harmonious rhythm. Every negative thought drew out a positive one to balance it out. They moved like waves, in and out, occasionally crashing into one another.

The city that descended from its fifth century BC perch appeared.

Genoa.

If Jack's hunch was correct, if he knew what the one finger raised meant, he'd see her by eight that night.

He ditched the car at a lot outside the city, caught a cab, got off on Via Roma next to the Louis Vuitton boutique. From there, he wandered to the old section of town, where narrow streets wound in no particular pattern. Breakfast tables were broken down for fruit stands, which later disappeared as outdoor dining tables were set up. Noble arrived during the transition to the latter.

Some found Genoa to be a grungy port town. Noble loved it there. The character of the city defined it. He could get lost in those narrow alleys. He could spend a couple hours riding the funicular up to the top of the hill, getting off at the last stop, then hiking back down on sets of old, rarely used steps overgrown with weeds that wound through neighborhoods. He'd find a little place to pop into for lunch or a drink. No one would speak English. And it was great.

He didn't have time for that today, but perhaps in the near future, he could share the experience with a friend.

The winding walk dumped him out on Via di Soziglia. He spotted a café and ordered a coffee. The courtyard in front of the Basilica offered plenty of places to sit, so he took up at a table in the corner, where he could see everyone. A small walkway between two buildings behind him offered a path to escape.

It never came to that. He sat there for an hour, watching the tourist line that looked like pawns on the black-and-white checkered tile as they entered the church, growing and receding several times over. At times, women were turned away for not having their shoulders covered. A few argued. Some went and bought scarves. A good business to have next door to the Basilica.

The desire to reach out to Brandon intensified. Bad idea. Sending out that signal could compromise the plan Jack had cobbled together. It was more of a rough draft drawn on the back of a napkin. It'd have to do. Time had run out.

The meandering walk back through old town cleared his head; helped him focus. Visualizing the evening, he developed a list of questions to ask Clarissa. Some designed to test her. Some for his own curiosity. Didn't matter how she answered. He'd help her. He owed her that.

An hour later, as the sun dipped behind the mountains and buildings cast long shadows that darkened the streets, he reached the seven-spoke roundabout in the middle of town and took the pedestrian tunnel running underneath. It deposited him on Via Assarotti. A steep uphill walk led to his final destination.

Enough sunlight lingered that Noble kept walking past the little restaurant, Osteria Pizzeria Nando, without looking inside because the glass only reflected the street. The balance of light inside and out made it too easy to spot him. So, he made four right hand turns, adding twenty minutes to his walk. By the time he approached again, the streetlights cast pools on the sidewalk. He stepped around them as he made his approach.

The door opened, triggering the chimes from bells hanging on a string. He heard laughter from inside. The air smelled of wine, homemade sauce, and freshly baked bread. The best bread he'd ever had was in that restaurant.

A man about Noble's age stepped out with his dog. The guy nodded at Noble. The dog drew the leash taut trying to get to Jack. The dog remembered. The guy didn't. He had translated the word swordfish for Arabella last time Jack ate there. The man apologized and dragged his dog across the street to his apartment building.

Jack considered another loop around the block, but it was too late. The door flung open.

"As I live and breathe." Arabella looked like the stereotypical Italian mother. Her wide smile forced her cheeks high on her face, nearly driving her eyes shut. Her salt-and-pepper hair was pulled back into a bun. She reached out. "Come give me a hug, Jack."

He glanced around to see if anyone had been in earshot; decided it didn't matter. He let the woman embrace him. "Promised if I was in Genoa, I'd return."

She released him partly from her grasp, allowing a little distance. Her right arm slid off his elbow and she held up a single finger. Her smile widened. "I knew you'd be here soon."

"You've seen Clarissa?"

Arabella nodded and winked.

Jack craned his neck to look at the dining area. There were six tables in total, two of which were viewable. "She's here?"

"No, she left—"

"Dammit."

"Let me finish!" She slapped his shoulder and gave him a stern look. "She left last night around nine and said to expect her back the same time tonight."

Jack glanced at his watch. Seven-forty-five.

"Come. Maurizio will want to see you." Arabella grabbed his hand and dragged him inside. "Let's get you a table and some wine and bread."

"Twist my arm."

She did. A little too hard.

"Been practicing that Krav Maga I suggested, haven't you?"

"I spend so much time fighting Nando off these days."

"You do look great." He whistled. "Bet you look better than when you turned eighteen."

"You're gonna get my husband upset, Jack."

"Bring Nando out. Where is the old bastard?"

"He's getting more meat ready." She pulled out a chair and gestured for him to sit. "I'll have him throw a special cut on for you?"

"Let's wait for Clarissa."

Arabella smiled as her gaze drifted past Noble.

"I'm here, Jack."

CHAPTER 53

CLARISSA LEANED ACROSS THE TABLE. HER BANGS SPILLED OVER her face and grazed the menu. The smell of her lotion mixed with the carafe of wine. Memories of the last time they were here flooded Noble's senses.

"You figured it out," she said.

He interlaced his fingers with hers. Her skin was soft and cool. She squeezed his hand.

"Took me a bit," he said. "Guess figuring out everything else helped lead me back here."

"I did my best with Brandon's server phone thingy."

"Actually, the correct technical term."

Smiling, she pulled her bangs back from her face. The lighting electrified her hazel eyes. "I knew he'd see my last position and relay that information to you, and while not obvious, it was enough." She paused a beat, continued. "What happened? Where's your beard?"

He lifted the hat and chuckled at the look of horror on her face.

"Oh my God. What did you do?"

"What I had to. This whole thing has been a cluster. Bear got roughed up that day we found you—which, I need to confess it was probably my fault that attack team showed up."

"How so? They were there for me."

"I had Brandon activate LPR on your plate. The one Beck gave you."

"When?" He told her and she shook her head. "It was already parked. Someone else knew that plate number, Jack. And I had to take the chance to prove what I've been told is a lie."

He eased back in his chair, confused.

She added, "Look, I'll get into all this, but first, tell me what else happened."

"Bear ended up in France after that. I was in southern Italy. They reunited him with Mandy, and Sasha came in."

Clarissa smiled and nodded, attentive to every word. But her demeanor changed as Jack paused a few seconds too long. Her eyes misted. "What happened?"

"Sasha's dead."

She clamped down hard on Noble's hand. Clarissa knew how much Sasha meant to Jack, and how Bear loved the woman.

"Bear was taken. Mandy escaped. We've been working with Clive and his people, including Sadie, if you remember her."

"I do. Tough as nails and sweet as cream."

"Something like that." Jack's laugh felt forced. "Anyway, their team destroyed the people that had Bear in custody. Big bastard was fighting his way out when they arrived. But he's hurt. Banged up pretty bad. All this after lingering problems following his tumor removal."

Clarissa cast her gaze down to the table and shook her head. A tear rolled off her cheek and landed on her empty plate.

"Brandon helped, got me on the path to Mandy. Rescued her and made an exchange in Nice earlier today."

"With who?"

"Sadie."

"Where are they taking her?"

"To be reunited with Bear, and hopefully, they can be free to return to the U.S. after. He doesn't deserve to take the fall for Skinner. That was all me. Once I right the remaining wrongs, find who the hell is running that organization that's been trying to wipe me out, I'll go home, turn myself in."

"You can't do that, Jack. Stay with me. I've got plenty of cash to keep us going. We can work with Brandon, and others, get access to your accounts. Just the two of us. Doesn't that sound great?"

His turn to stare at the table. "But it's not just the two of us, and it never can be, Clarissa. I've got Mia to think about. I have to find her, too. Guess that's one more thing to do before I go to jail for life."

"*We* can find her and the three of us will be together."

He reached across and ran his hand along her soft hair, around the back of her head, pulled her close and kissed her.

Arabella cleared her throat. "Might be time to take it upstairs?"

Clarissa covered her face and laughed. "Sorry."

"Why? You are in Italia. Be lovers!" She set two plates on the table. "But first, eat your dinner. You need your strength." She squeezed Jack's shoulder and sauntered to the front of the restaurant.

The door opened and the man with the dog came in and hurriedly spoke with Arabella. She led him over to the table.

"What's wrong?" Jack asked.

"I was sitting out on the stoop and minding my business, when I spotted this man staring into the restaurant. He snapped a photo on his phone and walked off. But then he came back. Did it again. He left and was talking on his phone. I saw him walk by twice more."

"Can you describe him?"

"I can do better." He lifted his phone and showed them a photo.

Clarissa gasped. "That's Beck."

Noble pinched the bridge of his nose as he scanned the restaurant; peered into the darkness on the other side of the front window. "He's probably been on the phone with someone back in Naples, working on getting a team here. Or worse, they're already here. Was there anything you said to Beck that would lead him to Genoa?"

Clarissa's eyes danced as she searched her memory. "It's been months since we were in constant contact, but, no, Genoa was never a thing for us. We stayed local to Naples, going to Rome occasionally, and Sicily once."

"Brandon didn't know, not for sure. Somehow, he tracked you, or me, to Genoa, and knew to come to this restaurant."

Clarissa's eyebrows knit and rose into her forehead. "Was he tracking us when you were staying with me?"

"We can only guess, and there's no time for that now." Noble turned to Arabella. "Can we go out the back?"

"Yes, follow me." Arabella led them into the kitchen where Nando and Maurizio broke into wide grins when they saw Jack and Clarissa. But those smiles faded when they noticed the look on the couple's faces.

"What's wrong?" Nando asked.

"I hate to ask you this question," Jack said. "Do you have a handgun I can use?"

He glanced at Maurizio and nodded. The taller, wiry man with matching hair ran through the dining room, presumably to go upstairs to Arabella and Nando's apartment.

Jack looked back and waved for the man who had warned them to come into the kitchen. He grabbed the phone and showed Beck's picture to Nando. "If you see this man, or he comes in, give him what he wants. Do not argue or fight with him. OK? He's a member of the U.S. Secret Service, but he may either be in danger, or wanting to bring danger to us."

Nando mocked stabbing motions with his chef's knife. "Let him bring it to me."

"This is serious," Jack said. "This guy could kill you."

Nando's demeanor shifted as he nodded and lowered his blade. "We'll tell him you were here earlier, and mentioned you'd be heading to Paris tonight. That'll throw them off."

Maurizio returned with a Beretta, and after a nod from Nando, offered it to Jack.

"I'll repay you tenfold, sir."

"Just stay alive. I must cook another steak for you."

Arabella led Clarissa and Jack to the back door. Noble cracked it open, waited, watched.

"Clear."

Arabella wrapped her arms around both of them, pulled them close, like the good Italian mother she was. "Be safe out there."

"We will."

Jack threaded his fingers with Clarissa's and led her into the darkness.

CHAPTER 54

CENTURIES-OLD BUILDINGS ROSE INTO THE NIGHTTIME SKY. Weathered facades spanning generations of design influence mashed together along the hilly streets of Genoa. Every street vastly different from the others, yet all looked the same in the soft light of streetlamps.

The alleys told another story. Trash strewn about. Homeless sheltering where they had staked their claim to a little section of the city. The smell of human waste and trash and used kitchen fryer oil mixed into a repulsive odor that the human sense of smell adapted to rather quickly.

The plan was to get to the harbor, where the metro lines ran, boats were available, and crowds lingered.

Jack led Clarissa through a maze of side streets, traveling clockwise, stopping when each spilled out onto a major roadway. There, they'd wait. And there, he'd ask her questions.

He leaned his shoulder into the wall and watched and listened. The breeze coming off the harbor chilled his clean-shaven face. An odd sensation, and one forgotten after having a beard for so long.

Shadows danced on the sidewalks, whipped into a frenzy when the gusts from passing cars rose through the trees.

"Let me preface this by saying I don't care if you stole two hundred million dollars."

Clarissa squeezed his arms. "Jack, I didn't."

"I'm not saying you did. But Beck had plenty of opinions on the matter."

"Did he tell you I have bank accounts that are topped off every time I make a withdrawal?"

Jack took his gaze off the street for a moment and questioned her.

"It's true." She pulled out her cell phone. The screen cast her face in a blueish hue, her appearance alien-like when she looked up at him. "You can see here."

"No, don't," he said. "It'll give our position away."

"This thing says I'm in Mongolia right now. Ain't nothing being given away." She tapped on the screen then reversed it so Jack could see.

He wondered if he looked like an alien now. After thinking it over, he had no doubt with his bald head and face. He ran his hand over his skull, glad that some stubble had already taken hold. *Just add water, ch-ch-ch-chia.* He doubled down on his focus and looked over the account. It sat at one hundred thousand exact.

"There's two more," she said. "And if I sent a message that I was concerned someone was on to me, they'd close these and spin up new ones."

"And *Beck* is doing this for you?"

She nodded.

"Why?" Jack glanced over at a braking scooter driven by a guy wearing a pink helmet with a faux-mohawk. A dog crossed the center line and raced to the sidewalk. The scooter continued on. "Do you have something on him?"

"Nothing."

"Do you think there's something there? Was he involved?"

"I do, and I think he believes he's buying my silence, but he's not. I'm going to figure this thing out, and when I do, God help him because I will come down on him with the fury of a volcano awakened after a thousand years."

"OK, look, you're gonna have to break this thing down to me. So far, all I know is that two hundred million dollars went missing. Was this money ever in the possession of the Secret Service?"

"Sorta."

"What kind of answer is that? Yes or no."

"I can't answer that way, Jack." She closed her eyes and sighed as her shoulders clenched up and then relaxed. "This goes really deep. The guys, they were a front for some organization, probably a shadow organization. They came across as terrorists, but there was nothing fanatical about them. That was just to throw everyone off."

"Who were the guys?"

They both snapped their heads back toward the other end of the alley as someone called out, "There they are!"

Jack reached for the Beretta. The textured grip felt like sandpaper against his palm. Clarissa placed her hand on his wrist, preventing him from aiming the pistol at the men.

"Not here," she said. "Follow me."

They turned right onto the street, downhill. This took the strain off their joints while allowing them to cover more distance in a short period of time. Footfalls rose from behind like galloping horses.

A scooter zoomed by. The driver wore a pink helmet with a faux-mohawk. This time Noble noticed a delivery bag on the back. The guy pulled over to the curb. Took off his helmet, set it on the seat, then opened the bag and pulled out someone's dinner.

"Over here," Jack squeezed out between labored breaths.

They slowed to a stop at the bike. Jack handed Clarissa the helmet as he straddled the seat. She pressed up behind him, her arm against his tightened stomach.

"Get to the bottom," she said over the hum of the engine.

"Clarissa!"

The shout came from behind and faded with the rush of wind on their faces.

Clarissa tugged on one arm or the other to indicate where to turn. Noble followed the directions, though questioned where she was leading him. What did she have planned?

At the bottom of the hill, the buildings thinned out. Over the elevated road and train tracks, Jack spotted the Genova Wheel, which stood over two-hundred-fifty feet high. In the background, the skeletons of cranes working on the shipping docks silhouetted the night sky.

Ahead, the red light foretold a disastrous tale. Thick crowds of pedestrians crossed the road in all directions, failing to stick to the lined walkways. Jack skidded to a stop, planting his foot at the end to keep from falling over.

Clarissa hopped off and backed away, into the intersection.

"Where are you going?"

"Get across the street and leave the bike, Jack, then meet me by the Ferris wheel."

"What are you talking about? We don't know how many people are out there. Beck seems to know your every move. I don't like this, Clarissa."

But she was gone, racing across the street and melting into the back half of the throng that had crossed.

Why had she rushed away? Was she supposed to meet someone there? Was this how she'd slip away from him? But where could she go with a thirty-second head start? Then other thoughts popped into his head. Had this entire thing been coordinated between her and Beck? Was she betraying Noble?

The light hadn't yet turned green when Jack rammed the throttle forward. The engine revved; the tire caught; the bike fishtailed until the tread gripped asphalt.

He never made it into the intersection. Not on the bike, at least.

The rear impact flung him off the scooter and sent him flying twenty feet in the air.

CHAPTER 55

THE THREE-HUNDRED-FIFTY-POUND MAN WHO BROKE NOBLE'S fall lay unconscious on the ground. The contents of his thermos inches from his outstretched arm trickled toward the sea, the traffic lights reflecting red and green off the image. Jack remained in a daze with his nose buried in the guy's armpits, which turned out to be as effective as smelling salts to revive him.

He popped up, careful not to move the guy's head.

The man's companion shrieked at Noble in Italian. He waved his arms defensively, but it only made her angrier.

Behind him, car doors opened. Heavy footfalls hit the road. He glanced back and saw two goons stepping into the intersection.

Jack reached into his back pocket and grabbed a wad of cash; tossed it to the woman while offering an apology.

The men rushed toward him. He looked past them toward the car. Were there more there? His question was answered when the sedan crept forward.

One of the men gained ground faster than the other. Noble decided to meet him head on. A quick strike, taking the guy out, might buy him some time.

But the first step in that direction told him he'd made a big mistake. Pain radiated from his calf to his hip. He stumbled to a knee. The first guy reached him. Jack didn't hesitate to deliver a groin shot with the pistol butt. He dipped his shoulder after and used the guy's forward momentum to flip him.

The next goon stopped short. The car's progress stalled in the middle of the intersection. The crowd paused and looked on with horror. The man's hands came up. Black gloves. Same guy from Luxembourg.

Noble raised the pistol and aimed it at the guy.

"I'm a member of the U.S. Secret Service, man. Don't do it."

"I don't care." Jack pulled the trigger. The bullet hit him in the right shoulder. He spun and dropped, clutching the wound.

The front doors opened and two men rushed to his aid. Neither were Beck.

Jack looked over his shoulder, spotted the man on the ground, scanned the crowd for signs of Clarissa or Beck. He turned as the first man got to his knees. Jack rushed forward, slammed the pistol across the bridge of the guy's nose, sending him flailing backward.

"Don't move," one of the others commanded.

Jack didn't listen. He busted through the red-rover looking line of tourists and locals out enjoying themselves before getting caught up in the mess.

The pain in his leg faded as he cleared the underpass. Adrenaline, perhaps. He didn't care if it was broken. Only had to last him a few more minutes. The base of the ferris wheel came into view as cries erupted from the crowd behind him. Sirens followed moments later.

This crowd remained oblivious to all that had happened and each step forward pulled Jack into a new atmosphere as the sounds of a reggae band on a stage at the other end bled into the night.

Laser lights reflected off the sky, the water, the wheel, and the crowd. Jack wove his way through, feeling the bass hit harder, pounding in his chest, lulling his heart into rhythm. He breathed through it, emptied his head of all the questions racing through his mind.

Doesn't matter what Clarissa's doing. Need to find her and get her out of here.

Not far behind him, yelling, cursing, and a few cries erupted as presumably one or two of the men pushed forward in pursuit. Perhaps there were more he didn't know about. At this point, anything was possible.

Jack continued to zigzag through the throng of people. He took off the hat, put on a pair of glasses. Might help. Might not. But if it bought him a few seconds before being recognized, he could take the other guys out.

A buzzing against his thigh filled him with dread. Had he left the phone on after his last transmission with Brandon? Were these guys here because of him?

He reached into his pocket and pulled out a Samsung phone. What? How did that get there? He dragged his finger across the screen and answered the call, shouting above the music and people surrounding him.

"Jack." It was faint and decidedly not Brandon.

"Can't hear," he yelled.

"It's Clarissa."

He turned in a circle, spotting one of the goons, the driver, he thought. Ignoring the guy, he continued scanning, looking for Clarissa. She was nowhere in sight. He remained on the line telling her to keep talking, even though he couldn't make out what she said. He pushed through the crowd on a line until he reached a platform that would give him a better view.

And make him a better target.

He vaulted onto the stage and looked over the crowd moving in time with the rhythm of the music. A cheer rose over the guitar solo at the sight of him.

A gunshot rang out behind him.

Time slowed for a moment or two, people and faces almost frozen, sound distorted. He saw her off in the distance at the entrance to a pier stretched out like a skeletal finger. The line went dead. The darkness concealed her as she turned and ran.

Noble dove off the stage. The awaiting crowd lifted their arms and caught him. He was passed along like a child caught in an undertow, unable to redirect himself to shore. So, he did as he was taught when he was a kid at the beach with his brother and sister.

Swim sideways.

And why not, the whole night had gone that direction.

A moment later, he found himself at the edge of the crowd, on his feet. He sprinted as fast as his legs could carry him with his pronounced limp. He heard the people behind him with all manner of accents, Italian, English,

American, German, yelling and cussing and complaining, as the two men chasing Jack pushed them aside.

The cover of darkness was mere feet from him. He strained to see beyond the last light. What awaited him was unclear. But the trouble coming from the opposite direction had obvious deadly intentions.

Noble slowed his pace after crossing the threshold. Not to a standstill, and not as though he was walking in the park. But he had to remain cautious. Clarissa had led him to this location for a reason. What was it?

A minute later he spotted her at the end of the pier, talking with someone. He strained to see but could only make out shapes. If not for her brushing her bangs aside, then he couldn't know with certainty it was Clarissa.

The sounds of the men behind him echoed. He turned, held the Beretta out, but couldn't spot them. And as he swung back around, a man descended upon him. He had no time to react as a hand latched on to his elbow.

"Come on, Noble," someone said. "We're running out of time."

Jack dropped the pistol and swiped down hard, breaking the connection. He jabbed the guy in the face, throat, diaphragm. Drove a knee into his gut. Shoved him to the ground. He scooped up the handgun and rushed forward.

"Jack, dammit, come back."

Noble didn't. He didn't pause to contemplate why the guy knew his name or had an American accent or said what he had said.

Clarissa appeared to turn and react. Did she call his name?

Another shot rang out from behind. Noble ducked, so did the people at the end of the pier. He heard more voices from behind. He broke out into a full-on sprint. Clarissa's face came into view. She appeared to be struggling with the man there. The man Jack recognized.

Beck.

Clarissa shoved Beck back, said something loud but indiscernible. Beck reached for her. She walked away and reached for something. He followed. Noble sprinted. They heard his heavy out-of-rhythm footfalls due to his injury. Beck turned to face him, his eyes narrowed, his mouth opened. He held up his hands as Jack launched into him.

Any other time, it would've been an unfair fight. And it was this time, just not in Noble's favor. Beck had him pinned; gained control of the Beretta. He aimed it at Jack, looked up, adjusted his sights, and pulled the trigger.

The blast left Jack blinded and deaf for a few moments, but he felt no pain. His vision cleared but his ears still rang. Beck was saying something, shouting perhaps, but not a word of it reached Noble's eardrums. The ringing got louder; the world swayed. Beck climbed off him. Jack struggled to his knees. He heard Beck curse, looked back, saw headlights.

"I gotta go, Jack."

"What?" Noble turned around to see Clarissa climbing over the railing at the end of the pier. She held on with one hand, leaning over the water. She looked back at Jack, held up a single finger, and jumped.

Beck and another man grabbed Jack and started dragging him away. An engine revved. The vehicle approached. A struggle ensued between Jack and the men. One let go, stepped back, pulled a pistol, and fired at the approaching car. Jack broke free from Beck, but as he raced toward the end of the pier to jump in after Clarissa, he stumbled, and though he caught himself, he couldn't stop his head from hitting the bicycle stand, painted black. The world went faded.

His last thought before succumbing to the dark was *she's gone.*

CHAPTER 56

BEAR WENT THROUGH THE CLOTHING AND OTHER ITEMS CLIVE had arranged for him and Mandy. The clothes weren't what Bear would've chosen for himself. Mandy's seemed OK to him, but she complained, too. They were each given a full-size suitcase, a carry-on, and a backpack. At least Clive had hooked them up with some technology in the backpacks. Nice Sony headphones and a MacBook for each of them, with matching iPads and iPhones.

He turned toward the knock on the door and said, "Come in."

Clive entered the room, a warm smile plastered on his face. "Appreciate what you did for us."

"Feel like I was a burden."

"Things happen. You never should've been involved. I only wanted you because I figured it would get Noble engaged. This whole thing has been a mess."

"I can help you untangle it."

Clive's smile lessened as he reached out and put his hand on Bear's shoulder. "The only things you need to untangle now are that girl's hair. It's time to head inside, Logan. This job is not for you anymore."

"How am I supposed to do that? Everywhere I go, goons are gonna be waiting for me."

"I've taken care of that."

Bear studied the guy for a moment, wondering what his intentions were. "What's that mean?"

"You don't exist anymore. Not the way you did, I mean."

"Not following."

"I deleted you. Your records. Replaced them all. You're an entrepreneur now. You and your daughter grew tired of the city and all the traveling and decided to live a peaceful life."

"What?" He straightened and tipped back a few inches while processing what Clive said. "I'm still me, right? Still Riley Logan?"

Clive nodded while reaching into his pocket. "And she's Mandy Logan."

"But none of the things I've done matter anymore?" It clicked. "Never a Marine, never in that CIA program. Wasn't there when Skinner died, or any other number of times crimes were committed. I'm not on any watchlists."

"You're getting the hang of it." Clive handed him an envelope and a keyring.

"What's this?"

"Title to your car and house. Keys to the same. You'll find the car in long-term parking at LaGuardia. Parking spot is inside the envelope, as is your new address. There's a private school there. Mandy is already accepted and enrolled. They understand she may need to catch up a bit, after having traveled the world for the past couple of years as you ran your empire from afar. All the details of that including the amount you sold the business for are in the envelope as well."

Bear felt a lightness he hadn't felt since, well, ever. He'd always pushed the envelope, even as a kid. Could've went anywhere for college but chose the military. Could've retired and done something productive but went into business with Noble.

Noble.

"What happened to Jack?"

Clive looked down; all traces of joy erased from his face. "We're working on that."

"I can't—"

Clive held up a hand. "I will always be able to reach you with this." He reached into his other pocket and produced a cell phone. Looked like one the military would issue. "Works anywhere in the world. Safe. Secure. All traffic runs through my server. I can contact you directly and no one will know. I'll also know if you contact anyone from it. That can be helpful, too. But do your best to keep it private."

Bear nodded as he accepted the phone. "But I gotta know about Jack."

"The moment I have something, you will know." Clive stepped back to the door, stopping to whisper something to Mandy, who laughed. "We've routed one of your accounts to one you can access in the States with no problems. You'll find the details in the envelope." He stopped in the hallway, looked back. "Sadie will be here to escort you soon."

"Wait." Bear met him at the doorway. "Are you close to figuring out who was behind this?"

"Maybe." He bit his bottom lip and stared Bear in the eye for a moment before continuing. "I think there're secrets that lie with Noble, and once we know those, we can figure out who's behind this and punish them for what they did to Sasha."

Bear held up the phone. "You know how to reach me if you need help."

Clive nodded and walked down the hallway, stopping in front of the elevators. Bear watched him step in, and Sadie step out.

She came into the room a few moments later.

"Kinda crazy, huh?" she said.

"What's that?" Bear said.

"Leaving the life."

"All I've wanted for a while now."

"Must be running out of testosterone or something." She laughed. "Doesn't sound like the Bear I know."

"I'm not the Bear *I* knew anymore."

Sadie reached out and pulled him closer to her. "Can't tell you how sorry I am about Sasha."

Bear choked on his reply before spitting it out. "Thank you. Me, too." He broke free from her grasp, and the memories of Sasha. "What's your take on Noble? Hear anything about Clarissa?"

The delay in her response told him what followed was a lie. "We've got a few leads. I'll be chasing them down soon." She reached out again and smoothed out his shirt. "Nothing you need to worry about anymore. You got that girl to take care of now. You raise her right. Got it? I'll show up if you don't."

"That a promise? 'Cause I can turn her into a hell raiser."

"Already am," Mandy said, not breaking her gaze from whatever game she was playing on the iPad.

Bear and Sadie shared a laugh that lingered for a few moments longer than he expected. Might've been the happiest he'd felt in a while.

"Come on, let's get you to the airport."

They talked about nothing in particular during the drive to Charles de Gaulle airport in Paris. Bear took in the sights, unsure that he'd ever be able to leave the U.S. again. Hell, he wasn't sure he'd ever board a plane again after today's flight.

Sadie dropped them at the curb. Their goodbyes were quick with minimal eye contact. The trip through check-in and security was a blur. Bear and Mandy waited at their gate until their group was called to board. During that time, he realized the opportunity ahead of him. A new life waited at the end of this flight. He and Mandy, living together as a family, with nobody and nothing to tear them apart.

And as Bear boarded the Air France Airbus A380 and climbed the stairs to the upper-level business section with Mandy next to him, he felt calm, perhaps for the first time in his life, on an airplane.

"What happens when we land?" Mandy asked after they were settled in their two-seat pod.

"We clear customs, then pick up a car, and drive to upstate New York, kinda near Buffalo."

"That sounds dreadful."

"Yeah, it does, but also wonderful."

"Whatever, man."

"You spent too much time with Jack."

Mandy turned toward him, grinning. "Don't worry, I'll end up like my dad."

"What do you know about him?"

She bit down, narrowed her eyes. "Quite a bit, but I guess I'm gonna learn a whole lot more in upstate New York, kinda near Buffalo."

CHAPTER 57

THREE MONTHS HAD PASSED SINCE JACK WOKE UP IN A HOTEL room with Clive and Sadie standing over him. The police found him at the end of a pier in Genoa, unconscious and wounded. There had been several shots fired that night. Somehow none had penetrated him. When Jack asked how they had located him, Clive declined to answer. When he asked if Clarissa had surfaced, dead or alive, they looked away and said nothing.

Clive arranged for Noble to leave on a private jet with a clean passport and identity. Like he'd done for Bear, Clive scrubbed much of Jack's past. Not everything, of course. There were some records that couldn't be erased. But all identifying information, all official records with his face, everything he could as it pertained to Skinner's death, had been removed. Worst case, temporarily. Enough to buy Jack some time to disappear for a while as Clive and his team regrouped to find who was behind the sabotage. Jack would be called up, Clive promised, to avenge Sasha's death and put an end to this once and for all.

The plane took him to Belize first, where, with help from Clive again, he located his brother, Sean. The reunion was short but fruitful. Jack turned over custody of one of his accounts so Sean could continue to remain away until it had been deemed safe for him to return to the country. Jack told him it might take a year, maybe even longer, but it would happen.

Mia warmed up to him after a few hours, and the next day, they got back on the jet and went to the Keys.

A rented bungalow had served as their home for the past twelve weeks. They got up early in the morning, talked, fished, swam, learned to paddle board, and sailed around the islands in the little Lido 14 Jack had purchased. Figured he had a dock behind the house, might as well have a boat, too.

Jack had slipped into the kind of life he never imagined possible but yearned for longer than he could remember. Something was missing, of course. Not a thing, rather a person.

The last image of her, looking back at him, telling him she'd find him with her finger gesture, haunted his dreams. She plunged into the sea and was never seen again. No body was found. He wished he'd have fought harder to dive in after her, but with Beck's team closing in, he tripped and cracked his skull. He remembered it all fading to black, then he woke up in the small room with Clive and Sadie staring at him.

"What're you doing, Jack?" Mia wrapped her arms around his neck from behind and hung there, her ten-year-old body pulling him away from the table. He threaded a few fingers between her arm to give himself some breathing room.

"Thinking about what we should do today."

"What about that market we saw from the boat? Can we go there?"

Jack lifted the lid of his Asus laptop and typed a search query into Google. "Looks like you're in luck, sweetie. Let me finish this coffee, and we'll head over."

They set off for the twenty-minute boat ride. The sea spray enhanced the humidity but the breeze kept them feeling dry. They docked near the market, tied off, made the short walk.

Mia's hair lifted in the gusts coming off the water, shining gold in the sunlight. He thought of what their time together would be like as she grew. The past three months had shown him this was the life he needed. And it had become the life he wanted.

The market was lively with several stands selling fruits and veggies, vintage clothing and items, and plenty of touristy crap. Of course, that's what Mia was most interested in. They wandered the twisting aisles. Every so often, Jack would get a feeling, the one that had kept him alive so long, telling him someone was watching.

He remained semi-alert to a threat, but the tranquility of the location, the hum of the people, the crashing of the waves, kept him relaxed.

Mia used her chore money to buy a few cheap items, then they found a stand selling conch fritters. He got Mia a lemonade, and a cocktail for himself. They found a table with an umbrella and sat facing the water.

The edge had faded. He no longer felt watched. And they enjoyed the time together.

As they left, two men with a young boy asked Jack to take their picture. He obliged, handing Mia his drink to hold. No one minded.

He stepped back to get the young family in frame.

Mia gasped.

He turned and saw that someone had grabbed her.

Noble tossed the phone back to the guys and sprinted after. The man ducked into a tent fifty feet away. Jack reached behind his back and wrapped his hand around the Glock holstered there. He reached the tent, stopped on a dime, ready to whip the pistol around and kill the man.

But the guy wasn't there.

Mia was.

And she was laughing.

Laughing with Clarissa.

"Heya, Jack," Clarissa said.

"What the hell is going on?" Jack choked on the thick, humid air. "What are you doing here?"

"Good job, Mia." Clarissa handed the girl some cash. "You got him to me like you said you could. Go ahead and buy something."

The girl walked past Jack, bumping him with her hip and giggling. The two men appeared and escorted her.

"Who are they?"

"Don't worry, they're good guys. On our team."

"Our team?"

Beck stepped out from behind a rack of clothes. "Sorry about Genoa. They were closing in on all of us, but it's Clarissa they really want."

Jack pressed his palms into his eyes; dragged his hands down his face. "Someone needs to fill me in because I'm lost."

"All of this has been about me, Jack." Clarissa stepped up to him, grabbed his hands in hers. "The reporter who was killed, the hospital massacre, Sasha, these guys are going after anyone who was tied to me."

He looked at Beck, who nodded. "We need your help, Noble."

"What about Mia?" He felt his heart splitting in two.

"Those guys will take care of her. They can get her back to your brother, too, and they'll protect him and his family."

"Are you in?" Beck said.

"They'll kill you?" Jack said to Clarissa.

"Eventually, yeah."

"I'm in." There was no internal debate.

"Great, let's talk about how two hundred million dollars disappears, and how that's not the most valuable thing they took."

Jack's story continues in **NOBLE LEGEND**. *Order your copy today!*

Join the LT Ryan reader family & receive a free copy of the Jack Noble story, *The Recruit*. Click the link below to get started:
https://ltryan.com/jack-noble-newsletter-signup-1

NOBLE ULTIMATUM / 303

ALSO BY L.T. RYAN

Find All of L.T. Ryan's Books on Amazon Today!

The Jack Noble Series

The Recruit (free)

The First Deception (Prequel 1)

Noble Beginnings

A Deadly Distance

Ripple Effect (Bear Logan)

Thin Line

Noble Intentions

When Dead in Greece

Noble Retribution

Noble Betrayal

Never Go Home

Beyond Betrayal (Clarissa Abbot)

Noble Judgment

Never Cry Mercy

Deadline

End Game

Noble Ultimatum

Noble Legend (2022)

Bear Logan Series

Ripple Effect

Blowback

Take Down

Deep State

Bear & Mandy Logan Series

Close to Home

Under the Surface

The Last Stop

Over the Edge (Coming Soon)

Rachel Hatch Series

Drift

Downburst

Fever Burn

Smoke Signal

Firewalk

Whitewater

Aftershock

Whirlwind

Tsunami (2022)

Mitch Tanner Series

The Depth of Darkness

Into The Darkness

Deliver Us From Darkness

Cassie Quinn Series

Path of Bones

Whisper of Bones

Symphony of Bones

Etched in Shadow

Concealed in Shadow (2022)

Blake Brier Series

Unmasked

Unleashed

Uncharted

Drawpoint

Contrail

Detachment

Clear (Coming Soon)

Dalton Savage Series

Savage Grounds

Scorched Earth

Cold Sky (Coming Soon)

Maddie Castle Series

The Handler

Tracking Justice (Coming Soon)

Affliction Z Series

Affliction Z: Patient Zero

Affliction Z: Abandoned Hope

Affliction Z: Descended in Blood

Affliction Z : Fractured Part 1

Affliction Z: Fractured Part 2 (Fall 2021)

ABOUT THE AUTHOR

L.T. Ryan is a *USA Today* and international bestselling author. The new age of publishing offered L.T. the opportunity to blend his passions for creating, marketing, and technology to reach audiences with his popular Jack Noble series.

Living in central Virginia with his wife, the youngest of his three daughters, and their three dogs, L.T. enjoys staring out his window at the trees and mountains while he should be writing, as well as reading, hiking, running, and playing with gadgets. See what he's up to at http://ltryan.com.

Social Medial Links:

- Facebook (L.T. Ryan): https://www.facebook.com/LTRyanAuthor

- Facebook (Jack Noble Page): https://www.facebook.com/JackNobleBooks/

- Twitter: https://twitter.com/LTRyanWrites

- Goodreads: http://www.goodreads.com/author/show/6151659.L_T_Ryan

Printed in Great Britain
by Amazon